I0595971

Songs of Autumn

Songs Series, Volume 1

Lauren Sevier

Published by Lauren Sevier, 2020.

While every precaution has been taken in the preparation of this book, the publisher assumes no responsibility for errors or omissions, or for damages resulting from the use of the information contained herein.

SONGS OF AUTUMN

First edition. November 21, 2020.

Copyright © 2020 Lauren Sevier.

Written by Lauren Sevier.

To my boys,

I love you the moon.

Chapter One

Knowledge, specifically grim knowledge, had the unnerving ability to plunge one's life into chaos while simultaneously giving it purpose. Liz's purpose had been, and continued to be, attempting to decipher the thousand-year-old prophecy depicting her fate that had been written in the form of a poetic riddle.

Her entire life, Liz had been raised for the singular function of being sacrificed in the false hope that her blood would save all the people of Aegis. She sighed deeply, sending motes of dust dancing through the shelves. She'd found yet another of a sundry dead ends. Rolling the ancient scroll carefully, Liz flinched as the stiffened papyrus crackled beneath her fingers. It had taken three weeks to decipher it, using a combination of ancient languages that had taken years to learn.

"Well?" The impatient tone startled Liz, nearly sending her crashing to the floor from her precarious perch among the faded tomes and cracked scrolls of the royal library. She clutched her chest in an attempt to contain her furiously beating heart. Liz glared over her shoulder at the grinning face of her best friend Tia.

"Well what?" she asked impertinently, the sting of her failure too fresh to admit to straight away.

"Did you find the secrets of the universe? Or the cure for my aching head the morning after a particularly wild revel?" Tia quirked one aristocratic eyebrow in her friend's direction. Holding out a flat palm to help Liz as she scrambled down the ladder and back onto more solid footing. Liz smiled despite her sour mood. Tia had a way of coaxing a grin out of her no matter the circumstance.

"The cure to your aching head is to stop drinking so much of the palace wine," Liz snapped playfully.

"Well, that's no fun at all." Tia looped her arm through Liz's and led her away from her usual dark corner. It was a sad little table with books piled high and quills strewn broken upon its surface. "Neither is all of this *study*."

Tia's nostrils flared and her upper lip curled in disdain that amused Liz to no end. The two girls couldn't be more different if they tried. Yet, it was a singularly grim sorrow that hung over them both; a heavy storm-like cloud colored their mutual existence in darker shades than the rest of the people of Silver City and bound them inextricably to one another.

Tia pulled her down the bright corridor, endless views of the bay sparkling bright along a wall of curved windows. The storm shutters were open wide to allow the last lingering summer breezes to filter in and ruffle long silken drapes.

The air was sweet with the smell of salt and fresh water lilies, it brought tears to Liz's eyes. Tears she tried to blink away, but Tia saw them despite her efforts. Liz couldn't help but feel the full weight of her helplessness squeezing her chest in a vice-like grip. If she was wrong and the prophecy hadn't been misinterpreted then her death was the only thing that would save every beautiful thing she loved. She didn't want to die, but she didn't want her kingdom destroyed either.

Cradling Liz's face in her hands, Tia leaned so close that their foreheads touched and breathed slowly and deliberately. Liz mirrored her, her lips trembling with the effort until it came naturally enough to dry her eyes.

"It was just another story about the gods." Liz admitted, feeling the flush of failure rise in her cheeks. "Another bloody story about the bloody gods who don't give a damn about any of us." Tia shushed her, a wrinkle between her brows folding deep in the rich ochre of her sun-kissed face. "It was my last chance to prove the prophecy wasn't translated properly, and I got it wrong." Tia had been spending far too much time along the white coast, and Liz could see the blistering of her cheekbones more clearly now than in the dim light of the library.

These were the things she chose to focus on, the rare severity of Tia's honeyed gaze turning to hardened amber. The way her willowy frame bent beneath the weight of Liz's words. Tia kissed her temple briefly, a soft brush of warm lips against her skin that served to ground her to this moment. Tia clasped her hands tight and didn't let go until Liz was more settled.

"You are the smartest person I know, highness. You will figure out another way. I have faith in you." Tia said, clearing her throat unattractively to rid herself of the unwanted sentiment that crept into her normally playful voice.

"There isn't enough time, Tia," Liz said, sniffling despite herself. With a shaking hand, Liz motioned to the windows behind her, where they both turned to see the billowing black sails of a three-hundred-ton frigate emblazoned with the sigil of a red dragon. The long, sleek lines of the ship belied her speed in the water. Maneuvering easily into the mouth of the bay, the ominous ship appeared to have the spirit of a sea monster, slick and deadly, cutting through the water more easily than the creatures who lived there. The arrival of the ship brought with it the promise of Liz's new husband, and the arbiter of her death.

At twenty winters, Lord Rikard LaMonte, known widely by his moniker 'The Dragon' was the only red-blooded man in the last thousand years to wield magick. Therefore, the Priestesses claimed he was the only person able to complete the ritual. All she knew of him were the dark rumors of his exploits across the seas in the lands to the west. Tales of his ruthlessness and cruelty carried back by crewmen with haunted eyes. Though there had been many blood moons before this one, Liz hadn't been of marriageable age until now. She could no longer hide behind her youth. He had arrived to kill her and, in the process, would gain the throne of Aegis as his prize.

"Princess!" Tia visibly cringed at the grating tone of Priestess Elba as she caught the girls staring wistfully at the slow progress of the frigate. "You must hasten to your evening prayers. The Queen will want you to retire early tonight."

Tia groaned loudly enough to earn a scathing glare from Priestess Elba, whose round sanctimonious face seemed even rounder in her cowl. When they were young girls, Tia used to say she looked like a pig in a dressing gown. Liz tried to put the comparison from her mind, but had to bite her inner cheek to keep from smiling at the memory. Sensing some hidden mirth and ready to stamp it out, Priestess Elba shooed the girls hurriedly down the corridor towards the water altar in the women's bathhouse.

The late afternoon sun blazed through the stained glass above the altar and flooded the marbled bathhouse in a myriad of colors, ranging from the deepest cerulean to a blush pink so faint it was nearly white. Courtiers, Priestesses, and Noblewomen gathered here to offer prayer and thanks to Seirah, the goddess of the moon and tides. As soon as Liz stepped over the threshold, the whispers began. With hair a garish shade of fresh blood, she could never enter or leave a room without garnering attention.

"Did you see him coming off the ship?"

"Only a few more days until—"

"... an awful color. Almost a scandalous shade of red."

"Good riddance, I say. This past winter lasted so long even the families that live on the East Bank nearly starved on her account."

Two days. They couldn't even wait two days for her to die? It was nothing Liz hadn't heard before, but compounded with her recent failure and the arrival of her husband and murderer, the unkind whisperings stung more today. Tia was furious, the set of her jaw too tight to hold her angry words back for long. Liz patted her elbow gently, a soft signal to let it go.

Priestess Elba and two others brought forth a large conch, the mouth wide enough for the anointing saltwater to pool. They began intoning the first of many prayer songs, echoing eerily against the curved marble walls until their voices became an otherworldly wave that carried Liz's thoughts away.

She should have been praying, not that she believed anyone was listening to her, instead she found herself taking stock of her life thus far. She had learned a great many things; she knew languages unheard of in the Kingdom of Aegis or long dead from the world at large, she could recite every epic poem or story passed down about the myriad gods and goddesses, and she knew more about Aegis's shipping and trading industry than most merchants along the west bank of the bay.

She knew a great many things, and yet Liz couldn't help lingering on the experiences her short life robbed her of. She'd never been to one of Tia's infamous revels, never danced barefoot on the beach, or dived from the white cliffs of Morr as other courtiers had done on hot summer nights. Liz had never fallen in love. Tia reached her hand over and linked their small fingers together, as if sensing her dark thoughts.

Glancing over, Tia's eyes rolled dramatically in the direction of the Priestesses. Liz smiled softly, sadly, her heart aching with happiness and sorrow mingled together. Happiness because of the time she had left, however little remained. Sorrow because of the doubt that refused to settle from her mind. An ominous belief that the Priestesses were wrong, the prophecy wouldn't be fulfilled with her death, and her life would be forfeited for nothing.

Tia was so brave and wild, dancing all night at revels and indulging in affairs with handsome knights and beautiful courtiers. She rarely had a thought or impulse pass through her mind that she didn't act on, regardless of the consequences. She'd fallen in love and broken hearts. She dared to dive off the white cliffs of Morr and swim in the open ocean. Liz was so jealous it churned her stomach at times, never begrudging Tia any happiness, only wishing she had been brave enough to defy her father and the Priestesses to join her.

She rose from her knees momentarily, dipping her fingers in the conch to anoint her temples and lips with the saltwater within. There was an audible scoff from someone down the row, but Liz ignored it and resumed her position before the altar.

"When the Blood Moon has reached its peak,
The Red Princess will see unseen,
The threads of fate of two entwine,
Her blood, the magick, then shall bind.
The North Wind will meet the flame,
Magick shall return or forever fade,
One by one the pillars will fall,
He who weds her, will rule us all. "

Tia stood and glared at the young priestess, the girl in the cowl too young to understand what it meant to give her life in service. The words were still ringing in Liz's ears, snaking around her body, imbued with a strange power over her. Eight pretty lines of rhyming poetry that dictated Liz's life, and her death. Her knees trembled and she worried they might give way beneath her.

"Did you think she forgot?" Tia ground out between clenched teeth. Liz only bowed her head, allowing her long crimson curls to cover her face and hide her expression for a few moments.

"She should be honored to give her life to the gods. As we are honored by her sacrifice." Another priestess admonished, before Tia sent them all away with a flippant flick of her dainty wrist. One of the noblewomen, old enough to be Liz's mother, spat at Tia's feet as she left.

"You shouldn't have done that," Liz whispered to her furious friend.

Tia turned her glare on Liz for a moment, before her expression softened. She held out a hand and helped Liz to her feet. Walking towards the large marbled tub, big enough for a dozen women, she snapped impatient fingers and ordered the servants to bring rose petals and buttermilk for a bath. Normally Liz would be quick to return to the library for more research, but today had been particularly difficult and Tia always knew how to ease her worries.

"It's like the closer the blood moon gets, the bolder they become. Cursed or not, sacrifice or not, you're still the heir to the throne and the crown princess of Aegis." Tia shook her head, her tight curls bouncing artfully around her face.

"It doesn't matter anymore. What matters is not making enemies when I won't be here to protect you," Liz retorted sharply, the realization of her own words forcing the sting of Tia's absence like a knife into her side. Just the knowledge that they would be parted was so bitter it stuck fast in her throat.

"As if they would ever see me as anything more than an Islander," Tia said, her face falling in a way Liz had never seen before. "No one sees me the way you do." She turned her desperate, amber eyes toward the bath.

Liz reached out and gripped Tia's hand tight, bringing it to her lips, tasting the sun and salt on her skin. "Idiot." Liz breathed out, a smile breaking the sorrow that had descended upon them both. "There isn't a person in Silver City safe from loving you. If they can't see you, then they don't deserve you." Tia's smile was shaky, but it stretched across the distance between them. A tenuous hold on barely contained emotions deeper than the ocean beyond the windows.

The servants moved toward the tub, sprinkling rose petals in the buttermilk bath, their eyes half-lidded and dreamy. The sweet perfume of oils scented the air and eased some tension lingering in the pit of Liz's stomach. Liz dropped Tia's hand and moved closer to the steam rising from the heated bath.

"The words could be romantic," Tia said, an edge of hysteria in her voice and a bold smile on her lips. Not once in all seventeen winters Liz survived had she thought of the prophecy as *romantic*. Tugging at the stays of her gown and allowing the servants to help her out of it, she stepped cleanly out of the pile of fine linen and silk.

"How exactly do you justify that?" Liz asked, an unruly chuckle escaping from between her lips. The serving girls helped Tia undress and unwind the golden baubles from her midnight locks.

"Well, it mentions the threads of fate, like in the old stories you've told me. Two *entwining* could be quite romantic indeed, and then at the end it speaks of marriage. Perhaps, the reason you haven't figured out the riddle yet is because it's meant to be a love poem and not a harbinger of death." She stepped swiftly into the bath without any hesitation. Liz sank to her shoulders in the restorative water, perfectly warm, enveloping her in a weightlessness that seemed to extend to her troubles.

She closed her eyes against Tia's desperate words; she'd felt that way earlier, too. Frayed at the edges, just desperate enough to hang onto hope that was fading faster than the scant light of the sun as it sank low over the bay. Liz tried to keep the tears from filling her eyes; she tried to stop her bottom lip from trembling. She held her breath in a last attempt to keep it from catching, but it was no use. She was a failure at everything tonight.

"If I could have just found some kind of proof. My father would have to listen to me instead of the Priestesses if I had some kind of indication that they got it wrong." Liz's voice broke and trailed away. Her nails dug into her palm as her father crossed her thoughts for the first time that day. She wouldn't allow the pious fool to ruin her time with Tia.

"I'm sorry," Tia said, struggling to contain her own emotions. After long moments, and the soft pressure of Tia's hands easing some hidden tension in her shoulders, Liz was able to regain the semblance of composure once more. They had been together as long as Liz could remember, the two of them, closer than sisters and more than friends. Liz tossed her hair over one shoulder and poured the buttermilk and water over her fiery curls. Dampened they were dark, embers instead of flames.

"It isn't romantic because my blood and the Dragon's magick are the only things keeping all of Aegis from starving in a winter that will never end. Or living short, hard lives in complete darkness when the sun no longer rises. Let's not forget drowning due to unpredictable tides. Take your pick." Tia's hands stopped. Liz leaned her head against the gilded edge of the marbled bath. "I'm the crown princess of Aegis, chosen by the gods and my blasted red hair to die in two days' time. What if the reason I can't disprove the Priestesses is because they're right? What kind of princess would I be if I let my people die out of cowardice?"

There was splashing, but no answer. Liz didn't open her eyes. Tia was never speechless, and Liz didn't think she could handle whatever expression she held on her pretty face. She would miss Tia the most. Out of everyone alive, she knew that Tia would mourn the girl she was. Not the sacrifice everyone else wanted her to be.

Each year it got worse. So many people died the last time winter descended. It reached Silver City, the bay freezing over for the first time in an age. Liz remembered thinking it had been so beautiful and crystalline. A great and terrible beauty, killing indiscriminately through starvation and illness.

Suddenly, Liz felt the biting cold, her breath fogging before her as she shivered in the steaming bath, freezing despite the heat. The mists rose and the bath was whisked away, until her mind took her to a far-off place.

Snow was falling steadily now, sticking to the ground and coating it in a fine powder. Black storm clouds of the first wild blizzard roiled overhead. As the mist cleared, Liz discerned the hazy silhouette of the Black Mountains in the distance, the clang of steel and the scrape of it against flesh. Men howled in the frigid air and soldiers surrounded her, twisting and tangling together, each desperate to end the other. Two armies marching beneath different flags, two sides of the same violent coin. The black banner of the Dragon's men rose above them, thrashing and gnashing, adorned with his crimson winged serpent. The other emblazoned with the Royal crest, a crown lifted on cresting waves.

A general screamed in silence, his words harsh and muffled together. His face, a frozen horror to behold. Eyes so black they may have been made from the harsh mountain stone, hair dark and tinged with blood. The only sign of life was the slash of red curled on his cruel lips. He pointed to a man astride a white horse, his face obscured by a helmet. The knight atop the horse raised his sword high into the air and a screaming howl ripped straight through her. A dark shadow passed in front of the sun, and the whole world went dark.

When the light returned, she was back in the bath, the mist faded into the wafting steam surrounding her.

"Where did you go this time, highness?" Tia watched her, dripping the warm buttermilk on Liz's moonlight pale skin. She felt as insubstantial as the mists that had carried her away. Liz gripped Tia's fingers to still her, needing her light to dispel the darkness encroaching on her mind. They were happening more often now, these visions of hers. Visions she didn't dare confess to the Priestesses, only to Tia. The last thing she needed were the Priestesses getting nervous and locking her away until the sacrifice.

"The same place. The same place every time," Liz whispered, the ominous cold still lingering deep inside of her, coiling in the pit of her stomach. When winter descended and the snow fell thick upon the ground, the Dragon would battle the white knight. Somehow, they would end everything, or perhaps begin something else. She trusted the certainty ringing inside of her, the low note of a temple bell resonating through her skin.

After a long while, Liz finished in the bath and donned her blue chiffon night robe. She padded on bare feet to her chambers, her mind whirring with renewed skepticism. Her visions never changed; the Dragon battled the white knight at the onset of winter. A winter that wasn't supposed to happen according to the prophecy. She couldn't prove it, but she knew the prophecy was wrong.

"Tia!" Killian, Tia's brother, scowling and handsome in his polished silver armor came barreling down the corridor. No doubt he was here to scold Tia for one of her latest escapades. Liz ducked out of his way and took a longer route to her rooms.

The fading summer breeze dried her scarlet curls as she stood on her balcony. She loved the palace with its wide, breezy walkways and endless ocean views. The stars were mirrored in the deep dark of the water below. The moon mocked her, shimmering and winking, kissing the peaks of the gentle waves lapping beneath. Her heart ached with the violence of its beauty. She wondered briefly if, when she died, she would miss this place so much her soul would wander back here.

"The kingdom for your thoughts, songbird?" Liz let her eyes shut against the musical tone of her mother's voice.

"I'm just soaking it all in while I still can." Her mother's long fingers twisted through her hair, untangling the wet, unruly curls. Her mother always had to fuss and fidget over her hair, every curl in its proper place. Liz preferred it wild and tangled. One coil completely indecipherable and clinging desperately to the next.

"Do you think father will even notice I'm gone? Or will he be too busy on his knees before Priestess Elba?"

Her mother clucked disapprovingly, her fingers rapidly moving to separate each wild curl from the next. "You know he will, Lisbet. Don't be unkind. His faith gives him comfort."

"Unkind?" She twisted to find her mother's weary eyes. "I'm the one you'll be burying. By his command, no less, your only daughter. I wish you were a little less kind, perhaps then I wouldn't have to die for his sake." Her mother's eyes, blue as the bay below them, hardened into ice.

Liz should've known better than to pick a fight. It was all they did lately. Perhaps if she were to live longer, to have a family of her own, these growing pains would have time to dissipate. As it was, she didn't want their last words to be in anger to one another. Sighing deeply, she prepared to forego her pride for the sake of peace.

"I'm sorry, I know you tried to convince him to give me more time." She heard sniffling and forced her eyes back out to the night sky. Liz wouldn't pretend that she was strong enough to watch her mother cry.

"You were three hours old when the Priestesses came to us. You hadn't even opened your eyes yet. What other recourse is there to take? We were all robbed of our choice in this."

It was the same questions every time, the same arguments, the same result. Only this time, her mother wrapped Liz in her arms like when she was a child and held her wet curls to her chest. Ruining the fine silk of her dressing gown.

"I know my duty. At least my death will save our people." Her words fell flat in the night air, spoken only to soothe her mother and not for her own benefit. The rattle of her mother's sobs reverberated through her chest. She buried her nose in Liz's hair and wailed to the night sky.

"I'm not ready for this, gods! I'm not ready."

In truth, neither was Liz.

Chapter Two

"We can't do this, Mara." Mat was breathless, shirtless, his hands clinging tight to the soft curves beneath his fingers. Her lips ran down his neck, and he gripped her so hard he worried that he might leave marks.

"Your mouth keeps saying no, but those hands of yours are saying something different." Her voice was throaty and deep. If he didn't leave now, he wouldn't leave at all. Mat wouldn't let a good girl like her get tangled up with a wretch like him. He clenched his teeth as her dress slid from her shoulder, exposing her soft olive-toned skin. Her dark hair fell loose and wild about her. A tortured groan wrenched from between his teeth, and she smirked wickedly at the sound. It took all his will power to loosen his grip on her hips and push her gently off of his lap.

"Mara, we can't. You know I wish it could be different." Her shoulders slumped. "It's not that I don't want to. Gods, you know I want to." He tried to reach for her hands, but she pulled further away from him. She sniffled behind her mask of raven black hair. He pushed a lock behind her ear, revealing the tears welling in her beautiful doe eyes.

"You're hateful, Matioch Steele. You're all I want. I don't care if you have a proper last name or not. What does a name mean to me? I'm a merchant's daughter, not a bloody duchess!"

He gathered his shirt from the floor and pushed the rough cotton over his head, ruffling his hair in the process. Soon she would work herself into a rage and begin throwing things. He rubbed the back of his head where she'd caught him the last time. It would be best for both of them if he left quickly.

"I don't understand! I don't understand why you keep doing this to me! Don't you love me?"

Did he love her? He loved her soft curves and the way she looked at him as if he were the only man in the room. He loved that when he stole into her room on chilly nights like tonight, she made him feel important.

Was that love?

He strapped his belt around his waist, securing his dagger and sword, and tossed his worn green cloak over his shoulders.

"I've told you many times, if you marry me, you'll lose all your prospects. Your dowry, your friends, and the protection of your father's name and money. What kind of life is that for you?"

Besides, he couldn't marry anyone when he had no last name to offer them. The only thing his father taught him about being a husband or father was how not to be there. He'd been broken long ago and wouldn't wish a life with him on any poor un-suspecting girl. He shook the thought away and offered her a crooked grin, taking one of her hands into his own.

"Come now, will you really let me leave like this?" He raised an expectant eyebrow and her resolve melted away. He pulled her roughly into his arms for a lengthy goodbye kiss.

The night smelled sweet, or maybe it was just the mead thrumming through his veins and Mara's kisses making him warm. A man stumbled heavily from a tavern down the alley, and the roar of laughter and cheers followed him on his journey home. Music and raucous revelry wafted on the breeze as the people celebrated the impending return of magick to the realm. Ever since he was a young lad, his mother told him the old stories. Months of summer without end, crops so plentiful they gave food away, no roaring at night from the mountain beasts. Tomorrow night, they would see it first hand; he would live through an endless summer. But at what cost? By all accounts The Dragon ruled his men through fear and violence. Not much of an improvement from a King who lavished each harsh winter in his seaside palace while his people starved. Even now he felt an unnatural chill to the night air. One that foretold of winter fast approaching.

A harsh winter it would be if it arrived too early and there wasn't enough time to replenish the grain stores at the keep. Mat strode up the cobblestone path through the city proper until the looming monster of Fangorn Keep eclipsed the moon's light. Sometimes, at night, he imagined the sprawling turrets and archways made the talons of a giant beast, slumbering on the side of the mountain. Mat twisted the signet ring around his forefinger, his mood dampened by his nighttime musings. As he approached the gate, he waved to the man atop the battlement. Soon thereafter, the gate raised, clanking in the darkness.

"Oi! Matioch!"

He grinned at the too-scrawny and too-tall silhouette of Finn, a kitchen lad a few winters younger than Mat who made quick work of following him around everywhere he went. Finn's second-hand tunic slid down his shoulder, ill fitted to his thin physique.

"How goes it, Finn?" he asked, clapping the lad on his shoulder as they walked together into the bailey. Finn fidgeted with his hands.

"What's the matter?" Mat asked.

"Nothing I can't handle, truly." He held his head a bit too far to the left, his unruly hair covering his left eye. Gripping the lad by the back of his neck, Mat spun him to reveal the red and purple bruise along his jaw and the socket of his eye. All the warmth and sweetness lingering from his night with Mara evaporated in the darkness.

"Who did this?" Mat's voice lowered into a deep baritone, belying his worry and anger.

"You have to stop getting so upset about it," Finn said. The lad shifted his feet, mumbling incoherently beneath his breath in the face of Mat's stern expression.

Mat found Finn on several occasions sporting bruises that he insisted were the fault of his own clumsiness. Only Finn wore his every emotion clearly on his face, and it was nearly impossible for him to lie.

"I will not repeat myself." Mat squared himself, staring the boy down as he squirmed beneath his imperious gaze. There was one man who Mat suspected could be dishonorable enough to put his hands on the young man. Most of the knights and soldiers garrisoned here would rather cut off their own hands than to dishonor the codes.

"Promise me you'll leave it, Matioch. I can't have you fighting my battles for me. I'll never earn the soldiers' respect if you keep treating me like a child."

The look in Finn's eyes confirmed Mat's suspicions. His mind conjured the arrogant face and cold, disdainful eyes of Gareth Black. The man held to no code but his own and made no oath to the kingdom or Lord Callum of Fangorn Keep. Despite Mat's raging urge to seek justice, Finn's shame and desperation tugged at his conscience. He wrapped a brotherly arm around his friend and pulled him close, rubbing his knuckles into his hair until he made his way back to the kitchens to finish his chores for the night. Mat didn't forget though. No, he ground his teeth and went to bed that night thinking of the ways he would make Gareth pay.

The next morning Mat was still livid. In fact, he spent most of the night tugging at his hair and stewing over the dilemma he found himself in. He promised Finn he wouldn't interfere, but his honor couldn't suffer the man to go unpunished. The memory of Finn's bruises shook his normally steady hands. He was tired of sitting back and watching as people he cared about suffered.

He tightened the straps of his leather tunic and pulled his gloves on, careful to make sure his gear was secure. His sword couldn't slip today. The familiar whistle of his claymore cutting through the air with practiced grace filled his ears as he marched onto the training ground. Mat smiled as the men ran through practice drills, paired off in sparring matches. Only a few of them bothered to look up at his approach.

The smell of leather and iron in the air, the thud of arrows in soft targets, the clang of swords, each detail of this place was pressed deep into him. It was the closest to home he's ever felt, and he'd never been allowed to train here, only watch from his place at the forge.

One day, Mat would belong here, training among these men. One day, his skill and honor would earn him a spot beside the second sons of lords and merchants. One day he would train beside knights of the realm. It was all he'd wanted for as long as he could remember. An impossible dream for an ordinary bastard. Mat didn't know how, but he was going to change that.

Mat remembered his first night at Fangorn. How full of hope he'd been that his position as the blacksmith's apprentice would somehow gain him entry into Lord Callum's legion. He'd hoped that the other boys could become what he'd always lacked. Comrades. Friends. Family.

Gareth Black made sure that would never happen.

"Gareth!" Mat shouted across the grounds, earning curious stares from men who fell silent at his approach.

Most of the men had the good grace not to mention his low birth, not rubbing the impossibility of a commission in his face. All but Gareth. He made sure no one forgot Mat's place. Least of all, Mat himself. His humors were callous. Though it had been many years ago, Mat could still hear Gareth's derisive laughter ringing in his ears and boiling his blood. No longer a helpless young boy, Mat became a reputable bladesmith by day and practiced with his wares by night.

Mat wouldn't allow Gareth to hurt Finn, not while he had the strength to stand between them. Across the way Gareth stood speaking with a Knight, an arrogant tilt of his head, bow in hand. As Mat approached, Gareth's grey eyes hardened to steel.

"What do you want, bastard?" His bored tone rankled Mat's nerves. The churning blaze of deep-rooted hatred pulsed in Mat's very bones. Gareth scoffed, his inky black curls falling into cold and unyielding eyes as he sized up Mat's intention.

"What do you think you're doing with that?" He motioned to the sword in Mat's hand.

"Give him your sword." Mat demanded of a soldier watching them from a few feet away.

Gareth raised a mocking eyebrow, his breathy chuckle a testament to his immediate assumption that Mat was ill equipped to challenge him. Whether or not he could win, Gareth wouldn't turn Mat down. He never backed away from a challenge; his pride wouldn't suffer it.

While most of the soldiers had grown close through the years and deployments, Gareth wasn't close with anyone. Though he'd been old enough to deploy with the others for two winters, at nineteen winters old he'd yet to serve once. At every turn he defied expectations, as capable of lashing out at enemies as comrades. His brand of quiet defiance isolated him from everyone else.

"You do not wish to fight me today, bastard." Gareth grumbled, ill-tempered as usual. Mat noticed something cold glinting in the darkness of his gaze. The memory of the red and purple bruises marring Finn's jaw from the night before pushed any warning firmly from Mat's mind. He could offer no excuse to justify his dishonorable behavior.

"Today, tomorrow, in the rain or shine, I love to watch you lose, lordling." The insult to his pride had the intended effect. A muscle in Gareth's jaw twitched as he tugged the offered sword from its scabbard, brandishing it recklessly. Something was seriously wrong within him. Gareth was never reckless.

There was a strange intimacy between people who hate each other. They thrummed through you, a discordant note within a song, impossible not to notice. Mat hated Gareth, but he knew the man. This lack of control made warning bells clang in the back of Mat's mind. A stillness came over the training grounds, dulling the normal cacophonous din of weapons clashing.

The soldiers flocked to the two men circling each other like wild mountain beasts. It was as if they'd scented the conflict in the air, palpable enough to taste, stinging and metallic like fresh blood. Gareth's stride was confident, his footwork impeccable, predatory. There was a rawness to him unlike anything Mat had seen before, and suddenly he lunged.

Mat raised his claymore just in time to meet Gareth's sleek blade before it could come down on his neck. Pushing him back with a grunt, Mat's step faltered. Gareth bared his teeth and struck again, this time aiming for Mat's leg. Again, barely enough time to push him back before there was another strike, and another, and another.

Gareth frenzied, roaring through combinations like a man possessed, rattling Mat's resolve. There was indeed a demon riding Gareth's back, something dark and twisted rearing its ugly head within him. Gareth's eyes, normally calculating, were glazed in a far-off place. It was as though he didn't even see Mat before him, and instead he was battling some unknown threat within his own mind. Mat often lost himself this way when training, overcome by his frustration at being unable to change his circumstances.

A hush came over the training grounds, and Mat raged to the beat of his pulse pounding in his ears. There was no doubt in his mind that Gareth meant to vanquish whatever foe Mat was taking the place of. Their ragged breaths mingled. Should Mat falter even once, it would be fatal. Just as doubt crept into his mind, Mat's ankle rolled beneath him and he fell to his knees.

With an enraged snarl, Gareth leapt on the weakness, his steel flashing. He sliced across Mat's shoulder, drawing blood with a hurried hiss. Mat thrust a parry, but Gareth's boot knocked him on his back. Then the same boot pinned the wrist of his sword arm into the mud, useless. With both hands raised Gareth stood over Mat, his eyes wild and unseeing, ready to drive his steel home.

In that moment, Mat realized he was going to die on his back in the mud. No last name. Nothing to show for his life to this point.

He took a shuddering breath and kept Gareth's gaze, refusing to look away in cowardice. At least he would die quickly, in battle, the way a soldier should. It was all he could ask for, an honorable death. He would not get to see the return of magick to the Kingdom of Aegis. He would never see Mara again, never get the answers he craved about his past. Gareth's nostrils flared as he plunged his sword down.

"What is the meaning of this?" The words boomed like thunder throughout the training grounds, seeming to shake the very soil beneath Mat's back.

Startled out of his rage, Gareth stopped his sword short. Eyes clearing, he blinked, his body slackening abruptly. The tip of his sword dragged in the mud. Mat curled a disgusted lip at the sight.

They'd crossed a line. It was forbidden for the soldiers to fight outside of a direct command or sparring during training. It was also forbidden for commoners to attack soldiers garrisoned here. In his gold threaded tunic and supple leather boots tracked deep in mud, Lord Callum of Fangorn keep glowered imperiously over the both of them.

"Clean yourselves up and meet me in the Great Hall. Now!" he barked, and they started. Mat scrambled from the ground, fumbling to grasp his claymore and shove it back into his sheath. He tried to wipe the mud away and only succeeded in smearing it further into his tunic. He would have to don his cloak to hide it. Gareth's eyes were fixed on the ground as he gathered himself and straightened his own tunic.

Mat didn't want to ask, but his honor demanded it. Otherwise, he wouldn't be worthy of a commission. "You alright?" Mat asked as he secured his worn green cloak around his shoulders and noted the sharp nod from the corner of his eye. No further discussion necessary, thank the gods. Gareth was normally the most composed of the entire battalion, too careful to lose control like that. This erratic behavior unnerved Mat more than he wanted to admit.

He wasn't sure what he expected to happen honestly. Mat had known it was a flogging offense to attack him. Perhaps he thought Gareth wouldn't risk his reputation. Perhaps Mat just hadn't cared in the moment.

Now they needed only to deal with the consequences of their actions, the wrath of Lord Callum. Mat had never been asked into the Great Hall, never singled out by the lord. Not in all his years.

Whatever happened next, Mat knew one thing for certain; he was in deep shit.

Chapter Three

The sunset over the bay was the most beautiful Liz had ever seen, perhaps because she knew it would be her last. It set the sky aflame, burning deep into her memory. She wore pearls in her hair and a crown adorned with so many shimmering diamonds it appeared to be made from seawater and starlight itself. Every inch of her porcelain skin had been cleansed and massaged with lavender oil. An extravagant lamb, headed for slaughter.

Each vision she saw in the days leading up to this moment solidified her belief that dying today wouldn't change anything. She couldn't prove it, but there had to be a reason she'd been haunted by the images of this battle. There was a clue within them, some secret that would unravel the prophecy and save all of Aegis. There *had* to be.

The silk and lace of her wedding gown clung to the curves of her body and flowed like water as she moved. Her figure, too curvy to be considered fashionable, was squeezed into an acceptable shape by a corset inlaid with whale bones. She'd never been more radiant, her flame-like hair mirroring the sunset outside.

Finally a woman at the age of majority, never more ready to begin, and it was her ending.

"Tell me again," she ordered Priestess Elba, adjusting the pins near her left ear.

"Your highness, it doesn't matter how—"

"Tell me again," she snapped. She turned piercing blue eyes on the priestess, whose words fell away in an instant. Liz's breath hitched and her eyes fell to the mosaic beneath her feet.

"You'll walk down the front steps of the palace to a boat waiting at the edge of the water. Your parents will walk behind you, and all the people of Silver City will be there to witness your descent."

Liz closed her eyes, imagining it, biting her lower lip hard enough that she worried she would break the skin. If she prepared herself now, perhaps she could retain some dignity in these final moments.

"The boat will carry you to the water temple near the west bank of the bay where your groom will meet you."

"My groom?" Liz scoffed, her eyelids fluttering open as she blinked back hot tears. "You mean the sorcerer you and my father sold me to."

Priestess Elba had the good sense to look ashamed, even a little wistful if Liz had the mind to be kind. "Yes," she acknowledged.

"Then what?" Liz asked. The Priestess couldn't seem to find the words, her mouth opening and closing several times as a flush creeped into her face from beneath her cowl. Death was a solitary journey and the truth remained that no amount of preparation would comfort Liz now. Tomorrow morning, Liz's mother would go to the altar and retrieve her lifeless body. Her wedding dress would become her death shroud. They would bathe her again, oil her again, her jewels and crown would be removed and traded for fresh water lilies.

"Then he kills you." Her father's voice came from the doorway as he strode into the room. The timber of his voice and the calm certain tone with which he spoke shattered what little composure Liz managed to gather. She wanted to laugh at her helplessness but found instead that heat was pricking at the corners of her eyes.

"Of course, Father." The smallness of her voice sickened her. She'd always made herself small and agreeable to him. Everyone did. Too afraid of his pious fanaticism and absolute power to risk his ire. Priestess Elba bowed low, backing out of the room at an uncomfortable angle, careful to give him a wide berth.

She felt the feather-light touch of his fingertips on her hair for the briefest second. The tenderness of the touch ruptured the tenuous hold she had on her emotions. Her eyes snapped to his face, deep lines etched into his brow and chin. Not one part of his face was familiar to her, nothing to connect them together.

"Even though this will be the end of my legacy, I am proud to end the suffering of my people. You should feel honored, daughter, to give yourself for Aegis. Your name will echo in the Halls of the gods for eternity." A hysterical bubble of laughter escaped her lips before she could quell it. Perhaps her mind had been lost in her desperation, but she laughed harder at the scowl on his lips. Tears blurring her vision she turned on him, all the fury of her seventeen winters finally released in this moment.

"You, great king, have done *nothing* for your people." Liz didn't raise her voice, instead punctuating each word with a confident step toward his looming figure. "I told you. For years, I begged you to listen to me, to heed the warning in my visions-"

With a scoff he dismissed her words turning his back on her and heading toward the door.

"I am your daughter!" She shouted at his retreating back, feeling the words all the way to the deep secret part of her so hurt it would never heal.

"You were supposed to love me." Liz whispered, clutching her stomach to try and keep herself from cracking open wide. She raised her eyes to the ceiling and sniffled, breathing slowly to rein in her sorrow.

"*I* love you." The voice came from the door to the sitting room where Tia stood, trembling so hard she could barely keep herself upright. Liz closed her eyes, her bottom lip quivering. Her resolve shattered as tears tumbled unhindered down her cheeks. Tia's hand gripped her hard, and they fell into each other's arms. Liz's eyes wrenched open as Tia's shoulders trembled with agony. They held each other together before either felt strong enough to stand on her own.

Tia had never been more lovely, tears clinging to her long lashes, embellishing her dark eyes like stars. Liz wiped away the salt tracks from Tia's cheeks, her hands brushing nervously over Tia's skin. She tried twice to pull the jagged pieces of herself into a semblance of respectability. Tia didn't fare as well, swallowing great gasping breaths, trying between the gulps to speak to her.

"Killian couldn't even... I've never seen him cry before... How am I supposed to...? I can't, Lisbet, I can't..."

"Everything will be alright, Tia," she whispered, not trusting her voice to stay steady.

"How?" she asked in a voice so small and broken it hurt to hear.

"When you see me tomorrow, it will be as if nothing happened." Liz sniffled, patting her own cheeks dry. "As if I were asleep." Tia shook her head, frowning at Liz and scoffing in disdain. "You will sing the song of my life. It will echo in the halls of the gods forever. You will sing me into eternity, my friend. And I will miss you; I will miss you the most."

Tia wept again at her words, holding her for a long time until she was steadied by a soft knock at the door reminding them both that time was short.

"It's too soon!" Panic raced up Liz's arms and into her throat. It was only sunset. The blood moon wouldn't rise for hours yet. Gods, she needed more time! She'd failed; there would be no more time to prove her certainty about her visions. Now, all she wanted was enough time to say goodbye. A servant girl hurried to answer the knock, grateful for any excuse to leave the girls to their maudlin weeping.

The door cracked open and Liz's mother peeked around the corner, taking in her daughter in all her splendor. A tight coil of fear released from deep within Liz's chest. They hadn't come for her yet. She still had a few blessed minutes of her life left.

Her mother didn't look like herself. Eyes rimmed in red, her hair a mess, and she wasn't dressed yet for the ceremony. It was unlike her. Always prepared, always poised, especially with this day so long in coming, Liz couldn't imagine a world in which the Queen of Aegis looked anything less than the epitome of regal confidence.

As she approached, the tears in her eyes rolled unhindered down her face and dripped off her chin. Cold dread spread from the base of Liz's spine, splintering out and fracturing the fabric of her reality. Her mother's hand was outstretched, reaching for

Liz. That same hand was covered in blood, thick and rust-colored, drying on her skin.

"Mom?" Liz took the sticky hand in her own. "Are you hurt?" She searched her mother's body for wounds. Her gown, especially the right sleeve, was covered in crimson stains. It soaked into the silk making the fabric slick against her skin, the stains so dark they were nearly black. Clutched fast in her other hand was a dagger, soaked to the hilt.

The world twisted beneath Liz's feet. It was as if she was seeing and feeling everything in a distorted way, from a considerable distance or from underwater. Her mind didn't make the connection right away, not until her mother unclenched her fist and let a dagger clatter to the ground.

"He was standing there with that *Priestess* in the corridor and I couldn't let them kill you. I couldn't let them kill my baby."

Liz's beautiful white silk gown was stained with blood, but she couldn't bring herself to care. Clinging desperately to her mother as her knees gave way, they sank to the floor.

"Who?" Liz flinched as her mother cradled her face in her sticky, blood stained hands, smearing it into her skin. It was still warm.

"Your father, the king."

No. Liz dug her nails deep into her mother's shoulders, not caring if it hurt her.

"It's treason. They'll execute you!" Fresh waves of tears rolled down Liz's face, worse than mourning her unspent life was knowing with certainty her mother would join her in the vastness of the frozen wasteland that awaited them all after death. "Why would you do something so stupid?"

"You have to run, Lisbet." Her mother's eyes were wide and frantic, scouring over every angle of Liz's face. Committing her to memory. "You can't save me now, but if you run you could escape."

Liz opened her mouth to protest, but her mother took her chin in a firm grip until she was forced to focus on her determined face, an older version of Liz's own. The shadow of a dream Liz didn't dare speak aloud hid in the gentle lines of her mother's face. She could almost see herself growing older, having thwarted the prophecy. Not the way the Priestesses insisted was true, but the way she knew was true in her own heart.

"Listen to me—"

I can't leave you to die," Liz argued. The courtiers' every whisper clanged in her ears. Every not-so-subtle look of oddity or strangeness she'd endured, reinforcing her belief that she didn't belong here. Liz had never been a person to the other members of court, merely a sacrifice. An object to be traded for their comfort, and a source of guilt when they thought too long about the implications of that.

"You can. If it'll help you find another way to bring magick back then you can and you will."

Liz shook her head again, not believing what this night had turned into. Instead of her own body adorned with water lilies on the altar of the water temple, it would be her mother's. They didn't sing the song of your life if you were branded a traitor.

"Where would I go? The entire kingdom knows I belong to the Dragon. I have nowhere to run, no one who would help me escape."

"I know a way out. A hidden passage in the caves below the palace." Tia's voice sounded stronger than before. Liz didn't turn to look at her friend but the wrinkles at the edges of her mother's eyes smoothed in an expression of relief. Screaming echoed from the corridor, her father and Priestess Elba had been discovered.

"Go to the northernmost point of the Kingdom. Winter is almost upon us, and the mountain passes will freeze. When it begins to snow, they will become impassable. It'll buy you time. Enough time to find a way to save Aegis." Her mother clutched her to her chest one last time, and then she pushed her away, set her chin, and pulled her shoulders back. Ready to face her punishment with unfailing grace. Liz clawed at her mother's dress, Tia snaking her arms around Liz's waist and hauling her bodily away.

"I can't run. I can't leave you here. Please." Liz could see it in her mind's eye. A mockery of her wedding tonight. They would beat her mother first, until her skin was more purple than its normal milky white. They would drag her down the steps of the castle, the entirety of Silver City watching. The Dragon would want to make sure the people saw her as he burned her in the open air. He would want to make sure they heard her beautiful, musical voice contorted into inhuman screams. Until it finally ended.

In silence.

There would be no one left to sing the song of her mother's life, no one to sing her into the halls of the gods, no one to remember her when they struck her name from all the histories. No longer would the queen exist anywhere except in Liz's mind, in Liz's heart.

"You can." Her mother smiled sadly.

The sound of boots clomping down the hallway resounded as fear pulsed hot in rhythm to her racing heart. Her mother tucked an errant curl back into place and smiled softly.

"Mother, I—"

"Promise me something." The firmness of her mother's voice silenced all of Liz's protestations in an instant.

"Anything." Liz couldn't help wavering as her voice broke on the word.

"Promise me you'll fight, until the last. Promise me you'll live well, my sweet girl. Live well for me." Liz felt Tia's arms tighten around her shoulders, but she didn't want to turn away.

"There are guards coming," Tia said. "If we're going, we have to go now." Liz shook her head. Not enough time. There was never enough time. She didn't get to memorize the shape of her mother's face. She didn't have enough time to say goodbye.

"Now, Lisbet!" Tia shouted, yanking hard enough that Liz nearly lost her footing.

"I promise."

Her mother nodded, resigned. She tilted her chin, giving Liz permission to go. Something inside of Liz's chest broke straight in half. Tia pulled her around the corner, through to the servant's quarters just as the palace guards burst into the room and surrounded the queen.

I promise.

Chapter Four

Mat stood at attention, awaiting Lord Callum's punishment. He wanted to believe that he exuded calm, stoic professionalism as he waited, but unfortunately that wasn't the case. In truth, he seethed at Gareth's casual confidence. Mat avoided looking at his foe, instead studying the worn leather near the toe of his mud-caked boots to hide the shadow of a snarl on his mouth. The dirty slice in his skin from Gareth's blade stung, and the fear of the lash itched across the skin of his broad shoulders and back. He had marks there already and didn't relish the thought of adding to the faded silver scars.

He fought the urge to lift his eyes and take in the opulent splendor of the Great Hall. Commoners weren't allowed into this part of the keep unless they were serving Lord Callum and his family. Gareth didn't seem afflicted with the same institutionalized obedience as Mat. Crossing his arms and sneering down his long nose with an entitled arrogance that rivaled royalty, Gareth didn't seem particularly worried about displeasing Lord Callum.

Mat's mind whirled as he scrambled to find an excuse believable enough for a commoner to attack a soldier. He bit down on his lip hard as his thoughts scattered in a thousand different directions, panic flaring in the deep part of his chest and thudding rapidly against his ribs. Gareth trained with the soldiers, was a valued member of the legion stationed here for the crown.

Mat was no one.

The oppressive silence of the stone walls set Mat's nerves on edge. The leather of his gloves creaked against his hard knuckles as he gripped his hands tightly behind his back. In that moment Mat decided he was tired of being no one. He lifted his gaze to study his surroundings, as Gareth's equal would. The Great Hall was long and the ceilings so high and vaulted that Mat couldn't quite see the top. Windows taller than any man lined the walls, arched and grated against the winter to come. The motes of dust shone like stars and danced in the fading fall dusk.

Lord Callum, Gareth, the knights... they all wanted Mat to learn his place. They wanted him to be complacent as a bastard, a man with no surname and therefore no value in their eyes, except to serve them. Mat felt a familiar churning in his gut at the thought. It was always there, pulsing just beneath his skin, his anger. A roiling hunger to prove them all wrong. They could beat him all they wanted, but with every blow they fueled that molten hunger within. What he wouldn't tolerate was anyone, no matter their station, tearing down Finn the same way. One day, Mat would rise above his station and claim his knighthood. One day, when people looked at him, they would see a man of honor. When they did, he would stop them from hurting anyone else.

Mat glanced at the other man, noting Gareth's lack of respect and his blatant refusal to stand at attention as they waited. His complete disregard for the nobility of the house didn't come as a surprise. Instead he seemed strangely unaffected by the grandeur of the hall.

Mat kept his soldier's stance, the epitome of contrition, muttering a breathless prayer that Lord Callum recognized Gareth's impertinence and took mercy on Mat. The minutes stretched and the longer they stood waiting, the faster the blood began to rush in his ears.

"Gentlemen!" The Lord's booming voice echoed in the space, the words themselves startling Mat out of his reverie. No one had ever called Mat a gentleman before, certainly not a man of rank. Lord Callum didn't look angry, as Mat expected. Instead his arms flung open wide in greeting. There was something distinctly feral beneath the saccharine expression in his eyes. Inviting Mat into his Great Hall, speaking to him as an equal, was unusual indeed. Lord Callum was hiding something.

"I hate to keep you both waiting." He said.

Mat glanced at Gareth whose expression was just as disbelieving. Enemies found on equally unsettled ground, muscles tensing and jaws clenched tight, waiting for the trap to spring around them both.

"I suppose you're wondering why I asked you here." Neither of them spoke, allowing the silence to blanket the hall. Lord Callum's careful words, his false congeniality, terrified Mat more than a lashing ever could. He shifted to move his arms to the side and suppressed a hiss as his shoulder throbbed from the shallow cut still bleeding freely from earlier in the afternoon. It wasn't deep enough to require stitches, only serving as a distraction.

"I'm told this isn't the first time you've caused trouble on the training grounds." Lord Callum's sharp eyes landed squarely on Mat's tense form. Mat stopped himself from lowering his gaze again in shame. "I'm also told that you've petitioned seven times to join the legion."

Mat nodded; his jaw clenched tight against the words on the tip of his tongue. Wind rattled the lattice of the windows as Mat fought to keep his temper in check. Seven times petitioned; seven times denied without the courtesy of showcasing his skill with a sword.

"It's been a long time without a war to fight." Lord Callum commented, taking his time to inspect the two men. Mat was self-conscious about his open, bleeding wound and the mud coating his pants and boots. He wondered if he'd made mud tracks on the floor. Lord Callum looked at them both expectantly but they stayed silent. Sighing, he rubbed a hand over his graying hair.

"Alright, I'll get right to it. Have either of you been to the Neither Wood at the crest of the Mylean Valley?"

"No, M'lord," echoed from both of them in gravelly, unused voices.

"My family owns a hunting lodge there, and I am sending the both of you to the southern edge of the wood to bring back as much hunted game as you can carry in a wagon. Skinned and preserved. And for the gods sake, take your time." Lord Callum stared pointedly at Gareth as he spoke. Something was wrong. The nobles bought whatever supplies they needed. Why would Lord Callum send them so far away on what was essentially a hunting trip? This wasn't a punishment.

"Lord Callum, permission to speak?" Mat requested.

His dark eyes widened in a way Mat was all too accustomed to, as if he'd forgotten about Mat's presence even after speaking to him. He extended a hand laden with rings to Mat who almost took it between his dirty gloves before realizing his mistake and pulling the leather off with a *snick*. He bowed his head low over the rings and cleared his throat, rising only to see a dangerous glint on Lord Callum's face.

Gripping Mat's fingers tight he pulled him closer, the pad of his pointer finger twisting the band of the signet ring resting on his hand. After a long, tense pause and another awkwardly cleared throat, Lord Callum's careful mask covered the danger Mat noticed peeking through his painted expression.

"Steele, is it?"

"Matioch Steele, M'lord. I'm a simple man, and while I appreciate your leniency, I don't understand it. Are we not to be punished for fighting? The blood moon ceremony is tonight. We should expect there will be a light winter at the worst. Why then should we need to restock the meat cellars?"

Lord Callum's face took on a grey pallor; in fact, he looked rather sick. He clapped his hand on Mat's shoulder, pulling him further into the room.

"What do you know about the half-bloods?" Lord Callum didn't seem to want an answer, instead he continued on. "Five of our grain stores were raided by the savages near the border of the Neither Wood. Even a mild winter could be fatal for many of us here if we do nothing."

Mat nodded, his head spinning from the news. Dread filled the pit of his stomach. When Lord Callum said this winter would be fatal, he didn't mean to his family. Hidden away from the slicing winter winds and threats of starvation, they would ride out the season in excess and comfort. No, it would be the villagers who died in their stead.

"Bloody mongrels, refusing to stay in their place." Lord Callum grumbled hatefully.

Mat nodded again, bored with his cruelty. After all, Mat refused to stay in his place too. He didn't like the circuitous way the Lord spoke. Mat preferred when men did not dress in velvet and gold threads and said what they meant. But simplicity never helped raise a man's station in life. If Lord Callum wanted to be cruel and manipulative, Mat was willing to let him so long as he benefited from it. Not very knight-like, but he could work on that.

"M'lord, I have one request." Mat said, pausing until Lord Callum waved his hand in continuance. "Allow me to take a few lads, commoners, to help us."

"It will be dangerous. The half-bloods traveling camps are always near the lodge. I can't guarantee their safety. You cannot fail to return before the first blizzard. The pass will be frozen over and impossible to cross after that and you'll be stranded. Do you understand me?" He peered imperiously down his hawk-like nose at the two of them.

"Of course, M'lord." Mat said with a bow of his head. Gareth stayed silent the entire time, assessing the situation with a predatory glint in his eyes. He offered nothing but a nod of acknowledgement.

"Steele, if you prove yourself worthy, I will grant your petition. You'll have a commission in the legion."

Immediately Mat knew this had something to do with the signet ring on his hand. There had never been a place for him in the legion before this meeting, seven times denied before today. Gritting his teeth, he let a smile stretch across his mouth, mirthless and cold.

Their meeting concluded; Mat shuffled back to the parts of the keep he was more familiar with. It comforted him to be in a functional space rather than surrounded by elaborate ornamentation. His feet were lighter now, gliding over the stone floor without caring about the mud that might be trailing behind him.

"What do you think that performance was truly about?" Gareth asked, his expression inscrutable. Mat's arm still hurt and he wasn't in the mood to suffer through a conversation with a man he hated.

"Who cares? He's given us official orders to take a few buddies and go on a hunting trip before winter descends. Its good fortune is what it is." Mat grinned wide as he realized he would at least get a long goodbye from Mara before he left and perhaps the opportunity to apologize to Finn for disregarding his wishes.

"You shouldn't trust him," Gareth said, his tone superior.

"I don't," Mat retorted pointedly enough to sting even Gareth's formidable pride. "I don't trust anyone laden with enough gold and jewels to buy all the grain and meat needed to keep all of Fangorn fed this winter, who chooses to send us on a *hunting trip.*"

"Then why are you going?" Gareth leaned against a stone column and crossed his arms over his chest.

"Why are you?" Mat asked in response.

"Do we have the option to refuse him?" Gareth asked, skillfully avoiding Mat's question altogether. Gareth wouldn't answer, for the same reasons Mat wouldn't have either. They were well-matched enemies at least. Gareth glared at him, a muscle twitching in his jaw. Mat refused to break the stare, and they stayed that way, locked together in silent fury, for longer than Mat cared to admit.

"Wharton Cove," Gareth said finally, shoving off the column and angling close enough that Mat could see the splatters of mud on his collar. When he didn't respond, Gareth's stony eyes flicked down to the signet ring resting heavy against Mat's hand. "I don't know what that symbol means, or why Lord Callum is so interested in it. But I've seen it stamped on crates coming from Wharton Cove. They're piled high in the stores." The wind whistled through the open archway to the training grounds and Mat struggled to contain the fury his casual words evoked within him. He didn't like the idea of feeling indebted to Gareth for anything, much less anything to do with his father. Mat had to remind himself to breathe normally, slowly, careful not to show any emotion as he processed the information.

"That reminds me." Mat hauled back and punched Gareth in the face, shaking off the blast of pain that radiated from his fist.

"Bloody afterworld! What was that for?" Gareth stumbled back, catching himself on the stone column. Mat felt the grin tug at one corner of his lips, his green eyes sparkling in mischief as he turned toward the forge.

"For trying to *bloody* kill me this afternoon. Next time, you better succeed, or I'll give you more than a sore jaw."

Without looking back, Mat left him there. It felt so *good* to turn his back on the entitled prick. Stopping briefly to tell Finn and a few others the good news about the hunting trip and to pack their things, he marched to his job at the forge.

The smith was drunk again, slobbering on the floor. Mat took advantage of the smith's inebriated state and the warm fall night. He climbed to the top of a parapet on the southern wall of the keep, his favorite view when he needed to be alone. He needed to be alone tonight, more than ever.

The night was eerie, perhaps because of all the celebrations that were raging in the local taverns below. He leaned against the weathered stone, watching the village begin to glow as the sun's last rays disappeared on the horizon. A gentle stream of starlight, trickling down the mountainside, a shining testament to the life below. Everywhere were signs of joyous celebration, lanterns being lit and set floating in the air, candles pushed down the river on makeshift paper boats and thick waxy leaves.

The entire world was celebrating the murder of a young girl tonight. The moon was high in the sky and would soon turn red and bathe everything in an otherworldly crimson glow. He shook his head, trying to shake off the chill creeping up his spine. He couldn't understand the tempestuous and grisly appetite of the sea goddess. Not when by comparison Eamon, god of the mountain, taught his followers to protect the innocent. Though, there were few who worshipped him and Mat was never allowed to participate in temple ceremonies. Bastards were not allowed to tarnish holy places.

He would have done the same, though, given his life to save the kingdom. In fact, he couldn't think of a better reason to die. In the service of the people. The Red Princess would have a warrior's death, at least. Quick and filled with glory. The glory of giving her life for the people of Aegis. He could respect her for that. Royalty or not.

"Oi! Matioch, what're you doing up here? I thought you were going to visit Mara tonight?" Finn stepped out of the shadows, all six and a half feet of long lanky limbs.

Mat grinned. "Oh, I'll be visiting her before we head out in the morning. Make no mistake about it, I plan to spend plenty of time with her before I'm stuck with the likes of you lot for the next few weeks."

Finn blushed.

Mat couldn't help but laugh at the look on the poor lad's face. He obviously didn't have a woman, or at least hadn't had a woman in the way that made one a man yet. Mat would have to remember to take him to a tavern when they returned to see if they could change that. Perhaps the goddess of luck and love would be with him. He ran his ring over the stubble of his chin, as he often did, deep in thought, twisting it around his finger obsessively.

"Oh no, not that bloody ring again. You get maudlin every time you wear it." Finn groaned. Distracted, Mat grunted in response, trying to close the gaping chasm stretching wide within him.

"It was my father's," Mat answered simply, the words scraping across an unseen wound that had never really healed within him. It had taken root and festered so deep that if he were to try to cut it out, his heart would come alongside it.

"I thought you didn't know who he was?" Finn asked, his voice soft and timid. He was reaching out to Mat delicately, careful not to chafe such an obviously sore topic while simultaneously offering to share Mat's burden. In moments like these, Finn became more family than friend. Mat closed his eyes and felt the wind against his cheeks, a chill creeping into the night air. The moon was a vulgar shade of blood red, bathing the world in the threat of violence and wild abandon.

"I don't. My mother refused to tell me," he admitted quietly before turning his best impression of a charming smile on his friend and clapping him congenially on his shoulder. "But that won't help me sneak into Mara's bed tonight, will it?"

Finn shrugged, taking an apple from the inside pocket of his cloak and taking a large bite of the crisp flesh. A flush crept up his neck and stained his ears nearly as red as the moon. Mat found that flustering Finn usually kept him from asking questions he would rather not answer. After ruffling Finn's hair, he excused himself and began to walk to clear his thoughts. They sat heavy on his mind tonight and would not let him enjoy the sweet summer breeze.

The night had grown more sinister, perhaps an effect of the murderous moon looking down on them from the realm of the gods. Mat hadn't thought about his mother in a long while, longer than it should have been. It must have been four winters now since he had last seen her. That last day his words spilled out hot and ugly, words that could never be taken back. He'd been such an angry lad when he made the decision to leave home and come here, refusing to lead the life of a scribe as his mother wished.

He'd been too young and impulsive to spend his life mired in texts beyond his station. Too angry to sit still for long. He came here to make something of himself in the only way that made sense to him at the time. His once all-consuming obsession with finding his father had been snuffed out with his mother's flat out refusal to reveal the man's identity. A thistle stamped in gold and a few furtive glances fanned the flames of that old obsession until it nearly consumed him.

As he strolled down the cobblestone street to find himself beneath Mara's window, Mat wondered if his mother had been protecting him by hiding his identity, or herself. How different would his life have been if she'd been honest with him? He felt shaken inside, as if his thoughts were swirling together and breaking apart again. Mat leaned against the wall opposite Mara's window and saw her candle flickering in the pane. A sign that she was awake and wanted to see him.

She would let him in, and if he showed her the depth of his suffering tonight, she would not let the petty rules of propriety stop her from comforting him. If he went to her window tonight, he would bed her. Mat was many things, but he wasn't a man who could bed a woman out of wedlock. How would that make him any different than the man who fathered him? Even if he wanted to give Mara more, he had nothing to offer. Not yet. Maybe not ever, if his trip to the Mylean Valley was unsuccessful.

Though being in her arms would comfort him, he turned around and began the long, winding trek back to his straw mattress on the dirty floor of the forge. In the morning he would pack his things and ride out with his friends and Gareth. He would have plenty of time to think as he rode, plenty of time to talk himself out of the impulse he had to track down this tenuous lead.

He wouldn't say goodbye to Mara. He owed her that kindness. Even if by some miracle he earned a commission, she deserved better than a broken bastard like him.

Looking up at the blood moon hanging low and wide in the sky, he said goodbye to her in his mind. He could have loved her. Maybe one day he would be man enough to love someone the way they deserved—with the entirety of his bitter, broken heart. Until then, he would remember tonight. He would remember the girl that he spent a wild summer with, and he would always remember that she wanted him even without a last name.

Chapter Five

"You have to eat, your highness." Tia offered Liz the last of their bread, but she shook her head, scoffing at the use of her title. There were no princesses here.

In truth, her appetite had disappeared in the fortnight since fleeing the palace. She needed to eat, as evidenced by the shakiness in her hands and the bone deep weariness setting in from the journey thus far.

In the chaos after the King's murder, Tia led her through the dark underbelly of the palace, and together they'd raced from the city. From there, they'd fled into the Neither Wood, a dense temperate forest inhabited by nomadic half-bloods and rumored to be a place of magick and death. No one would dare follow them there. Their fear of the nomads leeched away over the last weeks, beaten down by hunger and eclipsed by the threat of the Dragon's army scouring the surrounding lands for them.

She remembered ripping the pearls and crown from her curls. Shaking as Tia helped peel the blood-stained gown over her shoulders. Tia attempted to pick up the jewels and flowing silk but Liz screamed at her to leave them. The soiled garment remained discarded somewhere in the wood. If only the memories of her father's blood drying rapidly on her cheek could have been so easily cast away.

She couldn't blend in on the road in her under dress. Even her undergarments were too expensive to pass for a common traveler. They, at least, were less conspicuous than the lace and silk reminder of the life she fled. Even more pressing than wandering the countryside in her corset was the striking shade of her hair. The first morning, when the small fire had burned out, Liz poured precious drinking water onto the ashes and used the paste to stain her brilliant hair dark. The first week, Liz barely thought past the next mile, the next meal; she certainly didn't linger on thoughts of her cowardice or the consequences of it.

Tia hadn't spoken much. Mostly she gave gentle orders, and when they stopped at night, she held Liz when she awoke screaming. They didn't dare draw too near to any village or settlement, regardless of the cold and hunger they suffered. Liz would stay on the edge of the woods, hiding in the dark, as Tia stole or begged for whatever food she managed to scrounge up. If there were too many questions, the girls went hungry. No need to draw attention with the Dragon's own private army combing the nearby settlements searching for her.

The blood moon passed and would not rise again for two winters. If caught, the Dragon would make her pay for her impertinence.

Two days ago, they'd nearly been caught by a band of the Dragon's men, their black armor seeming to swallow the sunlight. Their only choice had been to disappear deep into the trees, far enough that the searching party couldn't find them. With no trails and no discernable landmarks, finding their way back to the edge of civilization had been impossible.

They were lost now, somewhere in the wood. Tia had dark rings beneath her eyes. Liz couldn't bring herself to eat the last of the food when her friend looked so scared. She'd taken so much for granted when she lived at the palace. Footwear, for one. Tia stole a too-large pair of leather boots for her after her impractical sandal succumbed to the snap of a strap and dangled uselessly from her leg for the better part of five miles. The resulting blisters lost them almost half a day.

"No." Liz shook her head, gifting Tia with a shadow of her former smile. "You take the bread. You have greater need than I do."

Tia sighed; relief evident in her expression. She ate slowly enough to savor the simple joy of having a full belly.

"How long until we come to the mountain passes your mother spoke of? We've seen the silhouette of mountains for a while now." Tia's voice was just strained enough to let the hint of her Island accent slip through the vowels and lengthen them. Liz hadn't heard the hint of Tia's past in a long time. It wasn't a good sign. Her Island tongue usually preceded great fits of anger or days of deep exhaustion. Liz worried about the toll the travel had taken on her friend.

"They're still too far away; we'll be in the shadow of those mountains for weeks before we're close enough to be safe." Liz shivered, rubbing her bare arms as goose-flesh rose on her skin, again. "It's getting colder. Do you think winter is already coming?" Liz failed to swallow the lump lodged in her throat. The consequences of running from her destiny were already catching up with her.

"No, that's ridiculous." Tia chided; her words rounded by her mouth full of the last bit of bread. Another cold breeze cut through the thin layers of silk and chiffon of Liz's under dress. At least her breasts were still bound by her corset; she wouldn't be able to stand the travel if she were so exposed, though one more chilly breeze and she'd gladly give it up for some sleeves.

The canteen wasn't full enough to waste any of their water to splash on her face or hands, so instead Liz just spat on her palms and rubbed them on the bottom corner of her skirt. She had never seen her fingernails so rough and broken, grime and dirt caked in thick rings beneath. Liz imagined the tender comfort of her mother's hands brushing through her curls and separating them. It soothed the rough edges of her desperation enough to allow her to settle in for another long night.

They had one wool blanket to share between them. At night they found the softest patch of grass and slept curled together beneath it. Oftentimes, Liz would find herself staring out into the night sky for hours. So many stars were visible here, as opposed to her view from Silver City. She dreamt every night of the knight on the white horse. The dreams mingled with the expression on her mother's face when she begged Liz to run.

Each day that passed, the dream was more urgent. The closer they got to the mountains, the more certain the events of the ensuing battle became. Snow piled thick on the ground, drenched in blood. The mountains bathed in darkness. The faceless knight from her dream seemed to be the key to everything. A battle raged against the Dragon's army; the knight fell, and when he fell so did all of Aegis.

It was clear what her dreams were telling her; that the knight, and not her blood, was the key to saving her kingdom. Instead of running away and hiding like a coward, she needed to find him.

The only notion she had of where he might be, was the mountain range they were traveling towards.

She hadn't been brave enough to confide these dreams to Tia, not when their own fate appeared to be so precarious. She didn't believe Tia would like the idea of Liz searching for the knight, not if it put her own safety at risk. They settled together at the base of a large oak tree, in between large roots that scored the earth around them. It seemed safe here, beneath the gentle owl calls on the night wind. Tia leaned her head against Liz's shoulder, and Liz clutched her tight. They'd always been this way. Leaning on each other silently, holding each other together as naturally as breathing. Liz could not exist in this world severed from Tia. She was an appendage, a second heart, beating in time with her own.

In moments Tia's breathing was soft and even, but Liz couldn't sleep. It was more than being plagued with shame and guilt for running. She missed her mother, yes, but something stirred beneath her sorrow. If she ignored her grief and her fear, ignored the haunting visions she had at night, she sensed something wild bubbling up beneath her skin.

Life.

Two weeks ago, she was supposed to die.

True, she was tired and hungry, a wretched thing not worthy to be a member of the royal family. She'd been taught there was no greater dishonor than to disobey the will of the gods and to abandon her people to starve in a winter without end. But, for the first time in her life, Liz was finally *awake*.

She felt every blade of grass tickling her legs and the warmth of Tia's skin curling around her. She surveyed each individual star in the infinite celestial darkness above and decoded the whispering songs of the trees. For the first time in her life, Liz's fate was in no one's hands but her own.

The morning sun filtered through fog-hazed air, the gentle rush of a nearby river attempting to lull her back to sleep. Liz rubbed the sleep from her eyes. A rustling noise sounded in the bushes behind her, she froze and scanned the foliage surrounding them. Nothing appeared. She shook the sensation of being watched from her shoulders.

"Let's find some breakfast." Tia's wide smile was infectious. She looked better this morning, more resolute. Liz was happy to bask in her brilliance.

"How did I never notice your ravenous appetite before?" Liz asked. She rolled the blanket and secured it to their meager pack, stolen from a farm two days outside the city gates. They took turns carrying it throughout the day, and Liz felt good this morning. Without asking, she pulled it on over her shoulders to take the first shift.

"Princesses have more important things to deal with."

Liz's easy expression fell sharply, worrying her bottom lip with her teeth. She'd spent her entire life dealing with important things. Trying to figure out an alternate interpretation of the prophecy and singing out prayers that she would find a loophole. All of it came to nothing. Instead of outsmarting the gods, she'd been punished by them. Her family was gone, her people doomed. She was a fugitive in the place she'd been ready to die for.

"How are you still so thin?" Liz asked, attempting a light-hearted tone and poking her in the ribs. Tia was slender and whip-like, gracefully so. Liz was curvier, ample bosom and hips that hardly fit into dresses without the constriction of her corset.

Secretly she had always been somewhat jealous of her friend's figure. Tia was able to exude the kind of effortless allure that bewitched knights, courtiers, lords, and kitchen maids alike. Her dark skin made her honey eyes and smile shine all the brighter, her gaze so mysterious it was no wonder that many Royal Guards would trip over themselves when she came near.

"Sheer force of will. For the sake of fashion." She grinned wide again, the action made something warm flutter deep in Liz's chest. Somehow in the midst of all this tragedy, Tia remained unchanged.

The rustling sounded behind Liz again. The smile slipped off of Tia's face and Liz knew by her expression that something was wrong. Liz felt it in her bones, a warning trilling up her spine. Tia opened her mouth, but Liz shook her head. Instead, Liz motioned with her hand to keep talking as though nothing had changed.

She chattered on as Liz listened raptly for anything out of the ordinary. After a few long, tense moments she heard it again. There, on her left, the snapping of a twig. Then what sounded like something large pushing past a low tree branch. They were near a river; it rushed in a cacophonous riot of sound beside them. The rushing river almost drowned out the sound.

Almost.

If it weren't for whatever sensitivity Liz had, niggling a warning in the back of her mind, she never would have noticed it. Tia stared at Liz, widening her eyes, asking wordlessly for an explanation.

"Run," Liz whispered. Tia took off into the brush. Liz bolted in the opposite direction, making as much noise as she could in an attempt to lead them away. Tia had to escape whoever was lurking in the bushes. The Dragon was not a kind or beneficent man. If they were caught, Tia would hang.

Liz wouldn't let it happen.

She *couldn't.*

She stumbled on, her dress catching against the brambles of the bushes. They tore into her arms and clawed at her face. Her legs worked harder, her breath coming in short bursts as her lungs burned with the effort. There was a crashing sound behind her getting closer and closer. Whoever they were, she would never outrun them. Not uphill in a dress wearing ill-fitting boots, at any rate. If she was lucky, she would draw them far enough away to give Tia time to escape unscathed. Her mother's words echoed all around her, repeating every time her heartbeat pounded in her ears.

Promise me... promise me... promise me...

She pushed herself harder, her hands reaching out to grasp at the wet moss on the hill in front of her. When she reached the peak, she vaulted over the other side and darted toward a large oak tree with massive roots that had hollowed out the earth beneath it, shimmying and scurrying until she was so far beneath it that she wouldn't be seen by her pursuers. She pressed her back against the hard-packed soil and stifled her breath with a dirty hand over her mouth and nose. Her chest heaved as a pair of worn black riding boots came into focus near her face.

"Come out yer highness!" The man's voice was deep and cruel. "We've been tracking ye ever since ye came into our forest." She closed her eyes tight against the fear rising in her throat at his nearness, burning like bile.

"Ye know I'll find ye. I promise if ye make it easy, I'll be kind."

Liz thought perhaps she could stay there, buried in the earth, all night if she had to. Eventually he would search somewhere else. He would leave. She just had to wait him out, bide her time. Even if it meant freezing, starving, lying in filth. She'd only just won her freedom; Liz was not prepared to give it away again so soon.

"Fine." His voice boomed around her like thunder, rumbling all the way to her marrow. "If ye will not come out on yer own, my men and I will search ye out. But not before we have some fun with that little *friend* of yers."

At his words, Liz's frantic thoughts ceased. They shocked her back into reality. Of course they'd captured Tia. Of course, there was more than one man after her. Her hand dropped from her mouth. She would have to acquiesce to him. There was rustling and muffled speech. The bottom of Tia's dress and three more pairs of boots came into her field of vision.

"She's a looker alright. It'll be a shame to scar up that pretty face o' hers." One of them grumbled and Liz heard the unsheathing of a blade.

"No!" She scrambled out of her hiding place, curls freed from her plait and falling into her eyes, dirt smeared over what seemed every inch of her. Tia was crying. A dirty, gap-toothed ruffian held her fast with a dagger to her throat.

"Do not touch her! You filthy mongrel, I'll have your hands cut off and your eyes gouged for even thinking about it." Liz spat at the man's feet, daring him to defy the authority in her tone. The man had a knotted scar over one eye that was dead, white, and unseeing.

He smiled at her, a cruel twist of his lips, reaching forward to grip her by her poorly masked red braid. He pulled slowly, forcing her to look on his hideous face as he snapped and one of the other men came forward with a dirty rope. Fear trickled down her spine as her hands were forcefully bound tightly enough that moving them caused her pain, but not moving them made them go numb.

"Willing or not highness, to the Dragon ye'll go."

Chapter Six

Wharton Cove was two days' travel by horse. *Two days.* It was the closest Mat would ever be, and yet the looming phantom of Gareth's presence anchored him in the mud. In the last few weeks, he'd tried to gain Gareth's trust, to ingratiate him among the men he'd brought along enough to lure him into letting his guard down.

Nothing. Worked.

Gareth slept apart, ate apart, trained in the mornings before the sun came up, and hunted alongside Mat when he ventured too far from the lodge. After a fortnight, he'd only said a handful of words to anyone else. When he spoke, it was direct and commanding, no sentimentality or frivolity leaking into the conversation. There'd been no hope of gleaning more information about the crates he'd seen, or slipping out from under his constant supervision to investigate them himself. To describe the man as practical would be putting it lightly.

Mat had been planning to steal away from this excursion and race down to Wharton Cove, returning in a few days' time and claiming he'd been lured too deep into the wood by the tree spirits. There were enough songs and stories about them in the old tales to convince the more superstitious men in their party. The goddess of luck and love didn't favor him this time, however, as Gareth volunteered to come with him. Now, he found himself setting snares and mumbling incoherent prayers that they would soon return.

He kicked the mud off his boots and stood, stretching his back. Though he would never admit it, the country was beautiful this far south. Everything thrummed with life. Soft moss covered the ground. The river rushed past him, and the tree foliage burst in a kaleidoscope of autumn colors as though the harsh winter months rarely touched this place.

Everything here erupted with inexplicable brightness. The chatter of squirrels in the trees and the gleeful tweeting of songbirds wafted on the rustling breeze. Though he didn't want to be in this wood, he would rather be here than at home pining for Mara. He knew he'd made the right decision, though that was hard to remember at night when he missed the feel of her fingers in his hair and her warm curves beneath his hands.

"I know you're up to something," Gareth said, startling Mat out of his musings.

"I don't know what you mean." Mat snorted, shoving past the other man perhaps a little harder than he intended.

Gareth's observation was too close to the truth. His piercing stare unsettled Mat enough to force him into changing tactics. "You seem to be the one keeping secrets. I saw how Lord Callum looked to you in the keep before sending us here. He wanted you out of Fangorn. That's why we're really here. Care to explain why?"

Gareth's silence never bothered Mat before, but he could feel his hatred simmering in the air between them. He narrowed his eyes in Mat's direction.

"Yes, well, it's my business. *Bastard*," he sneered at Mat but dropped the subject nonetheless, not digging too deeply into Mat's own deceit.

"Your business. Got it." Mat gave a mock salute and pulled more wire from one of the saddlebags for another snare. Gareth sneered again, but took the other side of the ridge to set his own snares, both of them glad of the opportunity to distance themselves from each other.

Mat didn't know what to expect should he actually manage to find his father. The uncertainty made it harder to stomach the thought of his friends knowing about his search. What if when he found his father, he was rejected. Or worse, blatantly ignored.

Mat's mother never gave him any indication of who he might be, or why he was no longer in their lives. Anytime he asked her about him, she would change the subject. When he grew older and became more insistent, she showed Mat his signet ring, offering only that it once belonged to the man. As a hotheaded teenager, ready to leave the sleepy hamlet nestled in a quiet mountain town just outside of Fangorn Keep, he insisted she tell him his father's identity or he would leave home and sever himself from her forever. She wept and begged, but wouldn't relent.

So he'd stolen the ring and left that night.

When Mat was very small, he imagined that his father would come home one day as if he'd always belonged there. Little Mat would stare out the windows toward the road, expecting his father to suddenly appear around the bend. Later he imagined his father was a very important man, someone a great lord or nobleman kept bound in service because he was indispensable to the household.

Now, he wondered if his father knew about Mat at all.

Whoever he was, Mat was not of proper enough birth to afford many rights. Not enough to justify ruining Mara's chances of finding a suitable match. He pulled the wire tight to rid himself of the vision of Mara's wide doe eyes in the face of a small child, perhaps her child with a husband who could provide for them. She would do well in a nice townhome, her wild spirit let loose in a city bigger than Fangorn. Mat had run away with his thoughts when Gareth came tumbling over the ridge in a hurry and pulled him down. He struggled for a moment, but the sight of Gareth's wide eyes were a clear warning.

In an instant, Mat was alert and tense, ready for whatever danger lie in wait.

"Wha—"

Gareth clamped a gloved hand over his mouth, eyes wide as he motioned to stay low and follow him. Mat's hand reached for the dagger in his boot, every muscle taut and on edge. If only he'd brought his claymore with him that morning. Fast and silent, they made their way up the hill to peer below. Just as Mat opened his mouth to ask again, Gareth held up a single silencing finger, pointing to the scene unfolding below them. Immediately he knew what had garnered such a response from him.

A woman.

A *beautiful* woman.

She was of noble birth, as evidenced by her tattered silk dress; the fabric too rich for a peasant by far. Even torn and dirty, he could tell at a distance that she was not of common stock; it was something about the defiant way she held her chin. She was probably the most beautiful woman he had ever seen. In fact, the sight of her in distress had somehow knocked the air from his lungs.

She was being dragged, hands bound, behind a mountain of a man with a scar over one eye. A bounty hunter, or worse, an Eastern slaver who had wandered too far from the shore he pillaged and found a beautiful prize to steal away to market across the stormy seas. Her captor snarled and yanked on the dirty rope binding her hands. She stumbled forward, and he laughed as she fell to her knees in the mud. Mat's jaw clenched as his mind whirred with the possibilities of rescue attempts, running through dozens of schemes. She smeared the dirt splashed onto her face with her bound hands, spreading it over her cheek.

At first, Mat thought she'd started crying. Her shoulders shook, and her dirty face was turned away. Then, a sudden southern wind carried her musical laughter to him. Tinkling and haughty, the sound forced a shiver down his spine. The bounty hunter snarled and the woman leapt, drawing blood down his cheek with her nails before he backhanded her roughly to the ground.

The sound of his blow thudded loudly enough to carry over the howling wind. Mat forced himself to breathe slowly and think clearly, the wind quieted and a plan formed in his mind. They had to do something. He couldn't watch this anymore. They were close enough to the river that the thunderous applause of the rushing titan would mask Mat's voice from the people below.

"If you draw them away, I can take the man holding her and help them escape."

Gareth's eyebrows rose in disbelief. "How in the bloody afterworld do you expect me to draw them away?" Gareth's fist clenched at his side annoying Mat to no end.

"You're good at making people want to punch you. Just do that." Mat rolled his eyes as Gareth nodded solemnly. He turned on his heel and, muttering something that sounded suspiciously like cursing under his breath, made off to create some kind of distraction. Knowing what little he did of Gareth, he didn't imagine it wouldn't be subtle.

Mat turned his eyes back to the prisoner, transfixed by her every movement. He had never seen a woman like her before. She was stunning. Her hair was dirty and dark, tied into a plait behind her except for a few wild curls that had come loose and stuck to her face. Her intelligent blue eyes were bright and wide with, not fear, but anger. Righteous anger. It was then he realized she was standing protectively in front of another woman. The second woman seemed smaller somehow, nearly folded in half and cowering behind the fearsome woman.

"You'll pay for that!"

Her voice was bewitching and musical; the wind slowed and the howl seemed to echo the tone of her ire. Mat grinned once he understood. She wielded her anger as a weapon, to protect the woman behind her, drawing their focus. The four men circled around them, and suddenly a shout echoed through the space. Gareth appeared over the ridge; hands cupped around his mouth as he caught their attention.

"Oi! Tree bangers! You sons of witches can only get women you abduct? Of course! Look at those ugly mugs. Faces only a mother could love."

Mat bit down on his glove to suppress a hysterical giggle. Tree bangers?

"Kill him." The bounty hunter scowled deeper than before, the white scar stretching taut for a gruesome moment. The others followed Gareth as he darted over the hill. The bounty hunter yanked hard on the woman's bindings, just as another man came up behind her and pulled the smaller woman away. She let out a blood curdling scream as she was wrenched away. The noble woman bared her teeth and threatened them all, much to their amusement.

"Our orders may keep you safe, but your little friend is fair game."

Mat saw his opportunity to strike as one of the horses broke free and the last of the bounty hunter's men took off after it. The small woman was tossed unceremoniously away, stumbling she fell into the rushing water and struggled to stay afloat and not get swept away.

"Tia!"

Mat leapt from his hiding place and with long strides found himself face to face with the screaming woman in seconds. "Hi there," he said, grinning as the scar-eyed man lumbered towards him menacingly. "Hello, big guy. How about we settle this like gentlemen?" Mat ducked and barely missed a fist whizzing by his ear. "Or not." Mat landed a blow to the man's stomach, which had no effect. He tried again, this time bringing his fist down hard against the man's jaw. Again, nothing. A trickle of black blood dripped from the corner of his mouth. The grin slipped off Mat's face as he realized he might actually be in trouble.

"Gods be damned! You're a half-blood?" Mat unsheathed his dagger then, knowing he wouldn't be able to beat the man in a fair fight. Not when he had magick running through his veins making him impossibly strong.

With a roar, the bounty hunter swung at him, refusing to let go of the bindings holding his prisoner. Ducking, Mat struck swiftly, burying his dagger deep into the man's thigh. It stuck there, and with a howl, he dropped the rope. Mat wrapped an arm around her waist, hauling her away from the fallen bounty hunter, now clutching his leg. She clawed at him as he pulled her further away from danger; he ignored her protests to drop his arm from around her waist. She did not relent, her nails drawing blood.

"Don't touch me. Tia! I can't leave her." She flailed and kicked at his shins, but he wouldn't budge. He couldn't see the other woman. She had surely been swept away by the froth of the river, the current too strong to resist for long.

"Don't touch me!"

Her wailing was going to do nothing but attract unwanted attention from the half-blood's friends, and they weren't yet a far enough distance to outpace them, especially not with her twisting and jerking like a wet cat. He brought his other hand up to cover her mouth; she slapped it away, so he covered her mouth again, holding tight to keep her screams muffled against his palm.

Beautiful, for sure, but definitely not worth the trouble.

Chapter Seven

Liz fought hard against the hunter pulling her farther from where Tia disappeared into the water. She'd lost everyone else; Liz wouldn't survive if she lost Tia too. As he tried to silence her with a hand over her mouth, her panic flared bright. As soon as his skin clamped down over hers, she would see things she didn't want to see. There was a vibration in the air, like a subtle harmonizing in the wind, the mists tugging against her mind. The threads of fate circled around the two of them, strong as steel bands, tightening around every inch of their struggling forms.

She sensed the threads in the electricity humming through her blood and shooting down her spine, setting every inch of her on fire. There was something unnatural about him, a discordant tone that terrified Liz. This was different and intense, a thrumming that threatened to shake her into pieces, a warning of what she would see when he touched her. His hand came down hard over her mouth anyway, his strength making a mockery of her struggles. The friction of his skin on hers sent her immediately to the place she dreaded, her eyes glassed over as the mist swirled against her skin and the snow chilled her.

Wordless screams and the clanging of steel against steel rang through the distant howling of a strong winter wind. She was here again, on the same battlefield with the white knight. This time she saw the battle through his eyes, from atop his white stallion. His hand gripped a large sword, swinging it confidently in a circular motion as he guided his steed through the writhing mass of men below.

With a swing of his arm, he beheaded a man. Another he trampled, and on and on and on, mindlessly. Disgust and horror thrashed in the pit of her stomach. So much death, so much blood. The violent throng surrounding her seemed to breathe. Sometimes there were more of the Dragon's soldiers desperate to kill her, and other times they beat back the tide. All the men had dead eyes, all of them merciless and killing each other. Until finally the general pointed out the man on the white horse, his command echoing out over the battlefield as he locked hateful black eyes on her.

Things became more jumbled, as she lost control of her sword hand. Hands reached for her from every direction, pulling at her and dragging her down, down, down. Her armor kept her too heavy to escape from them. Blades slipped in between her ribs and at the crook of her neck. Her thighs, her arms, her chest, nowhere was safe from the sting of them until the last of her warmth seemed to seep into the snow around her. Forcing her eyes down, she couldn't unsee the damage done. The snow was stained dark with her heart's blood. On her hand was a gold signet ring bearing a familiar sigil. An old sigil she'd seen in passing during her studies in the royal library. She couldn't remember its significance, but recalled it all the same.

As the mist faded from her eyes, she recognized the man who saved her staring at her with clear expectations. His handsome face could make a woman forget herself, most assuredly. She could imagine herself running her fingertips over the stubble on his strong, angular jaw. His lips were sculpted and his hair a golden mane drawing perfect attention to the clearest green eyes she'd ever seen.

"Oi! Did you hear me?" He waved a hand in front of her face in a frustratedly impertinent manner.

"What?" She pushed his hand away and frowned.

"I told you to get on the bloody horse."

He dragged her over a small hill towards a stocky work pony tied to a thin birch tree. She attempted to pull out of her tight bindings to no avail and scoffed at him in disbelief.

"I most certainly will not," she stated matter-of-factly. He stared at her for a moment before crossing his arms and narrowing his eyes.

"What do you mean you will not?"

"I won't leave Tia behind. You can't make me.," She wouldn't abandon her friend. Instead she dug her heels into the soft mud, refusing to leave.

"If you don't climb on this horse, I will tie you to it like a sack of potatoes." He used his hands to demonstrate his point, as if she were too stupid to understand him. When her resolved expression didn't change, he sighed, pinching the bridge of his nose before squaring off against her.

"We don't have time for this. The others will come back soon, and if they find you, I won't be able to help you escape again. So, climb on the horse, or I swear I will leave you to those men and I won't look back." He was serious, and as much as she didn't want to leave Tia, she couldn't be left to the bounty hunters. She couldn't be returned to the Dragon.

"Fine, but untie me first," she spat, brandishing her still-bound hands for him to see. Before she could protest, he hauled her over his shoulder and slung her across the back of his horse.

"How dare you! I was doing as you asked, you stupid—" She huffed dramatically, not daring to kick or squirm too much in case she spooked the horse beneath her.

"I left my dagger in your captor's thigh. No way to untie you yet." He mounted the horse and gripped her by the back of her corset to keep her from tumbling off as he began to ride. Every step knocked the wind out of her and made it hard for her to speak, which surely, he knew. He might have saved her from the bounty hunters, but he was no hero.

"I hate you!" she screeched out between breaths, though she regretted it. With the wind driven from her lungs, the clopping of the horse's hooves crushed her own weight painfully against her ribs. Without breath she couldn't even protest or groan.

"You're welcome, by the way. For saving your life," The man responded. She grimaced, unable to curse him again. Shouts came from behind them, and Liz craned her head to see what was happening. Two of the bounty hunters, one with an ominous black stain on his thigh where her kidnapper stabbed him, were running faster than any man she'd ever seen before, fast enough to overtake their horse.

"Hurry!" she shouted between clenched teeth. She felt the man dig his heels into the pony, and the wind whistled around them as they picked up speed. The bounty hunters gained on them so rapidly that she could stare into their eyes, reptilian and cold; blackness swallowed the whites of their eyes and crept down the veins of their cheeks.

The pony found its footing, and in moments they left the crazed men behind. The hunter didn't slow their mount for a long time. Low-hanging branches tore her clothes and hair. When he did slow, Liz tried to raise her head and shake the curls from her eyes to take in her surroundings. She had no idea how far they'd ridden or even in what direction. How would she find her way back to Tia?

Wherever they were, there was a meager camp and a fire that had burned down to nothing. The man swung his leg over the horse and dropped down fluidly, holding loosely to the pony's reins. His eyes flicked through the trees, as though looking for something or someone who wasn't there. Liz slid carefully off the horse and onto her feet while he was distracted, taking long slow breaths until her ribs felt less bruised.

He turned to her with a scowl, and Liz remembered the way the bounty hunters spoke about Tia. *Your little friend is fair game.* Liz wasn't a princess here; maybe she wasn't a princess anywhere anymore. Every person in Aegis, save Tia, now posed a threat to her. Should this man discover who she is or that she'd fled the sacrifice, he may want to revenge himself upon her. She shuddered, her fear crawling up her throat. When her rescuer took a step toward her, she hurtled down the path, her bound hands stretched in front of her as she crashed through the underbrush in a frenzy.

He swore, his voice so near to her back that she yelped. Before she could do anything else, he yanked her elbow hard enough to force her off balance. They tumbled in a painful heap of flailing limbs, elbows and shoulders colliding with softer parts as they slid down a steep embankment. They slid to a stop at the base of the hill, and he settled his weight on top of her.

Liz clawed at him, aiming for his eyes and neck, her legs kicking uselessly beneath him. Her nails found purchase against his skin, and he hissed. Small rivulets of red stained the collar of his shirt before he pinned her still bound wrists hard against the ground above her head.

"Gods be damned, woman!" he swore, unable to catch his breath as he stared furiously down at her. "That's the last time I try to help a bloody stranger."

"I didn't need your help."

"Well, if you don't shut your gob and stop screaming, then every half-blood for miles will be bearing down on us. I'd like to see how you'd fare then." He scanned the surrounding area, his green eyes glinting against the afternoon light. It was a look she was familiar with; the Royal Guards often had the same hawkish expression on watch. Assessing the area for threats.

"Get off of me," she said in a quieter tone. He looked down at her then, his eyes widening and a flush creeping up his neck to his cheeks. He scrambled off of her and cleared his throat, cautious to look only at her eyes. Liz sucked in a sharp breath; she'd forgotten in all the excitement that she was in her corset and underdress. She pulled her knees tight against her body to make herself small.

"My..." He cleared his throat again. "My apologies, M'lady. I hadn't realized you were... that you weren't wearing..." He shook his head, eyebrows furrowing deeply on his face. "Nevertheless, we need to find my companion and leave this area."

Liz tried to protest, but he pulled her up to her feet by her bound hands and began dragging her back up the hill behind him without another word or glance in her direction. She slid and whimpered at the wrenching pain in her wrists as the ropes rubbed her skin raw beneath them.

It was only a few minutes before they stopped. She stumbled at the sudden change of pace and fell straight onto her bottom with an undignified "oof."

They weren't alone.

A dark-haired man stood vigilant at the makeshift camp. Her smarmy rescuer crossed to him, speaking in low tones. The stark difference between the two men puzzled her. While her rescuer wore plain clothes and leather pauldrons, accentuating strong shoulders like those of a farmer or blacksmith; his companion couldn't have been more different. He stood a head taller in armor she did not recognize. There was an arrogant tilt to his chin and a rigidness to his gait that was all too familiar. What would a knight or nobleman be doing in the woods with a commoner?

He turned to fix bright eyes on her and suddenly Liz was jarred into an otherworldly awareness. The feelings and visions Liz experienced were a secret, one that only she and Tia shared. She didn't know how it worked, but she was sure this other man was just as tied to her fate as the one before. Who were these men? Her hands trembled at the confirmation that her visions and feelings were right. That meant, more death was coming.

Movement from behind his shoulder caught her eye and Liz nearly fell over in her attempt to jump up from the ground. *Tia.* There she was, soaking wet but thankfully alive. The dark-haired man with the austere expression also looked wet. Had he saved Tia from drowning after she'd been tossed into the current?

"Tia!" Liz wailed, holding her bound hands out to her friend who rushed forward and wrapped her arms tightly around her shoulders. Hot tears welled in her eyes. Liz's brutish savior scoffed at her tears, and to her great embarrassment, she wept all the more.

"Why are her hands still bound?" Tia asked, looking over her shoulder to the wet, exacting man. Both men shared a questioning glance, and Liz's rescuer sighed, offering a nonchalant shrug.

"Trust me, it's better that way," he grumbled under his breath, putting a hand to the streaks of red on his neck where her nails scored his skin. She huffed in response, infuriated at his arrogance.

"You will unbind her, at once." Tia demanded; her expression unyielding. Liz tried to contain her emotions but she felt shaken. She thought she'd lost Tia, but she was here. She was *here*. The well of her sorrow cracked open wide; her bottom lip quivered and her eyes grew hot. Her breathing came hard as she tried and failed to stop the wave of sadness enveloping her.

The man who'd saved her pulled a sword from the saddle of his friend's horse and reached out to her. She recoiled, tears tumbling down her cheeks, afraid of what visions his touch might show her this time. He reached forward again, more slowly and intentionally this time, but she stumbled back a few paces to evade him.

"I'm not going to hurt you," he said, his green eyes no longer bright with anger or mischief, but dulled with concern.

"I'm not going to give you the opportunity to try," she retorted spitefully, keeping her bound hands clutched to her chest.

He sighed, running a frustrated hand through his hair before squaring off against her again. He changed directions faster than she anticipated, and his hand gripped one of hers. He pulled her toward him until she hurtled into his chest. There were no visions, just the warmth of his skin. She sniffled, pushing her arms against the steel wall of him to brandish her hands.

He made quick work of the rope, and as it fell away, her cold fingers began to prick with feeling again. She rubbed the raw, bruised skin of her wrists and mopped at the tears on her cheeks.

"That wasn't so bad, was it?" he asked, the playful spark back in his eyes. She narrowed her gaze at him.

"Matioch, we should leave the area before the half-bloods return. I don't think their horse bolted too far."

Liz deferred to Tia, who was staring at the dark-haired man with ...*Matioch*. Tia had to be wondering the same thing Liz was. What happened now?

Nodding sharply, the infuriating man threw his leg over his horse and settled in his saddle. He looked down, holding a hand out to Liz as if she should know what the gesture meant. She raised a questioning eyebrow at him.

"Are you coming?" he asked.

As insufferable and confusing as she found this man to be, he'd rescued her once already. Although she didn't want to admit it, she felt a tenuous safety with him. She shuddered as she thought about the bounty hunters roaming the woods for her with their reptilian gazes, bearing down on them with superhuman speed. They were still out there, ready to bring her back to the Dragon in chains.

Her rescuer, Matioch, grinned at her with that same crooked grin from before, and she knew he was thinking of how she had been slung over the back of his horse. She pushed an errant curl away from her face and placed her dirty hand daintily in his calloused paw. Before he could pull her up, her eyes fell to the ring on his finger. The blood drained from her face as she recognized the gold signet ring. Stamped with the familiar yet elusive sigil of a black thistle. The same ring she'd seen on the knight's hand in her vision.

In one smooth motion, he settled her, somewhat inappropriately, on the front of the horse with his arms wrapped too familiarly around her shoulders. He clucked his tongue, and Liz clutched the saddle horn to keep her balance as they began to ride. A chill in the air breezed against her skin, and she wondered how long until the snow would stick to the ground. If her visions came true, winter would approach quickly and harshly this year.

When it did, this man, Matioch, was going to die.

Chapter Eight

A disgraced mistress? Kidnapping victim? Runaway bride? The possibilities seemed endless and the longer they rode the more outlandish Mat's theories became. They didn't speak, and the absence of conversation forced his focus onto every small detail before him. Her skin was cold when their arms brushed, so she hadn't discarded her dress out of discomfort. Had she been hurt?

The woman seemed frail pressed against Mat on the horse. She hadn't seemed frail at all when she was shredding him to ribbons earlier. He'd kept his arms wrapped tightly around her as he gripped the reins. As they closed in on the mountain range, the paths became steeper, more dangerous. He'd noticed her swaying on her feet earlier and didn't want her pitching off the side of the saddle unexpectedly. She hadn't spoken to him once since they'd set off. He didn't know what caused the change in her demeanor, but he knew better than to ask.

Obviously, the women had been through a traumatic experience. Mat couldn't leave them in the wilderness unaccompanied again, although he was at a loss about what to do with them now. They hadn't completed the task Lord Callum assigned them, and they couldn't leave the other men alone with half-bloods so close nearby. Until he could think of something better, he and Gareth were heading back to the lodge to regroup. A knight would know what to do. If he wished to be one, he should take this opportunity to prove he could handle the responsibility.

He glanced over at Gareth, astride his own horse with the other woman clinging to him from behind, her knuckles bleached white from the force of her grip. They would need to stop soon so the two of them could dry off. Or at least, build a fire so the poor girl could stop shaking and shivering. Mat was impressed she had the fortitude to keep her seat for this long.

"We'll stop over that ridge and build a fire." He pointed, and Gareth nodded in response. The woman tensed in front of him, her shoulders stiff and unyielding.

"Unless you want your friend to freeze to death," he muttered in her ear quietly.

"Is that a threat?" she asked in a low hiss, and Mat jerked involuntarily.

"Of course not," he said, shaking off the accusation. "Just an observation."

She turned to face her friend, and he felt her relax against him. Something dark churned in the pit of Mat's stomach at her reaction. He didn't like how easy it was for the women to think the worst of them. It meant they had been shown too much cruelty and not enough care. Mat would make sure they felt safe again, somehow. Too soon, she twisted in front of him to dismount.

"Wait," Mat said.

She stopped moving as he swung his legs to the ground and reached up to grip her around the waist. She recoiled from his touch as he picked her up and lifted her down onto solid footing.

"The path is steep here," he said in explanation, searching her eyes for some clue as to her identity.

They revealed nothing.

She turned from him to meet her friend as Gareth tied the horses off against a young sapling in the glade.

"What is your full name, sir knight?"

Her question surprised him as it rolled off her tongue in a clear southern accent. Too proper, too formal, less of a brogue than he was accustomed to hearing from the simple folk up north. Did she come from the royal court? The southern palace was leagues away. Too far for a noblewoman to risk traveling on foot. Then again, she was only in her underclothes; perhaps she was a courtesan.

There was no knight among them. Just a bladesmith and a soldier. Before he could correct her, Gareth laughed derisively. Mat glared at him, watching as the man pulled an apple out of a saddle bag and plunged his hunting knife into the ripe flesh.

"Him, a knight? Hilarious." Gareth grinned wickedly, as Mat squirmed under his arrogant scrutiny. The woman looked between them with those bright, blue eyes. They were so clear and piercing Mat swore she saw right through him, right into the places he kept hidden. He'd never felt more unnerved than he did under her intense study.

"What, pray tell, is so funny about it?" she asked, her tone suggesting Gareth had been laughing at her. Mat couldn't help the satisfaction warming his chest as Gareth squirmed beneath her ire. The man opened his mouth to explain, but no words came out. Gareth was infinitely more bearable when robbed of his ability to speak.

"He means because I'm bastard-born, M'lady," Mat told her with a grin, glad to have the upper hand back. He struck the flint again, and the tiny spark became a flame. Soon enough, a small fire grew. Meager, but warm enough for Gareth and the lady's friend to keep the chill at bay until they could dry off.

"Not M'lady. Liz." His eyes widened as she offered her name. He couldn't call her by her given name. It was too familiar. Too casual to be allowed by the rules of society.

"Elisabetta." Her nose wrinkled in disgust. "Most people call me Lisbet, but I would like it if you called me Liz. You have stabbed a man, rescued my friend, and delivered us from danger. I think we may have gotten off on the wrong foot, so to speak." She sat, very straight and still, right there in the dirt next to him. Once seated, she fidgeted with the way her skirt lay about her legs. Surprisingly she wasn't glaring at him. He wondered what she'd been thinking about during the ride that had softened her temper toward him.

"Matioch Steele, soon to be a soldier in the legion at Fangorn Keep. You may call me Mat, if it pleases you." He gave a short bow of his head, and she gifted him with a smile. Small as it was, suddenly he couldn't breathe. He coughed to cover the sudden awkward shifting of air in his throat. She shivered, and he pulled his worn, wool cloak from his shoulders and wrapped it around her. At least it could lend some warmth and preserve her modesty. He realized now, watching her wide eyes as he fastened it around her neck, the lines of propriety had blurred into near nothingness.

He touched her too often, too familiarly, and used her given name as if they were equals. Some married couples did not speak to each other so casually. Gareth's eyes burned dark across the fire at them.

Mat cleared his throat and sat back, creating some distance between them. "It isn't much."

"It's more kindness than I've been shown in far too long." Her eyes were suddenly so lonely. She twisted a strand of her hair between two fingers in deep concentration. The curl left behind dark stains on her skin. His eyes flicked over her hairline and caught the glint of copper hidden near her left ear. Mat's heart hammered in his chest and he schooled his features into a bland expression. A southern accent, fine clothes, half-blood bounty hunters, and copper hair? His outlandish theories were getting the better of him, surely.

"You have something in your hair," he muttered, reaching up and plucking a stray burr from the mess of coils knotted beyond repair in long strands. Her moonlight pale skin flushed pink, visible even in the shadows of the tree canopy. She opened her mouth slightly, a question on the tip of her tongue. Her eyes, now soft and liquescent, raised to his face briefly. She bit her bottom lip, and Mat felt a grin curl onto his lips as he watched her struggle not to ask.

"If you're a—" She stopped and his grin deepened as he noticed her frustration mounting. "What I mean to say is, if you don't have a—" She bit the words back abruptly, her lofty manners shackling her curiosity.

"Bastard. You can say it. It no longer offends me as it did when I was young. Ask what you'd like." His words came out in a rush, on a hot chuckle as her brow furrowed in irritation at his teasing.

"Well, I thought *bastards* had no surnames, but you do. Where did 'Steele' come from?" she asked.

He leaned back against the base of a tree, scratching the back of his neck sheepishly. "My mother. Her father was a blacksmith, and common folk are often named for their trades. Once I accept my commission I suppose 'Steele' will have another meaning." He eyed the simple hilt of the sword strapped to his belt. "Though, it isn't *proper* for a lady to know such things, is it?"

She had the most adorable wrinkle between her brows when she became annoyed. It enticed him to keep teasing her.

"I know quite a bit more than you might think," she retorted sharply, the tenuous peace stretching thin between them. Mat plucked a blade of grass and chewed it casually.

"Oh?" he challenged softly. "What does a lady know of commoners suffering?"

Her eyes grew dark and she turned away from him. "Enough."

The word was imbued with fathomless sorrow. It hung in the air between them for long, silent moments until Mat knew without a doubt that he was a complete jackass. He thought she would leave, but instead she took a steadying breath.

"What do you plan to do with us?" Her clear blue eyes sharpened into shards of ice.

The grin slipped off his mouth. "How did the two of you come to be in the woods, with those men?"

"You haven't heard?"

Mat shook his head. She pulled the cloak tighter against her throat, as if it could protect her from whatever secret was hiding away inside of her.

"The... princess escaped from the Dragon before the blood moon ceremony. His men have been hunting her, and anyone he thinks may be helping her." Every muscle in Mat's body tightened. The ritual to bring magick back to Aegis hadn't been completed. That meant winter would be upon them soon, and when it came, death would surely follow.

"The king is dead, and the Dragon is ravaging the kingdom unchallenged. Or at least, that has been the consensus at every town we passed through." The breath left Mat's body in a whoosh; a buzzing echoed flatly in his ears.

If she was telling the truth, then they needed to return to Fangorn Keep as quickly as possible. For the first time in recent history, the legion could be summoned to battle; he could be called to aid in the coming fight. This could be the first time in more than a lifetime that Aegis fought an open war. With no king, and the blood moon ceremony incomplete, there was a power vacuum and any Lord may gather arms to try and claim it.

"What of the queen?" he asked, his eyes far away as he waited for any details the girl could give.

"I don't know."

Liz had tears in her voice. Mat refocused on her and the others across the fire from them. Gareth and Liz's friend were both wide-eyed and unblinking at the turn of conversation. Mat clasped his hands together in front of him, rubbing his ring across the bottom of his chin. The repetitive motion helped him organize his wayward thoughts.

What would a knight do?

A knight would be bound by the codes. Codes of honor, chivalry, and above all else loyalty to the crown. But who will be wearing it? He pressed the heels of his hands against his eyes, the

muscles in his jaw working as he clenched and released his teeth. *Gods be damned.*

"Where were the two of you headed?" he asked, his brow furrowed as he thought over the consequences of the choices before him.

"North. As far north as we could get before winter descends."

Smart. She was buying herself time, that fact if nothing else confirmed his suspicions about her. Everyone knew during winter the far-north regions became isolated from the rest of the kingdom. The mountain paths became inaccessible, cut off from the rest of the country until the thaw came in the spring. She would not have the same luxuries up north as she would in the southern palace, but she would remain safe.

"You'll come with us, then," he said, clapping his hands against his thighs as he made up his mind.

"Mat—" Gareth interrupted, but Mat didn't acknowledge him.

"We're headed to a hunting lodge to get the rest of our party, and then we'll travel on to Fangorn Keep. You'll be safe there once the winter blizzards descend on the mountains." Liz's eyes no longer appeared empty and lonely. There was something in them that made the pit in Mat's stomach shrink. Something warm and wonderful; hope, he imagined.

"Matioch, you can't speak for Lord Callum. He wouldn't approve of you—"

Mat held up a hand to silence Gareth; ignoring him had become quite the talent.

"You're obviously a woman of noble birth, and as such, if you are seeking sanctuary, it is my duty to help you find it." Mat unsheathed his sword and lowered himself to one knee in front of her. He placed his sword before him, bowing his head.

"I give you the protection of my sword, and if necessary, my body. I vow to you, Lisbet, I will do all I can to see you safely to Fangorn Keep. I make this vow on the old codes."

Liz put her dainty hand against his cheek. "I can't ask this of you. You don't even know me."

Her friend whispered something under her breath, but Mat could only focus on the place where her hand rested on his skin. He was aware of the heat between them, the softness of her touch, each individual point of contact acted as a tether between them.

"You don't need to ask. Bastard or not, I'm not the kind of man who could leave you in the wilderness alone. If I cannot leave you, then, it's only proper we make things clear between us. I will deliver you to Fangorn Keep. From there you may do as you wish."

The Red Princess considered his words before nodding with a solemnity that would have given her away if the shade of her hair hadn't already.

"Call me Liz," she said again, as she removed her hand leaving him strangely cold. He rose and walked to the horses to gain some distance and perspective. He was transfixed by this woman. From the moment he'd laid eyes on her dirty, furious face he knew he was in trouble.

He thought of Mara. He should have said goodbye to her, should have explained things. It wasn't fair of him to leave her without a word. In truth, he was afraid she would somehow talk him out of leaving altogether.

Gareth followed Mat over to where they'd tied up the horses, silent fury etched in the set of his shoulders. He leaned against the tree he'd tied the horses to and glanced back at the fire.

"You're an idiot, you know that?"

"Funny, coming from you."

"You're going to get us all killed." Gareth's eyes remained on the women huddled together near the fire. Liz's friend gazed at him adoringly through her eyelashes, a clear invitation.

"You seem to have caught her attention," Mat responded, hoping to change the subject.

"Tia? Yeah, she's just grateful I plucked her out of the river. It'll pass. We need to discuss the foolhardy vow you just made and how Lord Callum is going to flay you until you have no skin left on your back. You'll be forcing him to choose a side."

"I'm going to get more than a commission when we make it back to the keep. I'm going to earn a knighthood."

Gareth's eyebrows rose in shock and he barked out a sharp, cynical laugh.

"You're mad," Gareth said, running a hand incredulously down his face. Mat tossed him the burr he'd pulled from Liz's hair. He caught it easily, more confused than before. Mat held up his hand, fingers smeared with black smudges.

"She's the Red Princess, and I'm going to deliver her to Lord Callum. Either she'll be grateful enough for our help that she'll bestow a knighthood on me, or Lord Callum will trade her to the Dragon and *he'll* be grateful enough to bestow a knighthood on me. Either way, we'll both be hailed as heroes of Aegis." Mat couldn't help but take pleasure in the emotions flitting rapidly over Gareth's normally apathetic face. Shock. Anger. Envy. Mat relished them all. His expression faded into stony silence, completely unreadable.

"It's not a very knight-like plan, bastard." Gareth said after quiet contemplation.

"Knights are above all loyal to the crown. How do you stay loyal to a crown when you don't know on whose head it will rest?" Mat asked.

"What until we get back?" he asked, bracing himself with a steadying breath.

"Until then, we keep them safe from outside threats. Bounty hunters, the Dragon's army, civilians who'll be tempted to turn her over. We get them to Fangorn."

Gareth nodded, his eyes straying back to where Tia whispered conspiratorially in Liz's ear. In response, a devilish smile flashed across Liz's face before she could stamp it down.

"We can't tell the others about her when we get to the lodge," Gareth said.

Mat nodded. It seemed, for once, he and Gareth landed on the same side of things.

"They'll figure it out, eventually," Mat said, a stone of guilt heavy in his stomach. Gareth's eyes darkened, and Mat understood what he refused to say out loud. There was no going back once this decision was made. They would protect the women even against their friends if need be.

"We'll deal with it when the time comes." Gareth's voice was deep with ominous intent. One fact remained true; she was alive. Alive meant suffering and death, and Mat had gone hungry enough times to know if he didn't do something drastic, he was dead anyway. So, whether they were hailed as heroes or hung as traitors, Mat had nothing left to lose.

Chapter Nine

As night fell, Liz realized she'd misjudged Mat and his friend, Gareth. Bastard-born or not, Mat had more honor than some knights and nobles she knew from court. Tia whispered to her about Gareth's daring rescue, how he selflessly dove into the rushing waters and dragged her out of the murky froth. He'd held her tightly in his strong arms, carrying her without any effort. She told Liz about how Gareth put his lips over hers and breathed life back into her.

"What did you see? Before he brought you back," Liz asked in morbid fascination. "Did you see the Halls of the gods? Did you hear the songs?" Tia shook her head, her midnight curls bouncing merrily around her face.

"Nothing. Just darkness and burning." Her eyes were far away and shadowed. Liz didn't like the dullness of her amber gaze and gripped her hand tight until her irreverent smile returned.

"Gareth is absolutely *delicious*," she whispered wickedly, her tongue running over her teeth briefly.

"Gods, help him please." Liz entreated laughingly to the sky as Tia smacked her shoulder good naturedly.

"He should be so lucky. I have it on good authority that being the object of my affection is a treasure for the ages." She waggled her eyebrows, and Liz felt her answering smile reach all the way to her eyes for the first time in too long.

Liz wanted to know how it felt to have a man's lips on her own, though she didn't dare ask. Tia would never let her live it down. There were many things Liz could endure, but Tia's relentless teasing might just break her. Tia continued to moon over Gareth, her eyes following him around the camp and smiling anytime he acknowledged her. Mat kept watch. There was no opportunity for Liz to speak with him again until the fire burned down to nothing more than glowing embers. She sat, shivering, as Tia wrapped herself in the saddle blankets Gareth offered them.

Gareth slept hard, emitting a rather grating sound that could've awoken the dead. Liz curled her knees up to her chest and stared at the stars she could make out through the foliage above.

"The divine twins." Mat's voice was low in her ear. It startled her out of her deep reverie. When did he come so near? He sat down next to her, his skin radiating heat that warmed her through the wool cloak he'd gifted her earlier. It acted as armor, shielding her from more than the chill in the air and prying eyes. It was a barrier against all the things she didn't want to let in. Her mother's bloody hands flashed in her mind before she could shake the thoughts away.

"Her bow and his cloak, see?" He pointed up at a constellation. She didn't follow his gaze; instead her eyes lingered on his face. She'd never met anyone like Mat before. She wouldn't have been allowed to meet anyone like him while at court. Even if she hadn't been betrothed to the Dragon since birth, princesses didn't often ride with bastards in the woods.

"Hak'ka's staff is just there if you look closely." She pointed without even looking in the direction of the constellation. He looked at her through the corner of his eye, the shadow of a sheepish smile fading as he found the stars.

"Huh. I've never seen that one before. You know a lot about the stars," he said with a hint of incredulity. She wasn't unaccustomed to being underestimated, but Mat's assumptions weren't malicious and she found that it amused her to no end.

"You don't have to sound so surprised. I studied the celestial bodies and events in Silver City." He leaned back against a tree trunk, far enough that he could see a large expanse of the sky unencumbered by the canopy above.

"Alright, show me," he said, the challenge clearly reflected in his eyes.

"Okay.," She tucked an errant lock of hair behind her ear and scooted along the ground until she was leaning back next to him, staring up at the same stars. Licking her lips, her eyes passed over familiar constellations. "You mentioned the divine twins?"

He rolled his head to the side to lock eyes on her face, impatient already.

"You're stalling." He rolled his head forward to gaze above them once more.

"So, the divine twins, Eamon and Isolt, God of the Mountain and Goddess of the Hunt were born when a star exploded." He made a sound that was a strange combination of a grunt and an exclamation of surprise. Liz grabbed his hand in frustration and directed his pointer finger across the sky in a wave-like pattern where a dark purple shape stained the heavens. She ended the forced motion to point directly at a star that was larger and redder than the others surrounding it. "This is where they fell from the heavens, and this is the mother star."

"That can't be the mother star, it exploded," he said, confused.

"What we see now is an echo of the past. The mother star has been dead for millennia, but her light is only reaching us now."

Mat sat up; his eyes fixated on the star. Their hands fell away; the unguarded expression on his face as he looked up made him appear younger than he was. She sat up beside him and wondered if he was thinking about someone he'd lost. Liz thought of her mother. She would have been horrified to see her cavorting with a bastard-born soldier half naked in the woods. This was definitely not what her mother would have expected by Liz promising to live a full life.

What made she and Mat so different? They were both slaves to the circumstances of their births. If she had been born without a father, like Mat, where would she be now? Not running for her life in an underdress, for certain.

Looking at Mat now, completely without obligation, she realized she envied his inherent freedom. He didn't realize how lucky he was to have been born a bastard, without the expectations of a family or kingdom to weigh him down. Sometimes Liz thought she could drown beneath it all. Running for her life these last few weeks had been the first time she could finally breathe freely.

"Have you ever loved a woman?" she asked, watching as his startled eyes fell from the stars and a crooked grin twisted onto his lips. "That's not polite to discuss, is it?" The heat built in her cheeks, and she was grateful the fire was dying, the light scarce.

"I suppose not." He rested an arm on his knee and pulled her chin up so her eyes met his, for a long time he just stared at her, searching for something. She wanted to kiss him when he looked at her that way. It was intoxicating, knowing he was one of the only people in the whole kingdom of Aegis who didn't know her as the Red Princess.

There were no titles between them, no prophecies, no curses, only given names. So, for tonight at least, they were equals. Tomorrow they would be at the hunting lodge, and when they arrived, lines would be drawn. In front of the others, they would be forced into contrived roles of propriety that Liz didn't know if she believed in anymore. But Liz didn't want there to be any barriers between them, not yet.

Her mother's voice echoed in the back of her mind, asking her to live well. She had never been attracted to anyone before, and Mat scared her on some level. She didn't know if it was because of the attraction she felt growing between them or because their time together was limited. Soon, much sooner than she wanted to admit, Mat would die.

In her visions, the battle happened during the first blizzard of winter after the snow stuck to the ground. Even now the air was getting colder, the leaves beginning to fall. Part of her longed to tell him. If she did, not only would he think she was crazy, he would never again look at her the way he was right now.

"What're you thinking about?" he asked her, and for some reason she couldn't think of anything other than the truth.

"What it would be like if you kissed me right now."

He sucked in a sharp breath and leaned his forehead against hers. She held her breath when his nose brushed her own, his eyes darkened with pain.

"Why would you tell me something like that?" His voice came out hot, raw; it set her heart pounding rapidly against her ribs. He leaned back and his clear, green eyes looked at her in agony.

"Because you asked." She bit her bottom lip to keep the rest of her thoughts from spilling out haphazardly.

"I vowed to keep you safe until we got you to Fangorn," he said, his voice coming out in a long, smooth groan.

"I don't understand?"

"I mean to keep my oath, even if it means keeping you safe from *me*." His thumb brushed her dirt-smeared cheek.

"I wouldn't have agreed if I'd known that," she told him, teasing. It elicited one of his crooked grins, the kind that usually infuriated her. Liz pushed a stray curl behind her ear.

"I've never been kissed before," she confided in him. He didn't look at her as if she were foolish, like she feared he might. "I was thinking about the last thing my mother said to me, about living well, and how there are so many things I want to try. Diving off the white cliffs of Morr, drinking spirits, kissing."

Mat opened his mouth to say something when she heard Gareth's voice from across the fire.

"Gods be damned, I didn't make an oath." Gareth rose from his spot and walked over to stand before Liz ruffling his hair and blinking himself into wakefulness. He held a rough hand out to her, and she allowed him to pull her gently to her feet.

"Oh, I—Um..." Liz cleared her throat nervously and faced Gareth. She hesitated for a moment, unsure. Then she felt the threads of fate winding tightly around them both. "Alright, I'm ready." She closed her eyes tight, puckering her lips.

"Open your eyes." Gareth put a hand under her chin, tilting her face up towards his own. She opened her eyes and really looked at the man who would be her first kiss. Dark curls fell into charcoal-grey eyes. They were just as mysterious as Gareth always seemed to be. She swallowed as he reached down into her soul with those bright eyes, tugging on some far corner of her mind and giving her permission to acknowledge the desire residing there. It was powerful and shattering.

"When you kiss someone, you do it with intention. Purpose. Don't hide from it." His voice was a deep rumble, it thundered into her skin. "You choose it." His words washed over her as he pulled her closer, his hand cupping her cheek and moving to entwine his fingers in her hair. His breath was hot on her lips. Her heart pounded in her chest as she was swallowed up by the darkness surrounding him.

He kissed her then, slowly but firmly, nothing messy or awkward about it. His mouth tasted her, until he breathed in deep and something shifted between them. The snapping of tension and a tightening in the threads of fate surrounding them both. His hand gripped her hard until he pulled away from her mouth with a groan, leaving her breathless. She was dizzy and warm and wonderful.

"I—That was—" She couldn't seem to make a coherent sentence, so she cleared her throat. "Thank you."

Mat wasn't looking at her any longer. Instead, he was looking up at the constellations, glaring up above them. Without a word, she crawled beneath the covers with Tia and turned away, closing her eyes but not sleeping for hours. Her last thought before succumbing to sleep was that Tia had been right.

Gareth *was* delicious.

Chapter Ten

Mat woke up that morning hating Gareth. He packed up their meager campsite, hating Gareth. He untied the horses, hating Gareth. Then he pulled Liz into his arms again, riding for the last stretch towards the lodge, all while hating Gareth. In fact, until last night when he watched Gareth kiss Liz, he didn't realize the true depth of his loathing for the man.

He wasn't jealous. The roiling in his gut and fury warming his blood wasn't from some misguided notion that he and the princess would somehow be together. No, Mat was furious with his audacity. He'd been under the impression that he and Gareth had come to an understanding. They made a plan to protect her, instead Gareth couldn't seem to control himself around her. Mat should've known better than to trust a man who pledged his loyalty to no one and nothing.

Other thoughts lurked in the dark corners of his mind. Thoughts he didn't want to give too much attention to. Thoughts about how warm her hand had been on his when she'd pointed out the stars. Or the simple pleasure of watching her mind whirl too fast for her mouth to keep up. Mat tried to force away the memory of his heart slamming against his ribcage when she spoke of kissing him, the night wrapping them in an intimacy that couldn't be manufactured.

It seemed that his molten animosity refused to dispel his pointed reflection of the night before. Liz shifted before him on the saddle, and his misgivings shattered with a brush of her body against his own.

His world narrowed to the feel of her back pressed flush against his chest, or the scent of earth and grass clinging to her fair skin. Though she was in a worn cloak and tattered under-dress, half-covered in dirt and her curls were haphazard around her face, she was beautiful. Beautiful in spite of her nobility. Beautiful the way Mara never could be to him, radiant from within. He continued to be enamored with the way she moved her hands when she spoke, or the shy way she smiled sometimes. Things he didn't usually notice in women.

Truthfully, she scared him. He could feel his resolve to turn her over to Lord Callum slipping the more time he spent with her. Mat tried not to think about the blood moon ceremony or the devastation that would be the result of not completing it. Just as he hadn't had a choice in being born a bastard, she hadn't chosen to be born a sacrifice. If he could change his circumstances, why couldn't she? But he didn't trust Lord Callum to hold up his end of the bargain they'd struck. Without her, Mat had no leverage. The sooner he could get some distance, the better.

"You've been rather quiet today." Her voice was melodic, lofty and proper. It sounded like the ocean, or so he imagined because she came from the southern palace near the sea.

"I only speak when I have cause to. I'm a simple man with simple thoughts, and not many of them on most days." He couldn't help his grin when he heard her tinkling laugh in front of him.

"Tell me—"

Anything. Mat would tell her anything.

"Your friend, Gareth. Tell me about him."

Mat's grip on the reins tightened, the leather creaking beneath the force of it. He took a deep breath and forced himself to sound calm, glad she was sitting in front of him, facing away from the dark expression in his eyes.

"He isn't my friend, but we've known each other since we were lads." Mat didn't want to lie to her. She was his sovereign, but more than that, she'd evaded capture by the Dragon's army and almost fought her way free of him by the river. Begrudgingly, he respected her.

"So then is he... like you?" Her question appeared innocent enough, but the whole conversation irritated him. Every time he closed his eyes, he replayed them kissing over and over again. Now, her continued interest in the man unnerved him. What had Gareth been trying to accomplish by making a move on her last night?

"He's *nothing* like me," he snapped. Liz's back stiffened in response to his venomous tone. He sighed, running a hand through his hair and starting again. "What I mean is..."

What *did* he mean?

"Gareth isn't a bastard. He's the son of a lord and makes sure you don't forget it. His family sent him to Fangorn on his thirteenth winter to earn a respectable living if rumor can be trusted."

Liz turned then to look over her shoulder at Mat, her blue gaze wise and sullen.

"That's incredibly sad."

Sad? Mat rolled his eyes and clucked his tongue to encourage his horse to trot along faster, forcing her to face the front instead of peering so intensely into the very heart of him. Gareth had parents, a name, and should something terrible befall his family, a title.

What about his circumstances could be considered sad?

He glanced back at Gareth and Tia on the other horse behind them. Their pony wasn't as sturdy and at least a turn or two behind, far enough they wouldn't overhear the conversation.

"Why is that sad? About Gareth, I mean."

Liz sighed, pulling Mat's cloak tighter around her shoulders. He liked seeing her wrapped in it, knowing it kept her warm. That *he* kept her warm.

"Well, his parents *chose* to abandon him. I can't imagine how hard that is for a child to understand," she said patiently. With those simple words, she left Mat speechless. How did she *do* that?

"I guess I never thought of it that way," Mat admitted, feeling somewhat ashamed for not trying harder to put himself in Gareth's shoes. In a moment, Liz managed to humanize his worst enemy and dull the sting of his enmity towards Gareth. "I always thought him lucky. He knows where he came from, who his family is. I would give anything to know my father, if I could."

"You don't even know who he is?" she asked, her words smaller than he thought possible. Mat cleared his throat, having unintentionally revealed too much of himself to her.

"No. My mother would never give me his name."

"I lost my mother recently." Her voice low as she spoke. Sad. "My father was cold and distant. He was so terrified of losing us that he pushed us away before he could. My mother was one of the only people who cared about me." Something in her voice caused Mat to grip her tighter as she spoke. As if his arms could somehow hold together all her jagged edges. "I always thought she would outlive me. It came as a shock when she was just...gone."

Mat hadn't thought about the fact that Liz was supposed to have died a couple of weeks ago. The blood moon ceremony and Liz dying somehow seemed separate in his mind. Now that he knew her, he couldn't imagine her just being gone that way. Suddenly he felt guilty for how he'd been acting, cold and aloof since she and Gareth kissed. She'd asked him first, after all, and he remembered now what she'd said the night before. Her mother told her to live well.

So what if she and Gareth kissed? They hardly knew each other; she and Mat hardly knew each other. Though he seemed connected to her in some inexplicable way, he couldn't fathom what her life had been like. He didn't know how she and Tia met, or why she was roaming the countryside without a proper dress. Mat knew nothing of her privilege or her pain, and he didn't want to know any more than he did now. He'd vowed to deliver her to Fangorn, and no matter his reasons, that needed to be his focus.

"Tell us one of your stories, Lisbet." Tia's voice was too sweet, like honey and secrets. Mat glanced over to see a calculating smile that didn't reach her eyes stretched across her lips. Liz sighed, and he felt the gentle exhalation more than he heard it. This was normal, a routine they followed; Tia asked and without preamble she obliged the request.

"What kind of story would you like?" she asked, tone indifferent.

"Mmm..." Tia dragged the sound out of her mouth, a decadent purr. "Something about the gods. Something *ethereal*."

"Once, in a time before men could remember, the gods walked amongst us," she said, and a derisive snort sounded from Mat before he had a chance to quell it. She tensed but didn't let his cynicism deter her. "The realms were all connected. The Halls of the gods as near to our mortal realm as passing through a doorway."

"Rubbish," Mat muttered, and Liz nearly unseated them both as she craned sharply to glower at him.

"It's not rubbish! It's true. I translated this story from a temple placard said to be the oldest living record of the gods."

Mat bristled as a cold wind filtered through the tree branches, the leaves rattling like insect song.

"You mean to say, I could've bloody walked into the Halls of the gods like walking into a pub? It's nonsense." He breathed a chuckle, the scent of ash heavy in her hair.

"Haven't you ever wondered why magick is fading from Aegis?" she asked with all the snobbish derision he'd expect from a Princess. The breeze that had been twisting between the trees began to bluster harder.

"I guess bastards like me just aren't smart enough to." His words were daggers, sarcasm slicing deep enough to force an angry laugh from her lips.

"I guess not." Her blue eyes were cold. "Even children know about how Hak'ka split the realms with his staff and stole magick from the world. When he locked the door to the Halls, he locked away the magick we needed to keep the world working. Clearly you never paid attention at temple."

"The only people I know that worship Hak'ka are his dirty half-blooded children who tried to truss you up in the woods. Perhaps they would be better company." Mat snapped; his anger nearly made him reveal he knew her identity. He *was* an idiot.

Tia's laughter pealed on the wind and Mat felt his face burn. He didn't dare look over at Gareth's expression.

"I haven't seen anyone ruffle Liz's feathers before. I quite like the sight," Tia said. Liz's whole body stiffened in front of him; her shoulders raised high by her ears.

They rode on in silence, listening to the chittering of birds in the trees and the quiet hum of life around them, following the river until the steepness of the path became troublesome and Mat held tight to keep Liz from pitching off the saddle. As soon as they finished climbing to the highest point of the path, they took a turn and the hunting lodge was spread out below them, smoke already coming from the chimney.

Liz sighed, a relieved sound, and Mat smiled behind her. If he were a nobleman, this would be where he spent all his time. He couldn't understand how Lord Callum rarely, if ever, visited. Nestled in the greenest grove of trees, with a babbling brook running beside it, was the wood plank cabin that acted as a hunting lodge for the Callum family. It was large and sprawling, but not overbearing. No, it fit the land surrounding it with its walls of windows and vaulted roof. The lodge sprang up from the mountain forest surrounding it.

As they approached, Mat shared a look with Gareth, hoping the men didn't look too closely into the women's poorly fabricated story. It was clear the two women had no experience with lying, or at least, lying well. A crooked grin twisted across Mat's lips when Finn burst from the stable at their arrival, calling out to the others that he and Gareth had returned.

Mat dismounted, then reached up and took hold of Liz around her waist, hauling her down onto settled feet. He turned to greet Finn but was stopped short by Liz's hand on his forearm.

"Mat," His name on her lips was sweet.

"I know, it was stupid of me to argue with you." Mat admitted, wishing to put the disagreement behind them. "I apologize for being an insufferable idiot, though, I cannot promise it will not happen again." He grinned but her serious expression didn't fade.

"There's something I should tell you—"

But her words were cut off by Finn barreling into his stomach and pitching him off of his feet.

"Matioch! You took forever to get back."

Mat's grin answered the lad as he ruffled the boy's hair and twisted him into a headlock.

"Get off you big lunk!" Finn protested.

Mat's eyes were bright and his spirits high now that he was reunited with his friends. He glanced back at Liz, whose eyes were wide and fixed on the lumbering bulk of Wallace as he returned the horses to the stable. More mountain than man, but gentler than anyone Mat had ever known. Wallace had an uncanny affinity for animals, in fact, he was the best stable hand at Fangorn.

"You shouldn't ride them so hard, Matioch." Wallace grunted disapprovingly before nodding a greeting to the girls and disappearing into the stable.

"Don't take it personally. Wallace prefers animals to people," Mat explained.

Liz stood, imperious and stiff, wringing her first two fingers around a stray curl. A curious habit he'd noticed and grown rather fond of.

"Ye slimy prick!"

Mat cringed at the crass language, normally it didn't bother him, but around the women it seemed more offensive than usual.

"That would be Smitty," Mat explained. Liz gifted him with a small smile as the short, stocky man punched Gareth in the arm. The thud caused Gareth to scowl and slink away, leaving them all to their reunion without him. "I would tell you that his *unique* demeanor becomes endearing over time, but I don't wish to lie to you." Mat turned to introduce Finn, but he'd left them all and was doting on Tia.

"What's your name, miss?" he asked. She giggled vainly, batting her eyes at him as she walked past. Gliding across the ground, she linked arms with Liz as Wallace waved them toward the lodge to be settled for the evening. Smitty smacked a hand on Mat's shoulder as he looked at their retreating forms.

"Aye, Mat. Ye've gone mad then? Ye bloody well know they're trouble, mate. Don't ye?"

He turned his eyes on Liz and Tia again. For the first time Liz's shoulders weren't drawn tight in fear. He made an oath to protect her, and even if he wasn't sure of the future or the plans he'd made, he would keep her safe. Did he care about the trouble they'd brought along with them?

Not even a little.

Chapter Eleven

Liz's guilt coated her like an inky film, soaking deep into her skin. She was keeping so many things from Mat. Seeing him there, surrounded by his friends with an easy open smile, she couldn't bear to tell him about her visions of his death now. What if, somehow, her words hastened his impending demise? As if speaking them aloud would spur the gods to action. Like a bad omen, she followed after him with a prophecy of her own. She would not wish such a fate on an enemy, much less someone she had grown to trust.

Tia tugged her inside the lodge, a familiar conspiratorial smile on her lips. Liz's heart ached beneath its beauty, evoking memories that had sharp edges. Pain and relief mixed together, indistinguishable from each other.

She missed her mother.

Somehow, innately, Liz knew the queen was dead. Perhaps the same way she could see through the mists and sense the threads of fate. The morning after she and Tia escaped from the palace, Liz woke up and the world was grey, her heart heavier.

Gone.

Now her mother only remained alive within Liz's memory, within her pain. Wallace lumbered towards them as she stepped into the thick warmth radiating from the river stone hearth and roaring fire within.

"Come." He kept it simple as he led them to a dark, curved staircase. Wolf carvings peered at them from the banisters, standing sentry for the family who was meant to reside above. Liz trailed her hand along the railing, marveling at the craftsmanship.

"You can stay here." A man of few words, and kind eyes. He lowered his gaze to the floor, bashful, pointing to three trunks near the grated window.

"Dresses," he said just as quickly, disappearing around the corner.

Tia giggled, and Liz caught her mirth and began to giggle as well. The giggles turned into howls and snorts of laughter, until they were both left clinging to one another to stay upright.

When the hysteria calmed, Liz took a few moments to inspect the room they'd been gifted. The furnishings were ornate, favoring golden trim and dark mahogany wood. There was a small vanity by the window and several crystal bottles of perfume. They caught the light and reflected dancing shadows on the walls. Liz reached out to one, curious of the scent, only to still her hand midway. Covered in muck and filth, she would smear it all over the pristine clear beauty of the crystal.

A knock sounded on the door, and Liz turned, catching sight of Tia lounging easily on the soft downy fur of the duvet, uncaring if her filth soiled the bed linens. Liz rolled her eyes and pulled the large oak and iron door open wide. The young boy, Finn, stood nervously before her. He shifted his weight from one foot to the other, giving the impression of a jerky sort of dance.

"S-sorry to disturb you, miss. I w-was hoping that—"

"Oh, for the gods' sake, come in already." Tia groaned, waving an impatient hand in his general direction. Finn shuffled in, his lanky form nearly halved by the hunching of his shoulders. Tia sat up, snapping until he shuffled faster and stopped directly in front of her.

Tia took his chin in one hand, eyes roaming over his face, turning his head back and forth.

"You're such a beautiful boy," Tia said, no hint of flirtation in the words. Finn looked as confused as Liz felt, not knowing how to respond to the statement of simple fact. He settled for ducking his head and glancing side-long at Liz for help.

"Why have you come?" Liz asked.

"I wanted to see if there was anything you needed, miss. I'll do my best to make sure you're comfortable." He bowed his head low.

"That's very kind, but unnecessary," Liz told him.

"No, miss. You've been through a great deal from what Mat said and... and I mean to make you feel welcome." Finn said it so seriously that Liz couldn't help but smile at the bowed crown of his head. She looked down at her hands again, covered in filth, just like the rest of her.

"We could really do with a bath, if that's not too much trouble," Liz said, and Tia moaned in delight at the mention of it.

"Gods, yes! Why didn't I think of that?"

Finn stood straight, his height dwarfing both of them easily. "No trouble at all, miss."

Tia caught him by the wrist and pressed something into his palm. Liz couldn't see what it might have been, but pain flashed briefly in his eyes before he all but ran from the room.

"What was that about?" Liz asked, mystified by the shadow that passed over Tia's face.

"You wouldn't understand," she replied dismissively, earning an annoyed huff from Liz. Tia tossed one of the down feather pillows at her and soon they were giddy once more, intoxicated by the unexpected safety of the lodge.

They stayed there, sequestered for the entire morning. They folded easily back into their routine from the palace, as if they'd never left. They pulled out the dresses, which must have belonged to Lord Callum's wife or daughter, all in thick velvets and brocades, fabrics she was unaccustomed to. They were bold in color—reds as deep as blood, greens almost black against her pale skin, and blues that reminded her of the bay at Silver City, deep and mysterious. Many suffocated her when she tried them, but a few could be let out enough to fit.

Tia laid and hung the dresses around the room until it looked the way Liz imagined the royal harem from the Eastern Isles would appear. Great swaths of fabric covering every surface, bright and whimsical. They didn't have bright or whimsical fabrics here, but she could almost imagine they were the same. Only the best silks and muslins came from the Eastern Isles, great golden ships filled to the brim with them. She could almost smell the spices on the fabrics.

Almost.

Tia must have felt the same way, because she began to dance a mo'tet, in great swirling motions. Her skirts bloomed around her, manipulated by the nearly impossible fluidity of her long limbs. She only saw Tia dance this way when she was homesick. Not for the palace or Silver City, but for her *real* home on one of the greater Eastern Isles. She didn't dance for onlookers, not even Liz; she danced to remember. She danced to *forget*.

Finn and Wallace brought steaming water in a caravan of buckets to fill the iron bath in the corner. Liz gazed down from on high through the grated window, taking in the wild beauty of the Neither Wood. This is where the doorway to the Halls of the gods was supposed to have been an age ago. Now, forsaken, it was a place of curses and shadows. Or, so Liz had been told. Liz knew what it felt like to be cursed, and looking at the woods now, she thought she'd never seen anything more beautiful.

Tia helped undress her with deft fingers, and she stepped into the scalding water to rid herself of the grime that had accumulated over the last couple of weeks. The cold seeped slowly into her skin, marinating her bones. She had almost forgotten what it was to be warm.

"We have to be quick so the water is still hot for you."

Tia smiled, all the way to her eyes. "Princesses usually care little about the comfort of lesser nobles."

"Lesser," she scoffed at the word. Disgusted. "Even before we fled Silver City you were more than a courtier to me. You're family. The only family I have left."

Tia's smile remained, but pain twisted onto her mouth, muting its brilliance. Whatever the cause of her pain, she did not give voice to it. It was enough that Liz recognized her suffering, enough to reach out and grip her hand to still it. Or so she hoped. She hoped that Tia knew without words that she shared the burden of her pain, regardless of its cause.

Liz bathed efficiently, scrubbing off the caked-on mud and grime beneath her fingernails. Scraping roughly against her scalp and through her wild curls, attempting to tame the unmanageable mess. Ash swirled away from her scalp like smoke. A far cry from her languid rose petal and buttermilk baths in the palace. She shimmied out of the water and into the fine linen chemise Tia kindly held open for her.

They avoided talking about what to do next, but they couldn't keep pretending they were in the palace. They weren't safe. Not yet.

"We don't have a way to re-dye my hair, Tia. They'll figure out who I am soon." Liz said, tying her chemise closed and shrugging into a dressing robe for the time being.

With clumsy fingers, Liz worked to open the laces at the back of Tia's dress until her friend was finally able to be submerged in the still-warm water. She sank down all the way to her chin, eyes closed in relief. Liz couldn't help but look at her, really look at her.

"We could tell them it was a custom at court to dye your hair to match the princess. You got scared when we fled and disguised the color?" Tia lied so easily sometimes Liz wondered what other secrets she was hiding.

"You think that'll work? Mat and Gareth are... unusually perceptive. I doubt it will fool them." Liz said, worrying her bottom lip with her teeth.

"The others are simple, superstitious types. But I fear you may be right about those two. What other choice do we have but to confide in them?" Tia said, amber eyes lit in mischief.

Liz picked up the soap and massaged the lather into her perfect, brown skin. Her shoulders bunched with knots; muscles tensed.

"You shouldn't be attending me, your majesty." The title rang in Liz's ears, and she dropped the cloth with a splash from the shock of it.

"Highness. Not majesty. I'm not a queen, Tia."

Tia sucked in a sharp breath and stood from the water, unashamed by her nakedness, her eyes afire. Liz didn't think she had ever seen Tia this mad at her before.

"We both know that's a lie." Tia's angry words, like arrows, struck true. Right into Liz's mangled heart. It had been an eternity it seemed since Liz felt anything so sharply as Tia's disdain.

"I might not even be considered a princess anymore. Not after running away like a coward and betraying my country and people." Liz's words were heavy with self-loathing and Tia's anger burned hotter as she spoke them aloud.

"Sometimes you say things that remind me exactly how *childish* you are." Her words sliced deep and Liz gasped at her audacity. Her cheeks burned in humiliation, eyes blinking hard in an effort to contain her hurt.

"At least I don't throw myself indiscriminately at anyone that smiles at me for more than *five seconds*." Tia's mouth dropped open wide. Liz had never spoken to her that way before. She'd most certainly never dared to mention Tia's less than proper behavior at court with her romantic liaisons.

"And you're so jealous it's killing you." Though she said it quietly, there was a particular viciousness to the statement. Maybe it hurt so much because it was true. It was easy for people to love Tia, but loving Liz came at a steep price. Too steep for almost anyone.

She felt frayed at the edges and too close to dissolving into tears. Though she realized it was childish, defensively she crossed her arms over her chest. "You're just jealous that Gareth kissed me."

Tia shoved her chemise over her shoulders. Her nostrils flared as she stomped toward her friend. Tia's palm made a startling crack against her cheek.

In the next moments, the silence between them was deafening. Angry, hurt tears welled rebelliously in Liz's eyes as Tia's ragged breaths and clenched teeth faded into regret.

"Apologies, Tia," she said quickly. "I didn't realize how deeply you cared for him."

Tia scoffed. "Sometimes I forget how little you know of the world." She sighed and took Liz's hand, leading her to sit on the bed. "I don't care about any man more than I care about you, majesty."

"I'm not qu—"

"Do not say it again." Liz listened immediately to her sharp words, stilling herself. "Your mother knew what would befall her, what she was sacrificing for you. It's time now to sing the song of her life and acknowledge that she's gone."

Liz shook her head, unwilling tears tumbling haphazardly down her cheeks. She couldn't be gone. Because if she was gone, then Liz had to acknowledge that she'd let it happen when she fled. She wasn't strong enough to do that, not now, maybe not ever.

Tia braced her hands on her shoulders, staring deep into her eyes. "I struck you because you aren't a common girl. Like it or not, you're a queen. Now is the time you decide what kind you're going to be."

Liz's lip trembled. Her father never intended her to live to adulthood, much less rule the country. She hadn't been prepared to rule. Queens didn't rule. They married men who became kings. She was unfit to lead. Unprepared. If she could find another way to bring magick back to Aegis, maybe she could rule them. Maybe then, she would be worthy enough to.

"I didn't leave my brother in Silver City to die at the hands of the Dragon so that you could drown in self-doubt. Killian would throttle you himself if he heard you talking this way." Killian's face flashed in Liz's mind. Was he gone now too? If so, it was because of her. Because she ran.

"Apologies," Liz said, realizing Tia was no longer angry, she was disappointed. Somehow that was worse.

"Don't apologize to me. Don't apologize to *anyone*. Just be better. Be the queen I've always known you could be."

Liz nodded but would only disappoint her again. She tasted ash in her mouth as the realization settled in the pit of her stomach. She was many things—a sacrifice, god-touched, a princess.

But she was no queen.

Chapter Twelve

The sound of a whetstone grinding against the edge of Mat's claymore was as familiar as the sound of his mother's voice. He knew this sword better than he knew most people. Blowing on the now sharpened blade, he balanced the length of it on the back of his hand. No small feat for a sword as long and heavy as this. He spun it by the hilt, testing the grip, sure that one day he would use it for something heroic.

"What's its name?"

Gareth had been quietly watching him work, and Mat tried to ignore him. At Gareth's question, Mat's brow furrowed in confusion.

"My sword?"

"Of course, your sword." They could never talk for long without arguing.

"You may be shocked to find out some men use their swords and don't bother to name them. They're tools. I don't name my hammers either," Mat grumbled under his breath. Gareth sighed, holding his hand out impatiently for Mat's claymore. Reluctantly, Mat handed it over, allowing him to take a few swings. As Gareth stretched out his arm and rolled his wrist, Mat thought he noted the beginning of respect creeping into his grey eyes.

"Not bad." He handed it back, clearing his throat in discomfort.

Mat stood, needing to work off some of the concern that began to plague him as of late. Moving to an open area away from the whetstone, he swung his claymore in a familiar rhythm. For years, after the smith passed out in a drunken stupor, he practiced what little he'd gleaned from the soldiers that day. By day he pounded metal; by night he swung swords.

He lost himself in the rhythm, the thrust and parry and footwork, completely forgetting that Gareth was there at all. Until he spoke.

"Watch your shoulder."

Mat faltered, breaking his form.

"Drop it, like this." Gareth unsheathed his own sword and showed him the same move, slightly altered. Mat repeated the move, begrudgingly nodding in approval.

They squared off against one another not in a duel but as drilling soldiers. As he faced Gareth, Mat couldn't help but remember him kissing Liz. As they moved mechanically through the drill, Mat's eyes stayed sharp on his opponent. Last time they fought, Gareth lost his calm facade and tried to kill him.

"Why are you looking at me like that?" Gareth asked, pushing forward to test Mat's reflexes. He met his sword and pushed him back.

"I'm wondering why you lost your mind during our last match." Mat said.

Gareth's jaw flexed, his foot slipped, obviously jarred by the turn in conversation. "I told you before; it isn't your concern."

Mat pressed his advantage, keeping him off balance. "It is when you hurt Finn. I won't stand for that." Gareth stumbled and Mat didn't hesitate. "I never thought highly of you, but he's young." Mat ground out between his teeth. He rushed forward and swung sure, pushing Gareth back. "Even a man such as you should have more honor than to beat a harmless lad." With a roll of his wrist Mat disarmed Gareth, watching as his sword clattered to the ground. He held the tip of his blade against Gareth's throat.

"I never touched the kitchen boy." Gareth's eyes were cold and lifeless again, no longer lit with curiosity. Mat shook his head, unable to reconcile that with what he knew of his rival. Gareth pushed the tip of Mat's blade away with a gloved hand, his steel eyes aflame with anger. His lips were curled back in disdain.

"Considering our past, I'm not inclined to believe you," Mat said, bored with the conversation now. Gareth, however, didn't let it go. He picked up his sword and leveled it at Mat once more.

"Again."

"No." Mat wouldn't give in to his arrogant demands. He caught sight of Liz, peering down from her window, that sad expression still in her lonely eyes. He remembered what she said about Gareth, how his family chose to leave him behind. He didn't want to like him, didn't want to forgive him for his past offenses. But Liz saw the world differently. She recognized the flaws but imagined a more understanding, kinder place.

He wanted to live in that kind of world.

Sighing, he raised his sword toward Gareth once more. They circled each other, looking for any opportunity to strike. Their surroundings narrowed to just the two of them, each step measured, every breath counted and weighed. Mat struck quickly to the left, then swung at the last moment. Gareth side-stepped his attack easily, his footwork masterful.

"Have you even asked the kitchen boy who hit him?" Gareth asked. Mat did ask Finn about his attacker. But the realization that he hadn't answered came fast and Mat faltered, giving Gareth enough room to disarm him and win the match. Mat didn't fight it either. Gareth's blade was pressed to his throat, and Mat struggled for even breath. He'd misjudged him terribly. Finn never gave him a name; he just assumed it must have been Gareth. Mat prided himself on his sense of justice, his honor, but his pride blinded him to the truth.

Gareth was innocent.

"I won't apologize for kissing her." His words clanged through Mat's mind before settling in the pit of his stomach. He'd hoped that he was able to hide his feelings about the other night well enough that it would never come up. No such luck. Instead of making an excuse or avoiding the topic, he gave Gareth the respect of facing him directly.

"What were you playing at?" Mat asked, wondering if he had to be worried about Gareth betraying him by revealing his plans.

"Playing?" Gareth chuckled darkly, running a hand through his long, dark hair. "I like her. She's... unexpected." The warmth of his voice rattled Mat, and he felt suddenly unsteady on his feet. He knew exactly what Gareth meant. "So, I won't apologize for kissing her. But I won't stand in your way either. It's clear there's something between you, and I'm a vain enough man that I don't like being *settled* for."

Mat felt too hot, and his breathing went funny all of a sudden. Gareth grunted to show the matter was settled between them.

"Apologies for making assumptions about you." Mat held his arm out. After a moment's hesitation, Gareth sheathed his sword and clasped his forearm, nodding in acceptance.

"I suppose it wasn't all bad. I got to kiss a beautiful woman, and you have promise as a swordsman. Your footwork is terrible, and you leave your left open too often, but you have promise."

Mat stifled the urge to smile and instead offered a cocky grin, earning a roll of Gareth's eyes.

"How do I improve?"

Gareth dusted off his breeches and chuckled. Clapping Mat on the shoulder, he said, "Learn to dance." Then he left, making his way back to the lodge.

"Wait, what?" Mat followed Gareth, catching up to him as they rounded the corner towards the hearth and fire within. Finn called to Mat from across the room, where he and Smitty were arguing over a pot.

"Oi! Matioch, do you think Tia would like rabbit or duck better in the stew for dinner tonight?"

Mat chuckled at Finn, watching the calculated concentration furrow his brow.

"I think she won't know the difference. It's a stew, mate." He turned back to Gareth, ready to question him further about this dancing business when the room that had been loud with the noise of bawdy men trying to co-exist in small quarters fell unnaturally silent. All of the men were staring at the top of the stairs. Finn in particular, was red all the way down his neck.

Mat's knees weakened and his breath escaped him in a heated rush. Liz had been beautiful before, but after a bath and wearing a proper dress, she was radiant. Her hair shone like a living flame; her pale skin as luminous as moonlight. She was wearing a simple dress, grey velvet with sleeves buttoned at her wrist. The simplicity of the garment magnified what was already beautiful about her. She descended with Tia in tow, her natural grace and fluid movements gave her an otherworldly quality.

"I-I..." Mat was stunned speechless. Gareth cleared his throat and bowed his head slightly as the women came to rest before them.

"I see that you've found clothes, at last." Mat clenched his fist tight at his side. Could he never say the right thing?

Liz quirked her eyebrow, a grin playing on her lips at his response. "I didn't realize my state of undress earlier was so distressing to you."

Mat's nails dug into his palm painfully at his embarrassment. Heat crept up his neck.

"I'll endeavor to keep buttoned up from here on out. I wouldn't want to offend your delicate sensibilities."

He was an idiot. Gareth chuckled and Mat decided he still hated him, after all.

"I should probably go check on Wallace and his progress in the smokehouse. It shouldn't be too long before we're ready to head back to the keep." Mat rubbed his dirty hands on his pants, ducking his head and heading outside cursing himself under his breath. He looked back through the grated window and saw Liz laughing at a grinning Gareth. His stomach lurched and roiled as he bit back the jealousy coursing through him.

He kept his eye on the tree line as he made the short trek to the smokehouse in the back, where Wallace was hanging a freshly killed and gutted boar. They'd been lucky thus far that the only half-bloods they'd come across were the ones who had captured Liz and Tia. They didn't take kindly to hunting in the Neither

Wood. No, it would be best if Mat's party left before tempting fate any further.

Wallace seemed to have everything in hand, so Mat stopped by the well to get a drink of cool water. He looked at his reflection for a moment. He was dirty, sweat beaded on his brow from sparring earlier. He plunged his hands in the water and pulled them out again, scrubbing futilely at the grime beneath his fingernails. An insistent breeze picked up, ruffling his blonde hair as he ran his wet, dirty hands through it.

There was a restlessness growing within him, some sense that things were changing more rapidly than he could comprehend. All his life he'd thought there was something bigger out there for him, some purpose yet to be realized. He'd never settled, never quit pushing forward. Then suddenly here she was, *Liz*, princess of the entire realm. He rubbed his hateful bastard hands over his face and turned back to the windows once more, watching her take a goblet of wine from Finn. Her smile lit up the entire lodge.

Why had she come down with her crimson hair on display like that? The answer was clear, but Mat couldn't seem to grasp it. She *trusted* him. All of them. He couldn't betray that trust.

"Gods, help me," he said to no one. "I have to tell her the truth."

Chapter Thirteen

Three days. Time passed too quickly during those riotous days, each moment filled with sparring matches, preserving game, and even firing a bow. Though, Smitty forbade Liz from attempting that particular endeavor again after a wayward arrow came inches from his throat and scared the daylights out of them both.

The men from Fangorn were a rowdy bunch, using crude language and indulging in simple pleasures. It was thanks to them that Liz learned how to separate tender meat from bone and shoe a horse. It was thanks to them she'd spent three days filled with more laughter and acceptance than she'd felt in a lifetime.

The nights, however, were another matter entirely. Since the passing of the blood moon her dreams and visions were more relentless the closer to winter they got. She woke sobbing, wrenched from dreams of mangled bodies on a field of thick snow. The smell of burning flesh acrid in her nose. The image of clear green eyes dim and unseeing. Her mother's voice singing a wordless song in the distance. These dreams, as horrific and paralyzing as they were, became worse the longer they stayed at the lodge. She could not determine if they were worsening because of the fast-approaching snow or because she was no longer traveling towards the mountains as before.

By the time evening fell on the third night, Liz hadn't seen much of Mat or Tia. The former spent nearly all his free time training with his sword, until sweat slicked down his face and stuck his golden hair to his skin. Meanwhile Tia spent her time with Finn, whispering conspiratorially and giggling during mealtimes. In truth, Liz didn't begrudge Tia spending time with Finn. It reminded her of the effortless charm she wielded at court more deftly than Mat wielded his blade. It reminded her of home. The ache of missing Silver City spread deep within her.

The sun dipped in the sky, its light filtering through the trees and offering a dim, receding glow. Liz watched from the balcony on the second floor as the stars winked into existence in the twilight sky. A terrible clanging and indistinguishable shouts echoed up the curves of the staircase. Smitty swore and laughter exploded in a cacophonous roar.

"Hurry up, Lisbet! You're missing all the fun!" Tia's voice was husky with barely suppressed laughter. Liz sighed; her heart too heavy for merriment tonight. It was easy to forget, for a time. Easier when she was focused on surviving moment-to-moment. Standing still allowed the gravity of her cowardice to settle into her bones and become an indistinguishable part of her. Her shame as glaringly obvious in her eyes as the obscene shade of her hair.

She'd left them all to die.

There was no perceptible motion, no noticeable sound. The air didn't shift. Yet, Liz bit down on her bottom lip and schooled her features into a mask of contentment.

"Good evening, Gareth."

He said nothing so she turned, surprised to see his hand in mid-air as if he'd been reaching out for her. The offending appendage fell heavily to his side as Gareth crossed to the railing and leaned against the banister. His eyes never left her face, as if he could see easily beneath her mask. It infuriated her.

"You think you're so *mysterious* when you just stand there, leaning against things and staring," she admonished him blackly. "You aren't." A smile she couldn't decipher curled wickedly onto his mouth.

"I came to see if you were—" He cut himself off sharply. "If you wished to join us." Liz raised an eyebrow at the slip.

"I don't know if I'll be congenial enough tonight," she admitted, hating how weak her voice sounded.

"Then don't be."

Liz looked over at him, half shadowed against the fading light. "If we can't be there for you in times of struggle, then we don't deserve to stand beside you in times of victory. No blood, No Glory."

"Where did you hear that?" she asked in a huff, shocked by his sudden wisdom.

"They say it in the legion," he said in his deep gravelly rumble. "When they pledge their loyalty to the crown."

Liz couldn't breathe. She swallowed hard and gripped her skirts tight to keep her hands from trembling. His still grey eyes gave nothing away, no hint that his words were more than a coincidence. He shoved off of his perch and offered a short nod, the approximation of a bow before returning downstairs.

"You should join us," he called back.

It was a long while before she was able to compose herself enough to glide down the staircase and take in the chaos before her. Tia wrapped Finn's neck in a fur and feather boa and left rouge-stained lip marks on his cheeks. His mouth was stained the deep purple of dark northern wine, brown eyes glassed over in drunken bliss as he clapped along to Wallace's bawdy tavern song.

Liz had barely taken two steps before Smitty stumbled towards her, shoving a pewter goblet of dark wine into her hands. He muttered something slurred beyond comprehension and then pulled Tia into a careening jig.

She heard Mat's laughter before she saw him. It was a good laugh, throaty and full-bodied, with an edge of playfulness that hinted at his young age. Turning the corner, she caught sight of him, radiant in his unfettered joy. She felt the thread between them, snapping taut, tugging her closer.

"You're here," he said, and she took a long drink of the wine in her goblet. The taste burst bright in her mouth, rich and spicy, warming her blood as it slid decadently down her throat. He laughed again, this time soft and breathy, at the expression on her face. "Smitty and Finn aren't shy about breaking into Lord Callum's wine cellar," he said conspiratorially low in her ear. She felt his breath on her neck and shivered at his nearness. She took another long swallow.

"They aren't worried about getting caught?" she asked, watching Tia's skirts flowing in woolen waves with each dip and turn. Mat shrugged, his eyes glinting merrily when she held her goblet out to him for a refill. He obliged her and raised his glass in her direction before drinking heavily. Liz felt too warm.

"You're quite the warrior," she said. "Not that I would be a good judge of that. I just mean, all you seem to do is practice."

"Train," he corrected gently. "Soldiers train. Lutists practice." She flushed at his teasing. The silence stretched between them comfortably. Perhaps it was inevitable that they would find themselves companions of sorts, familiar in a way that made the quiet between conversations feel safe.

"I'm surprised you noticed," he said, his voice hanging heavily in the air.

"I noticed." Her words were thin and reedy. Before she could say anything else, Smitty's meaty arms swept her into a lively country dance. Her head spun as her feet flew over the ground, and she lost herself in the rhythm. Her hair fell in waves from her careful plait, and she caught sight of Mat again over Smitty's shoulder. He ruffled Finn's hair, grinning that crooked grin of his, looking over with laughter dancing in his eyes. She couldn't help but think about what it would have been like if Mat kissed her that night under the stars.

Would she still fidget incessantly, driven to madness by this heat in her blood? Perhaps she'd drunk too much wine, but when Smitty clapped his hands and spun her around wildly, she laughed and danced without a thought to his hands wrapped around her waist. If he'd done this a couple of moons ago, those same hands would have been cut off for his impertinence. Tia pulled Gareth up and forced him into a stiff rendition of her twirling, her skirts spinning around her in a swish of thick brocade. Her beauty became luminous when she smiled so wide. Her light spilled over, filling up the entire room. At this moment, feet stomping and hearts beating in perfect synchronicity, they were infinite.

She squealed as Smitty picked her up and spun her around, her hands braced on his shoulders as the men stomped and clapped in rhythm to Wallace's raucous and bawdy tavern song. She was so dizzy, in fact, that she spun directly into Mat's embrace. He encased her in his arms and pressed her tight against his chest. Liz faltered, staring into those laughing green eyes.

Instead of spinning her as Smitty did before, Mat tightened his grip, and the rest of the room fell away. The same hunger she'd seen in Gareth's gaze the night he'd kissed her hid beneath the laughter in Mat's eyes now. He gripped her hand, taking care to hold her carefully.

Liz knew she was beautiful, it just never really mattered before. She'd felt smart, driven, desperate; but, in his arms, Liz *felt* beautiful for perhaps the first time. She couldn't hear the music or the other's laughter anymore. Mat took up the whole room, the whole world. She tasted his breath on her tongue. The beat of his heart thrummed through her skin, and she struggled to breathe. The calluses of his hand scraped gently against her palm and the sensation made her delirious. He surrounded her, enveloped her.

There were times when she felt safe with him, though nothing was safe anymore. When she and Mat were together, the looming threat didn't seem to matter. The shame and fear that became her every waking moment slowly faded away. She believed that with his help she would make it to Fangorn Keep. Perhaps then she could become someone else entirely. Maybe someone Mat could care for?

Like it or not, you're a queen. Now is the time you decide what kind you're going to be.

No, that would never be allowed. She had a destiny, written in prophecy by the servants of the gods. The Dragon would not stop coming, and caring for Mat put him in danger. His nearness made her dizzy and distorted reality. She would never escape those words, not until she returned magick to Aegis and the Dragon was disposed of. When Mat returned, he would have a commission at the keep. Mat was working towards a goal, making a difference, rising above his circumstances. He knew the future he wanted and pursued it. Who was she to stand in the way of that? She understood nothing about the world of men and romance. She tried to clear her head of the rampant thoughts, but he raised his eyebrow at her.

"Something the matter?"

"No," she said, a laugh falling across her lips. "I think I've had a bit too much of Lord Callum's wine tonight."

He smiled, holding her close. The way he gazed at her, studied her, made her burn inside.

"Haven't we all?" His soft voice somehow resounded through her, setting her skin afire. Warmth trickled down her arms, and she brushed her fingers innocently against the stubble on his jaw. His eyes grew hotter still; her mouth turned to ash.

"Ask me again." The bass of his voice rumbled through his chest.

It was different this time. They weren't alone in the darkness under the stars together. She couldn't bring herself to say the words. She wanted to, gods she wanted to. She wanted not to care about being in a room full of people, who would witness. She longed to be ignorant of the gap between their social classes. She wanted more than anything to be oblivious of every obstacle standing between them. Just for this one night, couldn't she pretend to be someone else? Someone less complicated. Someone who didn't live as an unwilling servant to the obligation of her birth.

"We shouldn't," she breathed into his mouth, drinking in the scent of the spiced wine on his breath.

"I know. Ask me anyway."

Damn the consequences, she thought rashly, peering up at his handsome face and no longer caring about the lines she shouldn't cross. She would tell him the whole truth of it, her real identity, everything. She would tell him, and he would be convinced it shouldn't matter. Mat would never turn her over to the Dragon. He would never harm her; she was sure enough to risk her life on it. He swore an oath, though they hadn't known each other long; his character made her believe he would not break it.

"Kiss me, Mat."

Without hesitation he pulled her tighter against him, crushing her mouth beneath his. He was not gentle, as Gareth had been. He opened her mouth beneath his in a rush of desperation, and his hand fisted at the base of her spine, pulling her to the tips of her toes. His other hand tangled in her curls, cradling her as she whimpered into his mouth. Helpless against the onslaught of him claiming her as his own. The world shifted beneath her feet as though if she didn't cling to him, she'd never find solid ground again.

When he finally released her, the men whistled crudely, but she couldn't bring herself to care. The difference between the two kisses staggered her.

She was undone by the way Mat kissed her.

Undone.

"Mat, I—" She couldn't think of what she wanted to say to him. What could she say when the world no longer made sense?

"I know," he responded, that wicked grin of his twisting onto his lips and making a mockery of the riotous feelings ricocheting in her chest. He released her from his iron grip, allowing her to stand shakily on her own. She shivered without his oppressive heat surrounding her. The cold washed over her skin, raising goose flesh as it kissed her flushed cheeks.

"Oi! Matioch, look, it's snowing!" Finn's excitement belied his age, his youthful exuberance infectious. The rest of the men made their way to the windows to watch the fluff of snow drifting lazily to the ground.

Pain lanced through Liz's chest. Her eyes felt hot as they tracked the swirling descent of a snowflake on the bracing breeze. She couldn't breathe. *Why couldn't she breathe?* Mat was smiling with his friends, gazing out the window at the start of what would be a long, harsh winter.

"I hate the bloody cold, but, the first snow of winter reminds me of being a lad." Mat said.

"Aye," Smitty agreed, "My ma used to make snow candies before the winters started gettin' so bad."

Finn rested his head on Matt's shoulder and the smile on his face was sadder than before, Liz felt paralyzed by terror. They were running out of time. The idiots were standing around reminiscing, when they should have been—

The sudden realization crashed through her. They were saying goodbye. These men weren't soldiers or courtiers, they were commoners. It was possible one or all of them could starve to death during this winter. They were saying goodbye to each other, just in case.

"What is it, Lisbet?" Tia asked, concerned eyes fixed on Liz's strained smile.

"I found the knight from my vision, Tia." The soft gasp in Liz's ear shuddered through her entire body, shaking her fragile, hard-won hope. Mat looked over his shoulder to gift them with a smile before Tia squeezed her hand and left her to her tumultuous thoughts.

Liz kept her visions from him. Mat had no idea that Liz's heart was breaking, that his time was running out. She knew exactly when and how he would die. He wouldn't behold another hazy summer. He wouldn't be here to see the Dragon reclaim her after the thaw, if there even was one this year. Her protector, a man that she cared about, would be gone. Just like her mother. Did they sing the song of your life in the mountains the way they did at home?

One day soon his blood would stain the white snow. His bright eyes would dim, and with them all of Aegis. It would be a lesser world without him in it. He looked over at her with that crooked grin she'd grown so fond of, not knowing Liz held inside of her a secret that could change his life.

She sucked in a shaky breath and approached Tia. Liz gripped her friend's fingers tightly, her only comfort. She turned away from Mat, knowing now that whatever happened next, she would not be able to ignore the visions any longer. She always pushed them to the furthest part of her mind, ignored them, pretended they didn't exist. She'd suffered the terrible truth of them in silence.

Like it or not, you're a queen. Now is the time you decide what kind you're going to be.

She wouldn't lose Mat the way she'd lost her mother. Mat promised to keep her safe, to protect her. She would be the kind of queen who refused to let him die. She was going to use her visions to change his fate.

She was going to challenge fate, and win.

Chapter Fourteen

Matioch Steele was a bastard. That was an irrefutable fact. He was a bastard bladesmith with nothing to show for the sum of his life thus far except for a beat-up claymore and a stolen surname. For all that the knights at Fangorn, villagers from his past, even his grandfather reminded him of this fact in a volley of cruel acts and insults, he'd never *felt* like a bastard.

At least, not until tonight.

Liz tasted sweet beneath the spiciness of the wine on her breath. The sweetness reminded him of wild honeysuckle that bloomed in the mountain valleys at springtime. The memory came unbidden, from his childhood spent tracing long winding paths between the forge and the small hut he shared with his mother at the edge of the wood. He'd carried baskets laden with food or supplies for the forge in leather packs and stopped to pluck the stamens from the center of the flowers to drink a drop of syrupy nectar.

Mat's blood pounded in his ears as Liz pulled him from the lodge, through the young snowfall, and into the stable. He felt like he was falling, tumbling through the darkness, praying for and dreading the sickening crash at the end. She smiled at him and the world faded away. He gripped her by the waist as she brushed the snow from her flame-like curls. They stuck to her eyelashes and soaked through his cotton shirt to send a shiver up his spine.

"You're beautiful." He couldn't help himself; he had to say something. She flushed, a pink tinge on the softness of her skin. His heart slammed furiously in his chest, hating himself more as each moment passed. He couldn't keep lying to her. She offered him a shy smile, pressing into his arms and rising onto her tiptoes to feather a soft kiss against his mouth. Mat closed his eyes and groaned, shuddering at the sweetness that tempted him to be a lesser man.

"Stop, Liz," he whispered, putting warm hands on her shoulders and pushing her far enough away that the cold air flooded between them and cleared his muddled thoughts.

"What's wrong?" she asked, her voice small in the inches between them. Mat knew that sound, the sound of a beautiful girl he'd disappointed. Only Liz wasn't just *any* girl; she was decidedly more than that. Fear shimmered in her blue gaze, and he could hear the words that rested on the tip of her tongue. *Did I do something wrong?*

He ran his hands through his hair, feeling the wind picking up outside and rattling the shutters. *Gods, no,* he wanted to whisper into her mouth as he kissed her senseless. But, he wouldn't. The wind howled like a ravenous mountain beast. He would never lie to her again. Swallowing hard past the lump in his throat, he retreated further.

"You deserve better," he said quietly, struggling to keep his thoughts together. She laughed, a scoffing sound, as if she couldn't quite believe his statement. She stepped forward, a hand reaching out to him, no doubt to soothe his fears. Mat jerked away, pressing the heels of his hands to his eyes.

"Mat," she called to him, but he couldn't look at her. "What's all this about? I don't care if you're a bastard. I don't care about your last name or the circumstances of your birth. You have more honor than the nobles I've known my entire life. That isn't nothing." Her pleading tone cut deep, mangling what was left of his heart. "It means more than you think."

"You think I don't deserve you because I'm a bastard?" His words carved through her good intentions, silence falling heavily between them as he leveled hot, angry eyes on her. It was childish to pick a fight now, but she was so *good* that it was almost impossible not to.

"I don't know what's happening here." Her tone was overly calm, attempting to diffuse the situation.

"You shouldn't have trusted me."

She held up open hands, inching forward so slowly that he didn't notice until she was close enough to reach for his hand. Mat felt sick, guilt roiling in the pit of his stomach. He wasn't strong enough to pull away again, so he let her grip his hand tight and lead him to a bench in the corner of the stable. The gentle pressure of her fingertips rested on his cheek as she turned his face toward her.

"Tell me." The whispered words feathered over his skin, leaving goosebumps in their wake.

"I planned to turn you over to Lord Callum at Fangorn Keep." The words came out in a hot rush. "There's a good likelihood he'd turn you over to the Dragon."

For a moment, Mat thought he hadn't said anything at all. She had no discernable reaction. It was possible he'd gone mad.

Then her eyes widened in horror. She opened her pretty mouth, then snapped it shut again just as quickly.

She recoiled, disgust curled onto her lips as she stood and backed away from him, pressing a hand to her stomach. The cold seeped into Mat's skin, especially where she'd been gripping his hand moments before.

"Say something," he demanded, but she only shook her head and refused to meet his eyes. "Liz, please." He tried to reach for her, but she pulled away. "*Please*, say something."

"I can't believe I was stupid enough to—"

She whirled on him, as furious as she'd been when Mat first saw her being dragged away by bounty hunters. This was Liz at her most beautiful, a fearsome beauty that defined her better than softness and shy glances.

"No!" She sliced at the air with a violent hand gesture to stop him from reaching for her again.

"Let me explain," he begged, but she shook her head. He chased after her as she plunged into the darkness and snow. The wind was so loud that he shouted her name at the top of his lungs to be heard above it.

"Stop following me!" She was racing toward the tree line without a torch or a cloak. In the darkness it would be easy for her to get lost and succumb to the elements. He jogged to catch up with her. She turned and shoved him, throwing her hands against his chest with the power of her whole body. He stumbled back, shocked. Before he recovered, her skirts disappeared in a swish between two trees.

Panic clawed up his throat, hot and acidic. "Liz!" he shouted, thundering forward haphazardly, oblivious to how far he'd strayed from the lodge. He searched the dark shapes of the forest as he barreled on, shouting and praying, each second lengthened until it seemed to stretch for an eternity.

"Mat!" Her voice drifted back to him, twisting on the wind through the trees. Where? Where? *Where!*

"Mat, I can't find you!"

He closed his eyes tight and listened hard. The wind ruffled his hair, seeming to tug him towards her voice. He snapped his eyes open and ran. He didn't know where he was, where he was going, just that he needed to get to her.

There was a flash of copper hair, and then she slammed into his chest. His momentum threw them both violently off balance, and they tumbled to the forest floor in a heap of elbows and knees. He was lying against the frozen ground, her hair spread around him in long, curling tendrils as dark as blood against the glaring white of the snow. She opened her eyes and they filled with tears, a small sob escaping her lips before they ran down her cheeks.

Mat pressed her into the ground beside him and ran his hands over her arms and the bones below her neck, checking her for injuries. She smacked his hands away, but he pressed them against her sides and searched her watery blue eyes.

"Where are you hurt?" he demanded, watching her scoff and smack his hands away again.

"Nowhere you can help." She shoved herself to sitting and mopped at her wet cheeks with the rough brocade fabric of her sleeve. Mat couldn't meet her eyes again after that. Instead, he shoved away from her, brushing dirt and wet leaves from his breeches. He stood and held a hand out to her, wondering if she would even accept his help. She placed her hand in his, and he pulled her up to her feet.

"Why?" she asked, turning on him with all the authority and entitlement her royal position entailed. He flinched beneath her withering gaze. "I trusted you, and I want to know why you were so willing to betray me." Mat's shoulders hunched against her imperiousness.

"You wouldn't understand."

"Try me."

The darkness of the woods seemed all-encompassing, and there was no sign of the light from the lodge. Mat gripped her by one of her folded arms and led her in the direction from which he thought they'd come. He didn't want to alarm her by revealing they could be lost, so instead he answered her question.

"Well, I'm a bastard, Liz. That might not matter much to you, but the rest of Aegis doesn't look kindly on people like me." The shame of it burned his face. "Even taking my mother's surname didn't help much. Growing up was lonely and confusing. I could never understand the names other villagers called my mother, or why we weren't welcomed at the temple on holy days." He helped her over the roots of a large oak tree, and she let him without complaint.

"They wouldn't let you pray with them?" He shook his head. "That's why you didn't know the story about Hak'ka."

To his surprise, he found no judgment in her eyes.

"I got older and learned what the names they called us meant, and then I started getting into fights." He grinned and rubbed the back of his neck sheepishly, but Liz didn't look surprised. "Mostly, it was hard for my mum to find work and feed us. She went hungry some nights so I could eat, and the thinner she became the angrier I got." Mat remembered those long nights, every guilty bite he swallowed down. Tasteless, like ash in his mouth, seeming to fuel the fire inside him.

"How could a man father a child and then just *leave*?" she asked. It may have been the cold in the night air or the darkness surrounding them like a cloak, but he felt her hand squeeze his harder. She shuffled closer to his side.

"I spent too long wondering the same thing. I wondered what I did wrong, if I was broken, or unlovable." He'd never said this aloud before. The thoughts had remained inside of him, festering with time and distance. "The truth is, Liz, we're all alone. Each one of us."

"We don't have to be," she said. He wrapped an arm around her shivering shoulders to encase her in his warmth.

"*You* don't have to be," he said. "The only differences between us are opportunities. You have them and I don't. I saw an opportunity, and I didn't think about what it would cost to take it."

She folded beneath his arm, fitting into the crook of his shoulder as if she'd always belonged there.

"So, what changed?" she asked. "Why tell me at all? You could have gone through with it, and I would have never been the wiser."

What *had* changed?

She stopped walking, and he was forced to look down into her eyes, a deep cerulean even in the darkness. Her gaze hid ocean depths. Wisdom that was solely hers, the kind that could fell him with a few words.

"I want to be the kind of man who deserves you." The air snapped tight between them and seemed to thin. Why had he said that? His breath came faster, and she looked at him demurely through the shadow of her eyelashes. "One day."

She stepped out from beneath the warmth of his arm. The wind died down to nothing. Stillness and silence wrapped them tightly together. Her eyes drifted over his shoulder, and she motioned to where the glow of lanterns was visible through the trees. A tight coil of fear released at the sight and loosened his shoulders with warm relief.

Slowly they made their way back toward the lodge, neither willing to break the silence or acknowledge the things they'd discussed under the cover of the trees. Mat held out a tentative hand to help her down the hill, catching her when she stumbled and praying he didn't mistake the flush on her cheeks as his hand gripped her waist. He didn't want to admit how horribly he'd messed up things with Liz, or that his deception snuffed out whatever spark had been between them.

"Mat?" Her voice was the kind of quiet he couldn't decipher. "How am I supposed to trust you now?"

He ached somewhere deep inside his chest and looked away from her in shame.

"I could tell you a million times over that it would never happen again, but they're only words." An understanding seemed to pass between them then. Neither of them needed to give voice to the regret lingering in the fogged air. Mat clenched his jaw as Liz shifted on her feet, reluctant to go back inside. It was as if she and Mat both knew that once she left tonight, whatever had been between them would never be spoken of again.

Liz's sullen eyes sparked with the light of an idea, and it seemed to illuminate her entire face.

"Tell me your deepest secret. Something you've never told anyone else. Perhaps then we could meet halfway?"

It was a hopeless wish, but also his last chance. Swallowing down any trepidation, Mat pulled her roughly into his arms and gripped her tightly. How could someone so small be so fearsome? Leaning his forehead against hers, Mat closed his eyes and the words fell recklessly from his lips.

"I found my father. Or, at least, a clue where to look... Wharton Cove."

Liz barely had time to widen her eyes before the rest of the story rushed out on a hot breath. Once it was done, all his fears laid bare before her, Mat felt lighter than he had in years. As if he'd somehow lifted a great weight from his shoulders, allowing her to share his burdens. She didn't speak at first, her eyes far away in thought. Was she reconsidering? Perhaps his secrets weren't enough to make up for his betrayal.

"We have to go. Mat, you've waited your entire life to find even a trace of him. I would never forgive myself if you—"

"I can't do that. Not until I know you're safe at Fangorn."

"Safe at Fangorn? Didn't you just say that you were going to turn me over to Lord Callum there and he would deliver me back to the Dragon? There is no *safe* for me anymore." She crossed her arms defiantly over her chest.

"It'd be easier to thwart fat Lord Callum than the Dragon and his whole bloody army." Mat argued. Her jaw snapped shut and she ground her teeth audibly.

"You want me to trust you, don't you?" Liz asked.

"Of course I do, but—"

"Then we'll go. I want to gauge your sincerity. Also, I wouldn't be able to live with myself if you didn't get the answers about your past." Mat was confused and cold. The wine had long since stopped warming his blood, and he didn't have the energy to keep arguing with her. "I don't know what this is between us, but I care about you."

Her words stopped his heart.

"I lived a sheltered life at court," she said. "With the exception of Tia, I wasn't allowed to get close to anyone. Not in the way that matters." She gripped her skirts so hard that her knuckles turned white; her eyes were boring straight into him. He wanted to dive into those fathomless blue eyes.

"Until you."

That caught his attention. A gentle breeze tickled the hair near his ears as his heart began to pound.

"You terrify me." His hands were shaking. He'd been pushed past his limit. She was always pushing, asking him to challenge himself in new ways. The wind blew harder, more insistently, swishing her skirts around her legs. "I don't know who I am, Liz. There's this whole part of me that's missing, and it's because of whoever my father is. Either he didn't want me and he left my mother to fend for herself, or he never knew about me in the first place and I—"

He trembled, and she pressed herself further into his arms, giving him something to hang on to. An anchor when he was adrift on a sea of uncertainty. She kissed him beneath his ear, her lips trailing to his jaw. The wind died again and it was unnaturally still.

"It makes no difference who he is. You're still the man who rescues strange women in the forest, the man that swore an oath to a stranger to keep her from harm. Whoever your father is, it doesn't change the part of you I care about. I have known my fair share of royalty, and there is nothing more kingly than to stand up for those who cannot do so themselves."

Angry tears welled in his eyes and he turned away, ashamed, but she held his face fast and didn't allow him to hide himself from her.

"What if I'm not strong enough?" He cleared his throat to keep his voice from breaking.

"You don't have to do it alone. We'll go together. Besides, it'll give us time."

She offered him a small smile, enough to let him mirror one in response. He nodded; he would have to tell the men tomorrow of their change in plans. He didn't know how he would explain it away. He clung to her, letting her hold him, until the night grew late and Tia called for her from the main lodge. The night was coming to a close, but he didn't want to see it end.

Tia's voice, giddy with drink, was coming closer, and Mat squeezed Liz tighter still. She sighed in his ear, and he felt her relax against him as she sank into the embrace.

"Tia will be so angry with me."

"Gareth is going to be furious." Mat smiled widely, completely unrepentant.

"Tell me everything is going to be alright. That I mean something to you."

Mat looked into her fathomless blue eyes, eyes that could see him like no one else in the world. Eyes that looked at him and saw someone worthy, regardless of his birth. All of Aegis was calling for her death, had celebrated when they thought her life was over. It turned his stomach to think of it now.

"More than you could ever know, princess."

She kissed him again, chastely, her lips a harsh push against his cheek as Tia marched towards them. She glowered ferociously at Mat, who peeled himself away from Liz and stepped back with a playful grin. Without a word, Tia gripped Liz by the wrist and dragged her away, giggling. He was alone now.

Just him, the snow, and the silence.

Chapter Fifteen

"You're thinking too loudly," Tia groaned, tossing a pillow at Liz who caught it easily. Liz attempted to smile at her friend but failed. She twisted her fingers through her curls until Tia deigned to drag herself from the sheets, grip her hand, and still her nervous fidgeting. Leaning her cheek into the crook of Liz's shoulder, Tia whispered lazily against the skin of her neck.

"My head hurts too badly for you to fidget like that. Tell me what bothers you or let me sleep away the lingering effects of the spiced wine from last night."

Liz sighed, unsure where to even begin. So much of what was said between she and Mat the night before felt personal. Too personal to talk about openly, even with Tia.

"It's Mat," she admitted, worrying her bottom lip with her teeth. "He looks at me and it feels like nothing else matters, but there are so many things that matter. So many things I can't be distracted from. He's the knight from my visions and I know he's going to die... soon. But, why have I been seeing his death over and over again unless it was to stop it? Tia, am I supposed to try and save him or am I supposed to lead him to the mountains?" Tia lifted her heavy head with a sudden clarity in her bleary eyes.

"Have you slept at all?" she asked. Liz shook her head, closing her eyes against welling tears that she refused to let fall. She crossed to the window, and her hands gripped the sill hard enough to bleach her knuckles white.

"What am I doing, Tia?" There was an edge to her voice that she felt all the way down to her toes. "What have I *done?* People are going to die because I ran away. My people." Tia's hand feathered onto Liz's shoulder; the familiar touch made her recoil instead of comforting her as it normally did.

"I know," Tia said in quiet resignation. "Ask me why I'm here, Lisbet." Tia's face was drawn and tight. Her warm brown eyes were not lit in honeyed delight; instead they were dark and unreadable. Liz swallowed hard past a lump in her throat.

"Why?"

Tia's eyes shimmered with tears. She gripped Liz's hand tight and brought it to her mouth, pressing her lips against her palm for a few seconds longer than normal.

"Because I believe in you," she said, her words broken and raw. "I believe in you more than I believe in the gods. I have watched you, every single day, fighting so hard to wrest your fate from the cruel grip of destiny. You made me realize I am more than the islander refugee they whispered about at court. I would rather starve in an eternal winter and die by your side than to live my entire life a slave to that sorcerer."

Liz sobbed openly; a weight buoyed from her shoulders by the strength of Tia's words. They wrapped their arms around each other until their weeping became teary laughter.

Time moved strangely; it could have been minutes or hours they lounged together on the bed. Liz placed her head in Tia's lap, hair splayed wildly over the furs. Tia twisted her fingers through the curls, deftly braiding the waist-length locks. Tia pulled small golden cuffs from her own dark curls and used them to secure the tiny braids.

"I saw how you clung to him last night," Tia said. Liz felt a furious flush rising in her cheeks. "I don't think I've ever seen you look so..." Her words trailed off, but she didn't have to finish the sentence. Liz knew exactly what Tia meant. It was unexpected and out of character, an impulsive and impossible relationship. Still, Liz couldn't find the words to express how much more herself she felt when she was with Mat. She couldn't explain the ease with which she forgave him or the instinct to get closer.

"Why didn't you tell me it could feel like that when you kiss a man?" Liz asked, keeping her tone light enough to elicit a giggle from Tia.

"Or a woman," she teased. "You're nearly as red as your hair. He must be a very good kisser." Liz's flush burned hot against her skin, but she nodded, unable to contain the smile overtaking her face. Tia leaned closer to Liz, a wicked spark lighting her eyes. "Which one of them is better?"

Liz gasped, sitting up so suddenly she nearly lost her balance on the edge of the mattress.

"Tia!" she whispered fiercely. Her friend collapsed in a fit of giggles, and Liz couldn't stay scandalized for long. It was another hour or more before either of them wanted to leave the warmth of their shared room. But after telling Tia about their plans to travel to Wharton Cove, it became evident it was time to prepare to leave the relative safety of the lodge.

Tia breezed down the staircase as if she hadn't been grumbling half the morning and hissing at the sunlight that dared to peek through the curtains. Liz watched her friend plant a loud kiss on Wallace's rough cheek before disappearing around a corner. She smiled and took note of the gentle way Wallace's fingers brushed over the place where Tia's lips had been moments before.

The smell of eggs and bread wafted in from the kitchens setting her mouth to watering. Smitty grumbled beneath his breath, heaping plates of steaming potatoes roasted with rosemary onto a plate. Finn's head was in the cocoon of his arms as he leaned on the tabletop, groaning every so often. Liz tried not to laugh, but the ridiculous smile spread wide across her face at the sorry sight of them all. This felt like home.

Mat marched into the kitchens and Liz's heart pounded wildly in her chest as he dropped to a knee before Finn, offering a water skein. Finn groaned more loudly than before but sipped slowly and Mat ruffled his hair affectionately. It tore something free within her, seeing the earnest concern Mat had for Finn and how tenderly he cared for the boy. Mat rose and offered her a smile, small and secret. Just like that she was back in the darkness with him last night, his jaggedness displayed plainly for her alone. He crossed the room to her. His hair was damp and his shirt was open at the neck, showing a small triangle of his chest below his throat. He smelled like soap, and she found she missed the scent of iron and leather.

"I hope you slept better than I did," he said, a wicked grin curling onto his mouth. "Finn spent most of the night emptying his dinner into a bucket, poor lad." Liz glanced over at the back of Finn's head again, grimacing when he groaned loudly once more.

"In truth I haven't slept well in days. I'll be happy to lay eyes on the sea again."

Smitty's head snapped up at her words, and she sank her teeth into her lower lip before she could reveal any more. Instead of waiting to hear Mat explain their trip to Wharton Cove, she slipped outside and sucked in a deep breath, filling her lungs with the lingering scent of autumn.

Shouting from inside and the banging of pots stole her moment of peace before Smitty and the others spilled outside.

"Ye've lost yer bloody mind, lad!" Smitty's brogue was thick and merciless when he was angry.

"It's just a couple of days. Gareth and myself will take the women to Wharton Cove to find out if Liz has family in the area. If not, we'll only be two days behind you to the keep." The lies fell too easily from Mat's lips.

Liz wrung her hands beneath the cover of her worn, green cloak. She didn't realize it would raise such a fuss for a small group of them to take a quick trip to the coastal town on the edge of the Northern Sea.

"I don't like it, lad. Why can't we all go together? It doesn't sit well with me, to leave ye all to yerselves. Think of the ladies!" Smitty threw his hands up in the air, exasperated.

Liz almost wanted to giggle at his childish chivalry but didn't dare risk angering him further. Mat rubbed his temple before explaining it all over again.

"You and the boys need to get this cured meat to Fangorn Keep. Lord Callum will not take kindly if any of this goes astray or gets ruined. With winter descending this quickly, the blizzards will be on us in a fortnight, and it'll be slower going with a wagon laden with supplies. I'll be right behind you." He clapped a hand on the man's shoulder before he complained that he didn't understand and Mat had to start all over again.

Tia sat in the corner; her borrowed dress of wool buttoned all the way up her throat. It was odd to be dressed in this manner, so many layers and skirts. It was odder still to see Tia bundled up that way. In the south, fashion was much less modest and formal. The thick brocade of Liz's emerald green dress scratched unattractively against her pale skin.

She held her hand out for Tia's and expected to feel her fingers in her palm the way they'd always done, since they were children. When Tia's hand did not find its way into her own, Liz looked over at her. Tia's brow was furrowed. She sat unnaturally quiet and still.

"Is something the matter?"

Tia didn't acknowledge Liz, but then, her demeanor had been rather odd all morning. She'd made herself scarce after they left the comfort of their rooms. Perhaps Tia was still battling a headache from the wine, or perhaps she was bothered by something else entirely.

"Tia." Liz moved in front of her, but Tia turned her face away. "Please, tell me what's bothering you."

Her friend looked up at her, big dark eyes filled with uncommon sorrow.

"After our conversation this morning I can't stop thinking about home. About Killian. I wonder if he's still alive, or if he allowed your mother to escape. I know he was in the hall when the Dragon came for you and—"

"What are you thinking?" Liz squared her shoulders, her jaw clenched to keep hot words from spilling out. Nervously her eyes flicked to the men on the other side of the stables, their voices still raised and argumentative. No one paid them any mind. "Keep your voice down. What if they heard you?"

"You said that Mat and Gareth already knew, I assumed they would have told the others."

"Of course not!" Liz whispered harshly, "You said it yourself, they're simple and superstitious. I don't like the idea of putting them in more danger."

"I didn't think—"

"No, you didn't." Panic settled into a staccato rhythm beating her pulse in her ears. Killian's kind eyes, always scowling at his tempestuous sister's antics, flashed bright in Liz's memory. She'd known him since they were children. His warmth was as familiar as Tia's. "I worry about him too. About them all. I shouldn't have separated you from him. He's the only family you have left, and—"

"Enough." Tia said the word wearily. Clearly, it cost her something to think of him now. "Killian owes you every-thing—his knighthood, my place at court, not being shipped back to the islands. He made his oath to the royal family, but he only ever performed his duties with your safety in mind. He would be appalled to hear you say we should have abandoned you in your time of need."

"Hush," Liz hissed, careful of the lull in the men's conversation. Tia paled, her weariness turning to humility in a moment at Liz's sharp tone. Liz leaned in, careful not to raise her voice and earn the attention of the others.

"We can't trust them," Liz said, hating the truth of it. Tia nodded, swallowing down whatever words had been poised on her tongue. Liz's harsh scowl softened. She motioned for Tia to follow her away from prying ears.

"I meant no harm, majesty," Tia whispered. Liz clucked in disapproval of the new title she had taken to using as of late.

"Do you remember when you said that I was a queen, like it or not?" Tia nodded, the motion slow and unsure. "I didn't like it. I've been trying really hard to just be Liz, nothing more or less than that."

"Mat is the only one who calls you that. *Liz*. It suits you." Tia's voice was still devoid of any of her usual levity.

"I've been thinking about my mother, about how she encouraged me to leave the ceremony and allow our people to die." Tia opened her mouth to say something, but Liz held up a silencing hand. "She gave her life so that I could have a choice. I'm just not sure what the right choice is anymore. I wasn't ready to die, but I hadn't considered that watching others suffer in my place may be even worse. What if I made a mistake?"

Tears welled in Tia's eyes as she wrung her hands against the stiff wool of her skirt.

"She didn't just give her life; she gave all our lives. Without magick, we'll all die. Maybe not today or tomorrow, but eventually all of us will perish. So, apologies *majesty*, but your choices will never affect you alone. No matter how much you wish it, you'll never be just Liz. I am a loyal subject and your friend, but I'm also a sister. I have sacrificed as much as anyone, and you have an obligation to hear me when I tell you that you are *wrong*. Fleeing that ceremony was the best decision you've ever made. If we could go back, I wouldn't have done anything differently."

"Tia, I—

"Everyone thinks there are only two choices. Die in a winter without end or live as slaves to a power mad sorcerer. But you and I both know there is another choice. The gods don't make demands, they present riddles. In every story you've ever told me, the mortals who have succeeded found loopholes. So, stop giving up and use that brilliant mind of yours to find one."

They stood then, neither budging, nor willing to compromise. Liz didn't want to be a queen; she also didn't want to die. She only wanted to be with Mat and the others. She wanted to unravel the mystery of Gareth and watch Wallace's gentle way with the horses. She wanted to laugh with Smitty and smile with Finn. She wanted to grow old with Tia and raise their children together the way she'd never been allowed to imagine before. Liz wanted to be herself, nothing more.

"What if I can't do this?" she asked, sniffling as Tia's hands relaxed against her skirt.

"Then we die. At least we'll die free." She shrugged and Liz breathed out a relieved laugh. Tia reached out and Liz met her, their hands gripped tight and their foreheads leaned against each other.

"Promise me that you won't forget who you are, Lisbet. After everything, I understand the appeal of hiding from your birthright. You don't have that luxury. You are meant for more; the gods have marked you for greatness. Never forget that." Tia looked deep into Liz's eyes and silently they came to an understanding.

Liz would have to make some tough decisions soon.

Tia left her to finish packing the few things that they would take with them on their journey to Wharton Cove. Only the things they both thought Lord Callum's family would not miss, and with the promise of compensation in the future. Tia didn't trust Liz to do the packing, fearing she would only bring practical items and nothing fashionable enough for her tastes. Liz leaned against the post of the stable, looking over the lodge and listening to the nickering of the horses.

She closed her eyes, letting her mind drift among the sounds of the forest. Only, it drifted too far, and before she realized what happened she was peering through the mists of another vision. This time she slipped into it without warning. They were coming more often now, more persistently. It frightened her.

Now that she knew who the knight was, she could make out the shape of Mat's lips and the strong set of his chin. Something was decidedly different about the battlefield this time. She recognized the shape of the man on the right of Mat. Wallace, with his lumbering bulk and kind brown eyes, was cut down by three men in black armor. Liz cried out, her screams echoing only within her own mind. Smitty, swinging a mighty axe was cleaved in two, his head rolling to rest at her feet. His eyes open wide and unseeing. His gruff cursing voice silenced forever. A cold wind blew against her skin and slowly she turned, mouth open in horror as Finn was brought to his knees, tears of resignation making tracks in the blood on his cheeks as a soldier came to stand before him, blade raised high, ready to cut him down. "He's just a boy!" she screamed to no one and nothing.

"Oi!" Her eyes snapped open to see Finn, smiling at her expression. "Didn't mean to startle you, M'lady. Do you know where Tia went?" He had a fist of wildflowers crushed in dirty hands.

"Our room, in the lodge," she choked out. As soon as he turned away, she clutched her thrashing stomach, which was threatening to spill the contents of her breakfast. She couldn't let what she'd seen in her vision happen. She gripped her shaking hands together hard enough for her nails to draw blood against her palms.

The lightly falling snow had turned the ground into a muddy, slushy mess. The heel of her boot sank into a pool of ice and mud and slid from beneath her, sending her stumbling onto the ground. Her gown was soaked. Tears rolled down her face in earnest. Her mother was dead. Her father had been murdered. Killian was just... gone. Everyone that she cared about would soon face a violent and bloody death if she couldn't figure out how to stop it.

She had to stop it.

A shadow crossed in front of her, and a pair of strong arms pulled her up from the ground. She moved to wipe her tears, but callused hands were already on her cheeks. When her eyes cleared and adjusted to the light, she peered up at Gareth, his grey eyes regarding warmly over her face. She didn't know what to say about her tears, didn't know how to explain them away.

He didn't ask. Instead he took her muddy hand and pressed the back of it against his lips. She sucked in a sharp breath as he lingered a moment too long. When he rose his head, his eyes held hers until the strands of fate that wound around them tightened perceptibly. Woven and knotted, braided into an intricate pattern of confusion and complexity. He bowed his head, excusing himself without words and made his way back to the horses.

Liz let out a ragged breath, her heart hammering in her chest. The trip to Wharton Cove couldn't come quickly enough. If her calculations were correct, and she'd checked them a hundred times the night before, bringing Mat to Wharton Cove should keep him from the Black Mountain Pass and the battle in her vision. By helping him find answers about his father, she could save his life.

All of their lives.

Chapter Sixteen

Mat couldn't keep arguing with Smitty. If he wasn't careful, their misunderstanding would come to blows, and Smitty always carried knives on him. Mat marched into the lodge, to the small room behind the kitchens he'd occupied during their stay. He needed to change and gather his things so they could leave for Wharton Cove. Mat was frustrated, trying to still the tempest raging inside of his mind. Not only did he have to prepare half of their party for a spur-of-the-moment trip, the other half needed to be ready to deliver the supplies they'd gathered to Lord Callum at Fangorn.

He was being pulled in too many directions. Gareth had been little help, his quiet stoicism rankling Mat's nerves and leaving too much room for him to doubt his decisions. He tugged his shirt off over his head and threw it on his cot. Crossing to the wash basin, he splashed his face and neck with water. He studied his reflection and grounded himself, sorting his priorities in his mind. Drying his hands, he caught sight of the signet ring.

He was so close. Answers to his past. Answers about who he was. Answers that would finally close the chasm of doubt residing deep within him.

He slid on a new shirt and then his leather tunic on top of that, fastening the buckles. He shoved his things into his saddle bag and slung it haphazardly over his shoulder. As he left the room, ready to alert Tia that they needed to head out and make good time, Smitty called his name from outside.

"Matioch! Come quick!"

Slamming the door behind him, Mat unsheathed his sword and tossed his saddlebags and his weapons belt into the dust. Gareth already had his sword leveled at the trees. Liz peeked curiously from behind Gareth's shoulder at the caravan stopped at the top of the ridge overlooking the lodge. Dozens of hate-filled, suspicious eyes gazed down at them.

"Half-bloods?" Mat asked. Gareth nodded but did not lower his sword. There were too many of them. From a glance he could count thirty, maybe more.

"Liz, pull up your hood," he demanded.

She looked over at him confused, but pulled the hood of her cloak over her scarlet hair, hiding it from sight. Panic clawed its way up Mat's throat, hot and acidic. He'd been lucky when he'd fought the half-blood bounty hunter who'd captured Liz. They had the element of surprise, and by the grace of the gods, the man hadn't landed any blows. Even a child could turn pain into enough strength to crush his skull one-handed. There were too many of them, every one imbued with the strange magick of their ink-black blood. They couldn't fight their way out of this. Maybe, they didn't have to.

Dropping his sword, Mat stepped forward cautiously. He glanced at Gareth, telling him without words not to leave Liz's side as he approached the traveling caravan. As he got closer, he could make out the faces of women and children, cowering in the wagons, peering from the windows, crouched behind the men leading them through the Neither Wood.

Mat raised his hands in peace. His eyes scanned the tree line as he waited to see which of the men would step forward to speak with him. To his surprise, a boy no more than eleven winters old stepped out from the caravan of half-bloods. He had pale skin and dark hair, freckles spattered across his nose, all the features of a young lad. But his eyes were ageless, wise beyond his years. The men with him parted, unwilling to touch him as he met Mat in the brush between the lodge and the caravan.

"We mean no harm to you," Mat said right away, loudly enough that the others could hear him. The boy smiled ruefully, amused by Mat's proclamation.

"If only that were true, *tin man,*" the boy said, looking past Mat pointedly to Gareth in his armor. "Your kind has been killing and persecuting us for centuries. Now that we have you outnumbered, suddenly you have a burning desire for peace? How... *convenient.*"

Mat cleared his throat, not adept at diplomacy and out of his depth.

"My name is Matioch Steele. Perhaps we should start there instead?" He held a hand out to the lad in a gesture of trust.

"I am Sylas, the blackblood traveler. It's been a long time since any man willingly offered me his arm." He took it, the bemused grin deepening on his face at Mat's confused expression. Sylas released him, and Mat took a shaky breath. They couldn't afford to battle these people; he had to protect Liz at all costs.

"We're leaving the Neither Wood," Mat blurted out, waving a hand toward the half-packed wagon and horses.

"Leaving it much richer than you entered it." Sylas raised an eyebrow before motioning to the cargo of the wagon, the cured meat Lord Callum demanded. "The Wood is sacred. People who kill more than they can eat are punished. Severely. Thieves are as bad as murderers here."

"It isn't just for us. We're bringing it back to feed the villages through winter. Innocent people. Women. Children. The sick and the poor. Surely, you can overlook our hunting this once?" There was a pregnant silence that followed. This boy didn't seem in a hurry to make any decisions. Instead, those ageless eyes skimmed over every plane and hollow of Mat's face, assessing him, judging him. When he was done with Mat, Sylas peered around him to Gareth, and beyond his shoulder to Liz. It was when he caught sight of her that the shadow of a true smile ghosted over his lips.

"Oi! Matioch! What's all this?" Finn shuffled toward them, not realizing they were in the middle of a delicate conversation. Mat closed his eyes and swore under his breath.

"Not now, mate," Mat said, hoping to still the lad's curiosity until he and Sylas could come to an accord. "I'm a bit preoccupied at the moment." Instead of reading the clear message in Mat's strained tone, Finn marched right up to Sylas and took his hand as if they were long friends.

"Name's Finn," he introduced himself, offering a deceptively shy smile. Sylas looked appropriately stunned, and Mat rubbed a hand against his now pounding temple. The fool was going to get them all killed. After a moment, Sylas broke into raucous laughter, bordering on hysteria. He laughed so hard he bent over and wiped the moisture from the corners of his eyes. Finn's eyes widened at the sound but a wide smile cracked over his face all the same.

"In all my years no one has addressed me in such a way!" He howled a moment longer before he regained control of his senses. "I shall allow you to continue on your journey, so long as you make your way quickly from this place. For a price." His tone deepened as he turned to gauge Mat's reaction.

"We have very little, almost nothing in the way of money—"

"I did not ask for money," Sylas said. "All I ask for is a favor."

"A favor? Name it. Anything in my power, I'll do for you," Mat said. Sylas waved his hand dismissively at Mat, stepping around him so that he could see Liz more clearly. With two fingers and little care he brushed away Gareth's sword, his rueful smile deepening into true mischief.

"From you. A simple request to be honored in the future, when next we meet."

Liz stepped timidly out from behind Gareth, straightening her shoulders and locking eyes with the half-blood boy.

"I won't kill anyone," she stated, her chin set and eyes defiant.

"Agreed." Sylas turned back toward the caravan, stopping only briefly to pull a pendant carved from wood from around his neck. He handed it to Finn, peering curiously up at him.

"Wear this to keep you safe. It shows you are a friend to the blackbloods. That you can be trusted." Finn gripped the pendant tight, a blush coloring his face as Sylas disappeared back into the caravan. They rambled on their way, weaving and dodging a path through the trees, leaving no trace of ever being there at all.

Chapter Seventeen

Wharton Cove was nothing like the southern coast. Everything appeared dark and awash in grey. The chill in the air was measurably worse than it had been in the Neither Wood. Liz's lip curled at the near constant scent of fish and the dampness that permeated everything. The salt spray was a biting kind of cold that made a mockery of her borrowed wool cloak and many layers. This coast was carpeted with rocks, instead of sand, with dark mysterious water that undoubtedly harbored the kinds of beasts she'd heard tales of as a child.

Instead of reminding her of home, she missed the southern bay of Silver City even more. The salt on the air may have been the same, but it was crueler here somehow. A farce of what she had known her whole life. She tightened her grip on the saddle horn in front of her, fidgeting in Mat's arms. In response his grip squeezed tighter around her.

"Quit squirming," he whispered in her ear. "You're making it hard to focus on where I'm going."

At the clear implication of his words, a blush crawled up her neck and lit her cheeks on fire. He chuckled near her ear. She hissed disapprovingly, and he laughed louder, enjoying teasing her far too much.

The clopping of the horse's hooves on the cobblestone echoed in the near silence. She was shocked by the lack of people on the streets. Surely it must have been the chill in the air driving them indoors. Nets hung from the doorposts of the fisherman's houses. An offering to the goddess of the moon and tides to help keep their loved ones safe as they traveled on the seas. She had seen something similar in the villages near the bay, but never to this extent. Nearly every home was covered with nets, obscuring windows and doors. As they traveled closer to the docks, she spied a woman begging a harrowed man to stay with her, gripping his arm tight. The sound of her wails rang in Liz's ears.

"Keep your hood up." Mat said, turning their pony away from the woman.

"I don't understand," Liz whispered to Mat.

"The tides and currents change in unpredictable ways now. It drags the small fishing boats out into the sea where most of the time they never come back." Every word he spoke was a dagger in her heart. Another consequence of her selfish flight from the sacrifice. Magick was waning here. These too-thin, gaunt-faced people were suffering because of her choice. She swallowed down hot bile as she thought of how cowardly she must be to let them suffer on her behalf.

Her traveling party didn't have to wonder which way to go; each of the streets seemed to lead to the docks and a large market just north of them. Many stalls were empty. Others were manned by women with weary faces or children far too young to be working at all. The silence here set Liz's hands trembling; it was a cocoon of absence that suffocated them, making each clop of the horses' hooves offensive by default. The air was too heavy, as if awaiting the riot of a storm any moment.

A new smell nearly knocked her off the horse. Acrid and almost sweet, rot and char warring for control, each worse than the other. Liz's eyes watered and she coughed as she took in the horror displayed before them. Four bodies tied to posts and burned beyond recognition. Eyeless, featureless, lips burned away to leave the remnants of white teeth still clenched in pain and terror glinting like pearls in the afternoon sun. The people at the marketplace took no notice of the gore, giving the impression of callous apathy. An eerie desensitization to casual violence and gruesome murder.

Mat swore and his heels dug into the horse's flanks, forcing the beast into a lively trot, maneuvering them to the other side of the market where the air was clear and fresh.

"Wh-what? *Who did this?*" Liz's thoughts fractured. Every emotion flashed across her expressive face. Shock, Horror, Outrage, Guilt. Mat made a sound low in his throat, a clear warning to keep her voice down.

"It's a warning," he said softly in her ear, too soft for the cruelty before them. "The Dragon's favorite intimidation tactic. You don't string up and burn men in plain view of the most populated parts of town, visible all the way down the docks if you're merely meting out justice. You make a spectacle as a warning to others." Liz couldn't help but nod at his logic, though she was loathed to think the men here died for something so fickle.

"We should go," Tia said grimly from the back of Gareth's horse. Mat turned their horse, and Liz craned her neck to keep the smoldering bodies in sight as long as possible before they disappeared from view.

She couldn't recall when they first saw the thistle sigil around town. At every turn they were confronted by the echo of the black flower stamped onto the top of Mat's signet ring. It still seemed so familiar to Liz, something from her lessons as a child, niggling in the back of her mind. The symbol was pressed into the stones in front of businesses. Plaques and statues had it embossed on them in delicate filigree. At a smaller market further from the docks, most of the large shipping containers had it stamped across barrels and on large casks of wine coming in from merchant ships. A dark thistle, spiked and ominous. The sigil appeared to be guiding them down the crooked streets to the base of a hill. They stopped at a brick-lined lane leading up the hill to a pair of ornate iron gates. The name of the manor displayed proudly on the gate; Greystone Heights.

The memory of where she'd seen the sigil slammed into her, nearly toppling her from the horse. The memory of a faded list of nobleman's estates and their masters. Greystone Heights belonged to Lord LaMonte, known better now as the Dragon.

Liz tightened her grip on the saddle horn until her knuckles bleached white, turning wide eyes to Tia who rode beside them with Gareth. Mat only paused for a moment before clicking his tongue and urging the horse to trot forward. Liz reached out for the reins and pulled them tight. The horse whinnied, prancing in place in frustration. Mat shushed the horse as Liz wriggled her way out of his grasp to dismount.

"What the bloody afterworld are you doing, Liz?" Mat asked, his tone irritated. She slid to the ground and stumbled, pushing a wayward curl from her face as she looked up at him in apology.

"I can't go up there. Not to Greystone Heights. I would explain, but I just *can't*." She pulled the cloak tight around her shoulders and tugged her hood low over her face, hiding as much of her hair and features as she could. Her boots weren't made for navigating the stony path set before her. She pitched to the side a couple of times, but refused to look back.

The sigil on Mat's ring mocked her now. It had been right in front of her all along. Not only did she realize now that he was the knight from her vision, the one whose death haunted her dreams for years; He was also somehow connected to the one noble family that wouldn't hesitate to end her life. The horse clopped along beside her as Mat followed without speaking. It irritated her. Didn't he realize that she was walking away so that he could continue on his quest? Finally, she turned on her heel, curls escaping from her plait as she fixed him with an angry glare.

"Why are you following me? Your answers lie at the end of that lane." She crossed her arms and huffed. He ran a hand through his hair, and offered his arm to her so that she could get back onto the horse.

"Let's find a tavern for the night," he said, ignoring her outburst. Being here put Liz in more danger than she'd been in since the night of the ceremony; but she'd already chosen to save herself once before. This is where that led; bodies burned in the street, people starving, and the possibility of a winter without end. This time she was going to choose Mat instead. She accepted his arm, and he swung her up to sit in front of him. She didn't understand him. His answers lay just down that path. Why stop searching for them now when he was so close?

They finally found what appeared to be the most respectable tavern in town, perhaps because it was the farthest from the docks. It was well lit with no women of the night hanging out of the stoop. They tied off the horses and Mat paid for the rooms while she and Tia found a semi-clean table near the back. Liz made sure to keep her hood up and pulled low over her face and hair. The glares of the locals followed them around, obvious outsiders wearing velvet and brocades. The women here were lucky if they got to wear wool. Most of them had their dirty hair tied away from their faces with what looked like scraps of linen, a fabric that wouldn't keep out the chill. The harsh winter approaching would devastate this place, these people.

Liz tried to ignore the hard stare from an intimidating man sporting blue tattoos along his jaw and the ridge of his nose. His long, dirty hair was matted in some places, braided in others, with metal beads tinkling together as he turned his head to follow their movement. Liz tried to settle into her seat. Her guilt made her too uncomfortable to relax her spine. Tia scooted her chair closer, her own cloak draped across the back of her chair as she surveyed the dingy room.

"Her majesty the queen, sitting on a dirty tavern bench getting drunk on ale." Tia giggled with wicked delight. Liz shushed her so loudly that Gareth turned to look back at them from his place at the bar several paces away, bright eyes furrowed in concern. Liz offered him a strained smile before he returned a confused gaze and turned away again.

"You cannot slip up like that. Not when we're right across town from Greystone Heights."

Tia offered no apologies. Her gaze kept traveling back to Gareth.

Her lingering interest and attempts to seduce him discomforted Liz in a way she hadn't experienced before. It wasn't unusual for Tia to have affairs. Liz had witnessed many of them over the years. Somehow the thought of Tia and Gareth together disquieted her, as if a discordant note had been struck and hovered in the air between the two women.

"Are you going to tell Mat why you can't go to the manor?"

Liz shivered just thinking about Greystone Heights. There was a curse on the house, the lands, and the family. Not in the way that townsfolk would toss salt over their shoulders or offer up part of their harvest and swear it helped their yield the next year. Utterly cursed by the gods, in strange and mystical ways. A curse Liz shared. One she could never quite escape, it seemed, no matter how far she ran.

"I'm not sure. He's been looking for these answers his entire life, a life that may be cut short too soon if I fail to keep him from the Black Mountains. What if I tell him about the Dragon's connection to the estate and he chooses not to follow through? I've been the cause of so much suffering, this place has only reinforced that. I want to do something *good*."

"Giving him a choice *is* something good." She replied quietly as the men headed their way.

Mat and Gareth came back to the table with mugs of ale and large grins. Liz sipped her drink, unaccustomed to it but finding that it warmed her blood. The taste got better the more she drank. The serving girl brought over their dinner, something hot and roasted beyond recognition. It was divine, and so were the oysters, and good gods had bread ever tasted this good? She drank too much ale, but her laughter came faster and fire began singing in her blood. Her body was loose and warm all over. More than once Mat tugged her hood up after it slipped.

Mat's green eyes sparkled down at her, and he whispered in her ear. "I wish I could kiss you, right now." The words sent a shiver of anticipation rattling down her spine. Why didn't he?

As the night grew later and the torches were lit, the tavern came to life. Musicians played and people roared with laughter. The room spun around her, but she stood and slammed her mug down until she earned the attention of the bleary-eyed patrons. Tia grabbed at her arm but Liz shook her off, her thoughts jumbled, not understanding why Tia looked so angry.

"Oi! Oi!" she called out, and the people turned toward her.

"Who knows the siren's lament?" she asked, looking around until the man she spied before with the tattoos on his face and braided hair stepped forward. "Sing with me?"

He nodded, smiling down at her affectionately. Why had she been so ill at ease around him before? The musicians began to play the same song her mother used to sing her as a child. The song was about a girl stolen by mermaids and forced to live in the sea. The girl realized that she would have to give up her soul and her family. Too late. Too late she realized what was truly important. Not the riches of the sea, but the riches of the love that once surrounded her.

When Liz began singing, she closed her eyes and swayed along to the melody until she was swimming in it, warm and languid. She heard the voice of her mother singing it with her, instead of the deep throaty bass of the sailor she'd enlisted. Liz's song changed from an upbeat tavern song to a slow, lonely ballad. The hood of her cloak had fallen but Liz was grateful for the cool air on her hot cheeks. She remembered the warmth of her mother's embrace. How cold the world seemed without her smile. She didn't know how long she sang, didn't realize there were tears making salt tracks down her cheeks. When her eyes opened and the music stopped, there was silence in the room.

Stillness.

It surrounded her until her chest tightened so hard she couldn't catch her breath. Mat gazed up at her in wonder, as if he'd never seen her before. Gareth's eyes were averted, locked on the wet ring of ale left on the table in front of him. She couldn't remember a time when his eyes ceased to follow her.

"What?" No one spoke. Not the musicians, not the man with the tattooed face, not her companions. Complete and utter silence.

Their stares of wonder changed into stares of horror. A chill crept up her spine, and she turned to find soldiers holding open the door and letting in a draft. The fire in her blood turned to shards of ice as she recognized the seal of the Dragon on their black armor, a great red winged serpent spitting a wave of flames. Her stomach dropped to her feet and her flushed cheeks paled.

The sailor beside her, with the metal beads tinkling merrily in his long tresses took one look at Liz's terrified expression and untied the deep blue scarf knotted carelessly around his neck. In the next moment he'd tossed it over her hair and muttered something guttural in a language she didn't understand. He made a swift motion around his own face, clearly indicating she should wrap her hair and without thought she obliged him. He smiled wide and tipped his head.

"Ma'lik Reggnai." he said quietly in the perfect lilting accent of the common Island tongue before offering a short bow and slinking into the shadows of the tavern. Liz understood that, at least. *My Queen.*

The general leading the Dragon's men inside the tavern had eyes as black as death. There was no life in them, and his gaze terrified her more than the lascivious eyes of his men. She knew the dark eyed general, had known him for as long as she could remember. He was the same general at the battle of the Black Mountain pass, the one who called the order that killed Mat in every single vision. She felt the possessive gaze of his men running over her chest and down the curve of her waist and hip.

"Well, you're quite pretty. Aren't you?" He walked forward, his black eyes calculating some equation that she couldn't comprehend. He reached a leather-clad hand out and gripped her chin to pull her eyes up to his. Her mouth gaped like that of a caught fish, gasping for air. Praying silently for deliverance.

He smiled. Just the corner of his mouth moved until it spread slowly and deliberately over his lips, exposing too much of his teeth. For one frozen moment, his grin reminded her of the burned away smiles on the charred remains of the men at the market.

She bit her bottom lip in an attempt to restrain a fearful whimper. He pulled her close to him, his nose tipping forward as he inhaled her scent. A predator, toying with his prey. She gulped; her head still fuzzy from the ale. Cold dread spread through her causing a shiver to race up her spine.

Mat shuffled over to them, his keen eyes darting between the men as his familiar heat warmed the air at her shoulder. For a moment, Liz felt wedged between daylight and night. Life and death were warring for attention, fighting for her hand.

"Lovely, innit she?" Mat said, expertly adopting the accent of the region. Liz forced her face not to react in confusion. "Me wife, the only pearl I'll ever need, eh lads?" He put a familiar arm around her waist and tugged her too close, suggestively close. "Met her in the southern bay, working the docks, and I loved her straight away. Now we have our own little boat, merchants, ye see?"

Liz nodded absentmindedly, allowing him to bury his head in her scarf-covered hair and grin goofily over at the soldiers.

"Your... wife?" The general looked Liz over, then scowled at Mat, seeming to find something strange in their pairing. "How long is it that you've been married?" Mat and Liz glanced at each other once and answered at the same time.

"Three winters." They echoed, turning to each other and allowing a warm smile to spread between them. It wasn't hard for them to pretend to be in love with each other. In fact, Liz thought perhaps it was too easy to pretend to love Mat.

"Let's get these soldiers here a round, will ya barkeep. To the Dragon!" Mat lifted his mug of ale, and the rest of the tavern shouted, echoing his bawdiness as the music began again. The soldiers settled into one of the long tables in the far corner. Mat dragged Liz back to their table and pulled her down onto his lap, laughing and clapping a hand on Gareth's shoulder.

"We have to get up to the rooms. Now." His voice no longer jovial, though the goofy smile remained on his lips.

"Tia, you and Gareth take the first room. Gareth, keep watch tonight." They worked together seamlessly, the way they always seemed to.

Gareth slung his arm across Tia's shoulders and up they went, away from the threat of the soldiers. Mat buried his head in Liz's shoulder, nuzzling his nose near her ear once more. He found excuses to be close to her, selling his charade while his heat permeated her skin. At least, that's what her ale-addled head focused on instead of the danger surrounding her, circling closer and closer, great as a sea beast, ready to swallow her whole.

Mat patted her hip and she stood, letting him pull her up the stairs inconspicuously as the general had his dark eyes fixed on his men while they drank. Mat rushed her into their room and locked the door. He held his ear to the door, listening as she twisted her hands together and nervously smoothed down her skirts.

"What do we do now?" she asked.

"We're going to stay in our room. If he bought it, we shouldn't have any problem tonight, but just in case—" He shoved an armoire across the room in great scraping motions, blocking the door.

"We can't stay in here, *together*," Liz said, looking pointedly at the one bed that engulfed the small room. It was nothing short of scandalous for them to stay together all night. She had only ever been alone with Mat a handful of times. Mostly, all they did was argue when they were by themselves. This was different and personal in a way that intimidated her.

Mat fixed her with an exasperated stare. "Are you serious?" Liz shrugged, her head still a bit fuzzy from the ale. She didn't think that she could stomach arguing with Mat right now. "You can be so spoiled sometimes. Do you know that?" Mat shook his head at her and turned away, shrugging off his leather tunic and unbuckling his weapons belt, carefully leaning his claymore against the wall. They were still in a significant amount of danger, but that was no reason for Mat to be rude. She huffed, taking off her cloak and tossing it at his feet.

"Well, sometimes you can be rather bossy." Crossing her arms over her chest, she sat indignantly at the end of the small bed.

Mat gaped at her, open-mouthed. "Bossy? I wouldn't have to be bossy if you would stop putting yourself in harm's way all the bloody time."

"Oh, and that's my fault is it?"

"Who else?" he asked, angrily untying the top of his wool shirt. A small portion of his bare skin was visible beneath his throat and Liz swallowed down her trepidation. "No one asked you to get pissed and start bloody singing in the middle of a tavern."

Liz sucked in a sharp breath, feeling the weight of his words hitting their mark.

"You think I asked for this?" she asked. "Any of this? I've had every single decision made *for* me, my entire life." She flung her hands wide, illustrating her point a little too well. "Don't attend parties, Lisbet. Don't have a mind of your own, Lisbet. Or what about the thought in every person's mind I've ever met... Can't you just *do what you're told and die already, Lisbet?*" Her hand covered her mouth the moment the vicious words escaped her lips. The ale had loosened her tongue too far and the stricken expression on Mat's face stilled even her breath.

He reached a hand out, a clear apology hanging on his lips, seeking to comfort her. She didn't want an apology from him, not yet.

"I'm not even allowed to openly mourn my losses, because how *selfish* would it be considering the suffering of the entire kingdom rests on my shoulders." Liz's hands shook as she unwrapped the scarf from around her hair, dropping it unceremoniously to the floor between them. Mat's hand dropped to his side and his eyes grew wide. She couldn't take the words back now; they couldn't ignore it anymore. The time had come.

"We've been circling around this for days, haven't we? Both too afraid to talk about who I am, the sacrifice, the kingdom." Hot tears burned in her eyes, distorting his handsome face. Mat nodded, and she noticed the deliberate way he swallowed his words. His Adam's apple bobbed as he sat in a spindly chair across the room from her. She fought hard to keep her face from crumpling.

"When did you figure out who I really was?" she managed to choke out, her voice thin and unnaturally high pitched.

"When I first met you, but when you didn't tell us who you were, I let you think we hadn't figured it out." His voice was rough, filled with unspoken regret. The knowledge that he'd known the entire time thudded into her gut. She reached up to wipe the tears that had fallen down her cheeks. Blinking rapidly, she raked in a shaky breath and kept going.

"Because you wanted to have the Crown Princess of Aegis indebted to you. Or to use me as a bargaining chip." It wasn't a question, he'd already admitted to it. Mat's eyes were wide hearing her full title ring in the tepid air between them. The clear green of his eyes darkened to jade, glassing over as he stared into some far-off distance. He didn't balk at her accusations. They both knew the truth. Instead he squared his shoulders and leveled his eyes at her.

"I bound myself to you with the oath I made. You could have used your royal status at any time to force me to do anything you wanted. Even when I admitted to you that I'd been planning to turn you over to Lord Callum at Fangorn, you could have still forced me to do anything you wanted. But you never did." A note of warmth crept into his words, and Liz closed her eyes to listen to him, her heart thumping erratically.

"In fact, you treated me... you treated *us* with respect."

Liz opened her eyes slowly, noting the wayward strands of golden hair sticking up at odd angles from where he'd raked his fingers through it too vigorously. "Why didn't you tell me who you were? Do you really distrust me so much?"

The questions came out hot, his eyes so unguarded and hurt that Liz's heart lurched and she bit back the urge to scream. He turned his eyes away, and no matter how she tried, he would not return her gaze. A sudden distance she'd never felt before yawned open between them, a chasm she couldn't seem to cross. Ragged and desperate she blurted out the truth without any thought to the consequences.

"Because I thought if you knew that I ran from my duty, caused the suffering of everyone in the kingdom because of my cowardice and selfishness, that you could never look at me the same." she said, tears now clear in her voice. Mat still refused to look at her, so she continued on, driving the dagger deeper, hurting them both because she didn't know how else to prove to him what she denied to herself all along. "How could you ever care about me if I told you that my entire life was a lie? That for years I'd been cursed by the gods, to see things before they came to pass. That I have seen your fate, and it's grim. That no matter how hard I've tried to escape this bloody sacrifice I seem destined to die, and no amount of studying or books is going to stop it." Mat looked at her then, his eyes wet.

"Don't say that." His voice was so low she barely heard him.

"How could you ever care about someone like that?" Her sniffles became sobs. Mat stared at her, silent for so long that she couldn't stand it any longer. She turned her face away to mop up the tears on her cheeks in her sorrow.

All at once he was across the room, pulling her up from her seat on the bed to stand on quaking feet. His hands twisted into her hair, and he crushed her against the armoire blocking the door. His fingers brushed at her temple and traced her lips. Clear, green eyes delved so deep into hers that she lost herself in them.

"I care nothing for fate. Damn fate, damn the Dragon, and damn the rest of the kingdom for all I care." His words were angry, angrier than she'd ever seen him. "I love *you*, Liz. Not for your crown or your curse. I love you because you infuriate me when you get pissed in taverns and sing until sailor's cry. I love you because you criticize your rescuer for not rescuing you properly. Because you refuse to save your own neck until you know your friends are safe. I love you because regardless of your station in life, you found a way to care about a bastard finding his father. You found a way to fill a void inside of me I didn't even know was there."

She sobbed again, her lips trembling, but twisted into a pained smile now.

"I love you, Mat." He brushed her tears away with his thumb as he pried her mouth open beneath his. She was whole when he kissed her, her breath and her heart stolen in a moment.

The same way she saw through the mists of time and felt the threads of fate, Liz knew she would never love another man the way she loved Matioch Steele.

Chapter Eighteen

Liz's high-pitched giggles melded with the crackle of the fire from the hearth in front of them. Mat didn't think she'd ever been as beautiful as she was right now. Her eyes crinkled at the edges in mirth, hair unbound and tossed carelessly over her shoulders.

"I asked Finn what the bloody afterworld he thought he was doing, introducing himself to the leader of the half-bloods. You know what he said?" Liz shook her head, eyes sparkling with joyful tears that she refused to let fall.

"He looked *lonely.*" Mat ran his hands through his hair, adjusting on the cushions they'd flung to the floor in front of the fire. He'd never spent an entire night just talking with anyone, much less a woman. The weight of the past melted away beneath her musical laughter. The longer they spoke, the lighter he became.

"How long have you and Finn known each other? When I first met him, I could have mistaken you for brothers."

"Since I arrived at Fangorn Keep, three maybe four winters ago." He smiled, twisting his ring around his finger, deep in memory. "He was only a lad then, recently orphaned yet still so optimistic. He made quick work of following me around, even though I shouted at him several times to leave me alone. I was quite surly in those days, angry at my mother for keeping me in the dark. Struggling to figure out who I wanted to be."

Liz settled deeper into the cushions, her eyes kind and curious, encouraging him to keep telling his story.

"I couldn't understand how someone who lost so much still saw hope in the world. In *me*. He still amazes me every day." Liz reached her hand across to still his fidgeting. "Of course, if you tell him that I'll deny it until my last breath." She smiled, and he breathed out a half-hearted laugh. "What about Tia? How did the two of you come to be so close?"

Liz's eyes darkened, worrying her bottom lip with her teeth. Mat tucked a curl behind her ear, his thumb brushing against her cheek. She was soft as moonlight, yet strong as steel. He tried to shake the disbelief from his shoulders that she was here with him, tucked together in the darkness.

"My father gave her people asylum when they were conquered by a larger island. Most of them never made it to Aegis. Tia and her brother Killian stowed away on a merchant vessel. They were lucky to survive. My father planned to question them as there was only a tenuous peace between Aegis and the Islands at the time. He forbade me to acknowledge her in the palace, as Islanders aren't considered part of *civilized society*." The marked disdain in her voice endeared her to him all the more.

"So naturally, I defied him and refused to eat until he gave her a minor title. Meaningless to anyone, practically made up, but it was enough to lift the stigma of our friendship. Her parents had been killed, and I always knew about the blood sacrifice. Death seemed to bind us together."

Mat stared at her incredulously for a moment, utterly baffled. "How is it that a princess, someone who grew up so privileged, can think of others that way?"

She shrugged, twisting a curl around her fingers. "I suppose, growing up the way I did afforded me a different perspective. I know what it feels like to have no control over your life or circumstances. I wouldn't wish that on another."

Firelight danced in her eyes as she pressed closer to him, allowing his arms to wrap tightly around her. Speaking quietly like this, enveloped by darkness and sharing their secrets, he had never been closer to anyone. She pressed her lips to his softly, her hands running through his hair. She tasted so sweet.

Earlier, when she sang her song, she'd bewitched him. Her beautiful loneliness broke his heart from across the room. He'd been so engrossed that he hadn't noticed the Dragon's soldiers enter the bar, putting her in danger. His heart had pounded then too. He would never forgive himself for that close call. He wouldn't be able to live with himself if anything bad happened to her. Even if that meant the death of every living thing and every person he'd ever known, he couldn't see her hurt.

Mat had never been in love before. He didn't realize it would grip him and hold him tight. It'd been there simmering beneath the surface since the beginning, but he'd been too afraid. Afraid that she would find him lacking, insignificant, worthless. Afraid that she wouldn't reciprocate his feelings because of his lack of surname. Even now, those oceans were hard to cross. Hard, but not impossible.

Mat would kill the Dragon himself to keep her safe. Or more likely, die trying. It should have terrified him how surely he would follow her into the desolation of the frozen afterworld.

The joyful thought of finding her there and holding her in his arms like this rang through him. A clanging bell of certainty resonated deep inside his heart.

She pressed harder against him, opening her mouth beneath his. He pulled away, leaning his forehead against hers. He swallowed her breath and forced himself to create distance between them. Mat wanted to get lost in her, could easily get lost in her, but he cared too much to rush. Her mind was just as beautiful as her face, and he wanted to know it better.

"How could anyone give you to that monster?" he asked, the thought of the Dragon spilling her blood over the altar cooling his feverish skin. "Much less your father. King or not, I don't understand how he could do it."

She laughed, though there was no mirth in her eyes now.

"Mat, have you thought about what to expect when you attempt to find your father tomorrow?" He sat straighter, rubbing a hand over the stubble on his jaw.

Mat opened his mouth but after a moment shut it again quickly. Had he thought about it? Sometimes, Mat felt as if all he'd ever thought of was this moment; yet he still couldn't seem to find an answer to her question. He was no longer the hopeful boy wishing to complete his family, neither was he a man who no longer needed the validation that he was wanted. Both? Neither?

"Three days before the blood moon ceremony, Tia and I were returning from our evening prayers." Her words were more solemn than he expected them to be. Her features appeared gaunt as the firelight flickered in the hollows beneath her eyes and her high cheekbones.

"He said if it were up to him, I wouldn't have made it out of the birthing room. Better that I had been born dead than to live long enough to disgrace his lineage with my shortcomings. Not only was I born a girl, I spent all my time studying and trying to outwit the gods and the prophecy he held so dear. Not content with humiliating me, he ordered the guards to lock Tia in the dungeon. She's terrified of dark and small spaces, ever since she was on the ship that brought her to Aegis. The entire court could hear her screams."

Mat felt sick, thinking of how the entire village celebrated at the thought of Liz's death. How he had been drinking mead and kissing merchant's daughters, ignorant of her suffering. Though he'd never had any sort of opinion of the King, he couldn't imagine a father using his daughter's friend to punish her. His stomach thrashed and his jaw clenched. He reached toward her, but she shook her head, pulling the blanket tight around her shoulders.

"Don't you dare pity me." Her words were sharp, her eyes sharper. "I told you so you might understand something." Mat tugged her into his arms, needing to have her close to him. "Fathers are just men. Men who can be cruel, indifferent, flawed. Whatever happens tomorrow, remember the man you are. If I dwell on who my father was, as a person, I would learn to hate myself. The way I sometimes hated him."

"You know you didn't deserve that, right? Neither of you," Mat pressed a kiss into her curls, inhaling her earthy scent. She nodded, before tangling her fingers with his and leading him toward the bed. They had avoided the issue of sleep arrangements, but now his mind was whirling as the heat from his flush crept up to his ears. She sat and patted the quilt next to her, awaiting his decision.

"I shouldn't," he said in an exhausted rasp. She sighed and tugged him forward, until he was seated next to her.

"Could you have done it?" she asked after a long moment. "Sacrificed your child to save the rest of the people of Aegis. Would you be able to make that choice? To kill one child in order to save millions?" Her eyes were so blue when she spoke like this, wise beyond her years. They saw right through him, to the insecure young man who didn't have those answers, because he had never asked himself those kinds of questions. Could he do it? Was he strong enough to put the welfare of the people in front of his own flesh and blood?

"No." His voice broke on the word. "Aegis be damned, I would let the whole world burn to keep you safe."

It was the hard truth; he would never be strong enough to watch her die. Not for the sake of anyone else. But then, he wasn't a king. Mat would never be asked to make that sort of decision. It was easy to give convictions when he would never be held responsible for the magnitude of the consequences. She smiled, small and shy, and leaned back onto the pillows. Mat followed suit, watching her eyelids flutter shut and snap back into wakefulness as she fought sleep.

"I feel safe with you." Her whispered words bolstered him. Until the sound of her even breathing lulled him into a gentle slumber.

Chapter Nineteen

Liz lay there, half-delirious, watching Mat's face as he slept. She brushed a lock of his gold mane from his eyes and feathered her fingers over the scratchy stubble on his cheek. She didn't think she'd ever seen him clean shaven. She loved that about him. She loved his crooked grin and his noble heart. Her heart fluttered just looking at his handsome, sleeping face.

It'd been a while since she was pulled into a vision of the knight falling. Maybe she had changed his fate by bringing him here to Wharton Cove. She'd watched the sky for storms, noted how cold the nights became, and tracked the leaves falling from the tree branches. The first blizzard was only days away, a week at most. She breathed a mumbled prayer to the gods that she'd prevented it from coming to pass. Even if it didn't end the world, it would end her world to love him and then lose him forever.

He stirred, his eyes cracking open and drinking in the sight of her face, a grin stretched across his lips. He looked happy. She smiled at him in return, her hair streaming wantonly around her shoulders. She nestled into the crook of his shoulder as he ran his fingers through one of her curls, separating it into many more.

"They'll think I've ruined you," he said, kissing her temple softly.

Liz scrunched her face at his words, a giggle escaping unbidden from her lips. Mat blinked a few times, and Liz raised onto one of her elbows to peer down at him with a teasing smile.

"You cannot be serious." She said, "That is so... *old fashioned.*"

"Old fashioned?" Mat grumbled, pulling her down on top of his chest to feather a kiss over her shoulder.

"Well, yes. To think love could *ruin* a woman. Besides, you haven't... you know... ruined me." A blush burned all the way down her neck.

"Haven't I?" he asked, and she knew what he meant. Though they hadn't taken advantage last night, falling in love with him ruined her for any other man. She smiled again, wondering about the threads of fate binding them together. Like the steady beat of his heart against her cheek, the coils pulsed rhythmically within her until she resonated in perfect time with Mat. They would have to wake soon and face the day. It was time to meet with their friends and discuss what to do next.

Mat needed answers.

Liz had to tell him about the Dragon and his connection to Greystone Heights. She hadn't wanted to talk about it last night, hadn't wanted the Dragon to leech away her happiness. But in the hazy light of morning, Liz needed to set aside her childish fears. The trust they'd built the night before was fragile and would easily crumble with more half-truths. She pushed her long hair over her shoulder and out of his reach, the curls separated and frizzy now. Gathering her courage she brought her hand to rest on Mat's signet ring.

"I recognized this symbol when I first met you." She confessed, watching Mat's expression sharpen. "I never said anything because I couldn't remember where I'd seen it or why it felt important. When we came here, it started coming back to me. That's why I ran from the manor house. Because I remembered that it's the Dragon's ancestral home."

Silence.

"Greystone Heights is the name of the manor at the top of the hill," she told him. He raised himself up onto one of his elbows, resting his jaw on his hand, giving her his undivided attention.

"When I was young, my mother told me my fate. That I was marked by the priestesses from the water temple as the princess in the Dragon's prophecy. She told me I was born only to be sacrificed when I came of marriageable age and the blood moon reached its apex in the night sky." It didn't bother her to speak of it, not anymore. "Naturally, I had questions and was unafraid to express my concerns." She told him, a grin playing on her lips.

"I can only imagine." He laughed, both of them picturing her, freckle-faced and demanding answers of the queen. The strained laughter was a nice break in the tension that had been building and shimmering in the air between them.

"She told me a little about the man who would one day be my murderer. How he *became* the Dragon." Mat sat a little straighter, and it was no wonder. There was a lot of mystery surrounding the notorious sorcerer and how he gained his powers. He was the only red-blooded man to have wielded magic in the last thousand years.

"His mother lived at Greystone Heights. She was a noblewoman from a respectable family. She couldn't bear a child, no matter how hard she tried, and she prayed to the gods every day, offering them gold, pearls, the finest silks. Nothing worked. Her husband was a great nobleman, Lord LaMonte, a good friend and confidante to my father. He was highly decorated for his service to the royal family during the harsh winters when the famine reached the southern shore."

Liz rolled out of bed. The story was as familiar to her as the pale planes of her face. The words were woven into the very fabric of her. They shaped her, intertwined with her beating heart, twisted and coiled in every breath and movement. She straightened her clothes and sat down in front of the clouded looking glass to brush and plait her unruly hair.

"The Lord became disinterested in his wife, and there was talk of him seeking council with my father to dissolve the marriage."

Mat pushed to the end of the bed and began to lace his boots.

"Wouldn't she have been shamed?" he asked. She forgot sometimes how little he understood the nobles and their machinations. She cared little for the devious lot of them, and Mat's ignorance only endeared him to her more.

"Yes. She would have become a considerable burden to her family. Unwelcome at court. Never able to marry again. She was said to have been seen walking along the rooftops of Greystone Heights, her eyes unseeing, muttering to herself. Some people said she had been forsaken by the gods, driven to madness, her sacrifices bankrupting the once wealthy family."

"You nobles are a strange lot," he said, shaking his head.

"A serving girl fell pregnant; the Lord of the manor had fathered the child, and the noblewoman lost whatever sense she had left." Liz tossed the finished plait over her shoulder and turned to face Mat who seemed invested in the story now.

"She watched the woman obsessively, the entire pregnancy. When the child was born, a boy, an heir to the nobleman's house, she knew her husband would legitimize the child and dissolve her marriage. So, she stole the babe in the middle of the night and used him as her final sacrifice to the gods. They say she fell pregnant before the night ended, and when the babe was born, she took one look at his sleeping face and threw herself from the rooftops she'd once been fond of walking. Something about the babe was so evil his own mother couldn't stand bringing little Rikard, the Dragon, into the world."

Mat shivered and she grinned, amused with his reaction to her tale.

"Now all the people at court maintain the Dragon's family, and Greystone Heights, is cursed. That sometimes they hear the wailing of a babe at night, or see the figure of a woman walking the rooftops. It used to wake me at night, thinking of the accursed place. That's why I jumped down from your horse and ran."

"That's where the answers to my past lie? The Dragon's home." He looked dazedly at the ring on his forefinger. The sigil of the nobleman's house engraved clearly and mocking her from across the room.

"Greystone Heights is the Dragon's *ancestral* home. That's an important difference to consider."

She knelt in front of him, covering the sigil etched into his ring with her hand until he was forced to look up at her.

"I love you. I'll go anywhere, risk anything, and face any fear if it means you'll get the answers you've searched for your entire life." Mat pulled her up by her hands and wrapped her in his arms, before pulling away.

"I can't. I thought discovering the truth about my past would bring me comfort. But, if it's a choice between my answers and your safety, I can't risk you."

Liz raised a defiant eyebrow, silencing his protestations. When she pulled back, his green eyes hardened into furious jade. His jaw clenched tight against her stubborn defiance and for a few long moments they stood there at an impasse. Neither admitting defeat or willing to compromise.

"You can, and you will. The Dragon hasn't lived at Greystone Heights since his father died. Almost twelve winters now, I believe. The LaMonte family crest is the dark thistle on your ring. They own many of the merchant vessels and businesses at the docks here. Rikard outfitted a few such vessels after his father died and spent many years sailing the unknown regions of the Western Seas." Mat huffed, crossing his arms in unyielding stoicism before her. "When he came back, his magick was stronger than ever and he had a private army."

"I swore an oath, Liz. I may not have lived up to the codes during every moment of this journey, but I plan to keep you safe. Come what may."

Liz's heart fluttered as fast as hummingbird wings in her breast at the protective rasp in his voice.

"If you love me, you'll let me make my own decisions," she said gently. She saw the moment the fight left him, wind disappearing from his sails.

"I'm not ever letting you go now that I have you," he said. "You know that, right?"

She nodded, feeling a bit lightheaded. He pushed the armoire back to its proper place and tugged her by her hand out into the hall. He rapped three times in quick succession on the door to the room next to them. There was a heavy scraping sound, and Tia and Gareth emerged from the room, looking no worse for wear and much more rested than she and Mat did. For some reason, that eased a tight feeling in her chest, to see Tia looking rather disappointed. Odd.

"We're going back to Greystone Heights," Mat said, looking to Liz for confirmation. Her nod settled things, and the four of them set out from the tavern.

Chapter Twenty

Bastille, one of the Dragon's generals stood in the shadows, waiting for them to ride away before issuing an order to the rest of the men to follow at a distance. The princess was smiling, her mahogany hair caught aflame in the light of the morning sun.

Soon she would be delivered, and the altar of the goddess would run red with her blood.

The Dragon would become more powerful than any red-blooded man had ever been before, and the world would be saved from the ravages of fading magick. The general smiled, a white grin in the darkness of the shadows, ready for his name to echo in the Halls of Eternity, his glory tied to his master's.

Chapter Twenty-One

The brick lane was lined with trees that had long since lost their foliage, which must have once been lush. A discernible fog clung to the ground, exacerbated by the nearness of the sea. The horses whinnied and fought against Mat and Gareth holding their reins, until they were forced into compliance as they trotted forward. Mat's heart beat a staccato rhythm in his ears, indecision and fear coursing deep through his veins.

He was afraid of the danger that may lurk at the Dragon's estate, afraid of what he might find there. He'd believed his father was a valued servant at a noble house, gifted with the signet ring for his exemplary work. Someone like Mat, someone common. The thought of somehow being connected to the sorcerer destined to kill Liz writhed inside him, leaving a sliver of deep self-loathing behind. Mat heard nothing but the echo of the horse's hooves surrounding them, mirroring the rapid beat of his heart as they ventured forward towards the iron gate.

The grounds were unkempt, the building mired in black lichen that hadn't been removed from between large grey bricks that met in neat lines. There was a distinct lack of servants or guests. It was, by all assumption, as abandoned as Mat had been. As if the curse had driven all life from this place.

Mat dismounted, pulling tentatively on the iron filaments until the gate creaked open, no lock needed. He swallowed hard before he swung himself up again behind Liz, urging his pony forward with the click of his tongue. Liz's shoulders were drawn tight, her body tense in front of him.

The skeletal limbs of the trees stretched outwards as they approached the manor house. Clawing at them, begging them to stay away. Liz began to breathe rapidly, her fear palpable through the material of the cloak held fast around her. If there was anyone still on the grounds, they could be loyal to the Dragon and a threat to Liz. The manor sprawled out before him, dark and unwelcoming in the scant daylight. He dismounted again, the sigil of the house proudly displayed on a solid gold knocker. Seeing it here, clearly emblazoned on this place, sent a wave of revulsion through him. As if his body rejected any connection here before his mind could catch up. The front door was as tall as two men, arched and carved from solid black oak.

Mat squared his shoulders, gathering his courage to knock. He looked over his shoulder, his eyes fixed on Gareth, who stared disbelievingly out over the lands and house. His mouth hung agape at the ornate dormers and the four stories of dirty grey brick and columns.

"I thought this would lead to someone who worked at the docks, not... *this*." Gareth said, his tone oddly humble instead of his typical arrogant drawl. "But, we came all this way." Gareth fixed his gaze on Mat then, the steadiness found there oddly reassuring. With one grave nod, Mat swallowed down the trepidation rising in his throat and faced the door once again.

Could Mat's father really have lived here once? It seemed impossible to imagine. Doubts and questions swirled around him, making him dizzy and unsure of himself. He stood, hand raised to use the knocker, frozen by his uncertainty.

His father could be dead. Or worse, he could be one of the Dragon's soldiers, tasked with dragging Liz to her death. What if he didn't want Mat at all? What if he did? The possibilities were endless and roared in his ears, like a harsh winter wind coming off the south side of the mountain. Could being loved by a father loyal to the Dragon be worse than being abandoned? His hand shook.

He looked back over his shoulder again, this time to look at Liz. She sat astride his horse, smiling down at him. He couldn't go back, not now that he was standing here. Not with Liz watching. He wouldn't be a coward in front of her. He'd come here for answers; Liz had risked her safety to be here for him.

He knocked.

The sound echoed through the house and reverberated down into his bones, shaking the foundation of his identity. Mat waited with baited breath for someone to come to the door. When nothing happened, he knocked again. After another long wait, he pushed on the door gently and it opened with a long, loud creak. Surely a family this well connected wouldn't leave the entire estate empty? It was unthinkable. Someone had to be here.

Coming this far, risking so much, he couldn't leave with *nothing*. He fisted his hands at his sides, hard enough that his knuckles strained against the leather of his gloves. It was the only way to stop them from trembling. The inside of the foyer was dark, the ceilings so high he couldn't make them out. He took a few tentative steps onto the marbled floor, covered in a thick layer of dust and memory.

"Hello!" he called out, listening to the echo of his voice as it bounded around the room. The distortion of his voice gained momentum before falling into an eerie silence. "Is anyone there?" he called out again, curious now why a house this grand would be deserted.

"Oi! What're you doing?" A gruff voice shouted behind him from beyond the empty doorway. Turning sharply on his heel Mat walked outside towards an old man, perhaps a groundskeeper, hunched over a rake. The man took one look at him and clutched his chest, stumbling backwards. His face paled and his mouth gaped open, like a fish out of water.

"It doesn't look like anyone has lived here in a long time," Tia said. Liz hushed her, waving at Gareth to back the horses away in an attempt to give Mat some space.

"Do you know me?" Mat stepped forward, watching as the groundskeeper scrambled away, leaving his rake behind. He sprinted down the lane as if demons from the afterworld were nipping at his heels. Liz dismounted, as did Gareth, the both of them circling around Mat in his confusion.

"It looked like he recognized you," Gareth said. "If he's one of the Dragon's men we need to be cautious. I'll keep watch with Tia."

Gareth took the reins from Liz and led the horses away with Tia still astride, graceful and solemn, staring down at him with pity clearly mapped in her dark honey eyes. Mat was grateful for the moment alone with Liz, needing her warmth to ground his scattered thoughts.

"I don't understand." He confided in her.

She gripped his hands to keep him from running them through his hair in frustration.

"Did you see where he went?" She peered in the direction the man fled. Mat shook his head, disappointed at the ramshackle state of the house and grounds. How would he get answers if no one had been here in years? Liz grabbed him by the hand and began to lead him back up the front steps and into the grand foyer.

"Perhaps they left something behind that will give us a clue." She squared her shoulders and jutted out her chin in determination, and led Mat back inside the house. Her brow furrowed as she looked around the darkened space.

"Where do we start?" he asked, pulling back a dusty curtain. He let some daylight filter in through the massive windows. It dispelled the shadows and cast a harsh light upon the dilapidated remains of the family estate.

"Let's try the sitting room." She said. Mat fixed her with a puzzled stare. "What do people do in sitting rooms?" She asked him, tugging him along by his hand as they navigated shadowed hallways.

"They sit." He replied dryly. She turned and smiled at him, bright enough to lift his dark spirits momentarily.

"Yes, they sit and talk. They sit and read. They sit and *write letters.*" She said, smiling mischievously in the scant light. "It's a bit of a long shot, but, we aren't out of options yet." He grinned sheepishly in response, though he held no hope of learning more. Without any staff or family here, and the threat of the soldiers in town making it too risky to question villagers about the family, it would be impossible to try to piece together his past.

This entire search had been a waste. A waste of time, resources, and worse still it had put Liz in danger. That battalion of the Dragon's soldiers could come after them at any moment. They shouldn't be here. Liz turned a corner, gliding into a large sitting room with sheet-covered furniture. A cold draft forced a shiver down Mat's spine. The fireplace was massive, sprawling, and had an ornate portrait of a nobleman above it. It was hard to make out in the dark room, so Liz tugged at the thick curtains until she had exposed the dirty windows and enough light filtered into the room to illuminate the man's features.

"Well, I think I understand now why the groundskeeper ran from you," Liz said, studying the face of the man above the fire. It was Mat's own. Exactly. Golden hair and green eyes. His features were the same as Mat's, a perfect mirror image. Though something in his manner, in his stance, was decidedly different. He held himself the way Mat thought a nobleman would. His eyes cold and chin tilted, as if he were looking down his nose at him. Judging him silently with flat, green eyes. Mat recognized himself in this man and yet, did not recognize himself at all.

"What does this mean?" Mat asked, sinking onto the sheet covered settee. He ran his fingers through his hair, pulling at the scalp before huffing in exasperation.

"I can't be—" He motioned to the portrait over the fire. "I mean, I just can't be." He looked over at Liz who raised a disbelieving eyebrow in his direction. "Can I?"

Why did his voice sound so small?

"Be the son of a nobleman?" She looked between Mat and the portrait. "Of course you could. I have seen innate nobility in you. Mat, you possess kindness that rivals kings." She sat next to him and nestled her cheek into the crook of his shoulder as he absentmindedly wrapped his arm about her.

"That doesn't mean I'm related to *him,* does it?" Mat asked. He watched as it dawned on her what he meant, and her face twisted into an expression of horror. The sliver of self-loathing from before solidified into a shard that sliced deep and took root inside him. He'd never felt anything as sharply as her fear of him.

"We need to leave this place," she said, just as the clomping of boots sounded on the marbled entryway. He rose quickly, Liz stumbled over her skirts and went sprawling to the floor. He spun on his heel, drawing his claymore from the scabbard at his hip just in time to brandish it at the general from the night before.

"The shade of her hair is really quite striking," the general said, slick and domineering all at once. His black eyes slithered to Liz as she pulled herself up from the floor. "How kind of you to deliver what my master needs to fulfill his prophecy."

Mat shielded her, swiping at him with his claymore until he backed away. Holding his hands up, the general smiled at the pair of them. A shiver raced down Mat's spine, the hairs at the base of his neck standing on end. He had the distinct feeling of being watched, dozens of the general's men were closing in around them. Yet, they held back, waiting for something to happen. The general's too-wide wide grin unnerved him.

Dread filled Mat's stomach. He sensed someone lurking in the darkened doorway behind him, and he turned to confront a bulky shadow, a man who seemed to be cloaked in darkness itself. As he stepped out into the light, Mat noted his familiar clear, green eyes. When the stranger's curiosity appeared to be satisfied, his gaze slid past Mat to Liz, trembling behind him.

Could this be Lord Rikard LaMonte? The Dragon himself, in the flesh. He was younger than Mat thought he would be. From the tales of his accomplishments and cruelty Mat imagined he would be middle aged, but he couldn't have been much older than they were. Twenty at best. If his recent assumptions were right, this man was Mat's *brother*. Other than his eyes, he didn't resemble Mat at all. He was dark from his head to his toes; his long nose and angular jaw were sharp, his mouth a cruel twist above a strong chin. His black hair fell about his shoulders, his skin an olive tone.

The air surrounding Mat crackled, like the air before a wild storm. The stranger had thunder lurking inside of his cruel, green eyes. Mat tasted something metallic on his tongue as the man stepped too close, invading his space. The thick wind of a storm swirled faster with every step, though they were indoors and it shouldn't have been possible. As impossible as it was, this storm was familiar in its strangeness. Mat felt a rushing inside his skin.

"You're in my way." The deep bass of his voice rattled Mat down to his marrow. When Mat didn't move, the Dragon sneered down his long nose, his lips pulled back to bare his teeth in a cruel imitation of a smile. "Who was your mother?" he asked, mockingly. "I thought I'd found all my father's bastards. I'm curious. Who did I miss?" His callous words sent Mat reeling. It couldn't be. How could he have gone from no father, no family, no history, to one that he despised in a single moment?

"Leave my mother out of this." He raised his claymore up to shield himself and Liz. Mat didn't want to believe it. He couldn't accept that the family he'd been searching for all this time, had been this man. This murderer. The image of the burned bodies at the dock flashed in his mind. His stomach thrashed and his skin began to crawl.

The Dragon laughed at Mat, and the darkness in the room came alive. They all knew that this would end in death. Mat couldn't fight magick with his claymore. Liz would be lost, all because of his selfishness, his stupid need to know where he came from. Now, he wished he could go back, stay ignorant of the truth. His mother sacrificed so much to protect him from all of this.

From *him*.

His half-brother in another life. The sorcerer who held all the world's dreams and nightmares at his fingertips. The Dragon brushed Mat aside and extended his long fingers toward Liz's pale face.

"Don't touch her!" Mat shouted, and the wind inside the room picked up, howling and rattling the crystal chandelier above them sending dust raining down from above.

"You're more beautiful than I imagined," he said to Liz, ignoring Mat's protests and the gathering wind around them. "If only I could kill you for your impertinence. The blood moon will not rise again for two winters. I'll just have to hurt you in *other* ways until then."

"I didn't mean—" Liz's beautiful ferocity lent steel to her spine as she tried to defy him, but her face was pale and stricken. The Dragon pounced on her wavering strength in an instant.

"Didn't mean what?" His murderous gaze lit from within as he fixated on Liz's quivering lips. "Didn't mean to defy me? Didn't mean to deny me of my gods-given *birthright?*"

When Liz shook her head, Mat felt her curls bouncing and tumbling from her plait, her terrified breath feathering rapidly across the skin of his neck.

"Your voice is so musical." The Dragon closed his eyes for a moment, luxuriating in the sound of her whimpers. "I wonder if your screams will sound as beautiful as your mother's when I burned her alive."

Liz's nails bit into Mat's skin. Her body folded in on itself from the force of her sudden pain. Mat wished he could wrap his arms around her, hold her together. If for nothing else than to give her an anchor to something real.

Mat clenched his jaw and swung his claymore, but the Dragon stopped the blade in midair with a look. Straining with all his might, shoulders burning with exertion, Mat couldn't force the blade to move. The Dragon stepped out from beneath the sword's path. His bemused expression shifted into annoyance.

"You know, it's a shame." The Dragon circled him, keeping Liz in his sights. "You have potential. Too bad you won't live to see it flourish." He snapped the fingers of his other hand, and the general and his men surrounded them. Liz cowered behind him. Her hands gripped Mat's sleeve, the tunic's leather creaking beneath the pressure of her fear.

"Let him have me, Mat," she whispered, ripping his heart into jagged pieces at the resignation in her voice. The kind of resignation that belied a lifetime of preparation to be this man's sacrifice. Maybe Mat would never be able to win this fight, but he wasn't going to give Liz up without trying.

"Never," he ground out from between his clenched teeth.

"That's the wrong choice."

The terrified cries of a woman trilled in the air as two of the soldiers pulled forward Tia and Gareth, swords to their throats.

"Tia!" Liz covered her mouth with shaking hands, tears springing into her eyes as her friend whimpered against the soldier holding her. "*Please*," she begged, her bottom lip quivering. "I'll go with you, just please don't hurt her."

Tia stilled in the soldier's arms, her honey eyes hardening to amber. Mat noticed a shift in her stance and faster than he thought possible, she slipped from beneath the soldier's arm. He blinked and she was across the space, kissing Liz. Hands tangled in crimson curls, breaths mingling. She pulled away from Liz's shocked face and said simply, "Make sure my song is *wild*."

She rushed at the Dragon then, a piece of broken vase clenched in a bloody hand, arcing towards the Dragon's apathetic form. With a glance from the Dragon, she was frozen in place, the sound of wind rushing in Mat's ears. The strange sense of familiarity folding over him once more.

Tia reached toward Liz, clawing through the strange air desperate to reach her friend. Mat held Liz back, her fingertips all but touching Tia's across the charged space. Not quite an inch apart, their racking sobs echoing in his ears.

"You," the Dragon growled to Liz in his deep bass, his voice so low it rumbled around them like thunder. "Are." He turned toward Tia, still held fast in the rushing wind, his eyes never leaving Liz's face. "Mine."

With a flick of his finger Tia's head snapped back. The room filled with the sound of bone cracking and her sobbing silenced. A moment. A millisecond. Barely a twitch of his finger and Tia was gone.

Just gone.

Liz fell to her knees. Mat stood numbly in shock. He'd failed them. All his promises to protect them were falsehoods; he was too weak to protect anyone. They could only watch as the wind died and Tia's limp body slumped to the floor; her arms crumpled at an unnatural angle as she lay there, honey eyes staring wide and unseeing.

Liz broke.

Broke straight in two.

Even if they survived, she would never be the same again. Never laugh or smile the way she did before. Maybe she would never trust him again. Mat bared his teeth and roared at the Dragon, earning a smirk as he swung his claymore. Gareth twisted from the grip of the soldier holding him.

"The princess will never be yours," Mat snarled. The Dragon dodged every swing of his sword without breaking a sweat, a bemused smile playing on his cruel lips. Mat couldn't see straight anymore. Blinded by his anger, his ire, his need for revenge.

The man before him had a father, a home, a name to fall back on. Maybe he did wield magick; maybe he'd convinced almost everyone in Aegis he was some kind of savior. That only meant he had something to *lose*.

Mat would be damned if he let this abomination kill the woman he loved. Toss her away as callously as he tossed away Tia. Loyal, warm, *wild* Tia.

The wind shifted again, gaining intensity. It rattled the chandelier hard enough to snap the crystals. The curtains flapped wildly like the wings of gulls. The wind mirrored Mat's roar. Somehow, he was *controlling* the wind. His anger fueled the gale. Incredulous recognition thrummed through the hollow part of his chest. This wind belonged to him, had been there all along, mirroring the rushing of the blood in his veins. He focused and the wind rose again. The Dragon laughed maniacally, flicking his finger. The settee flew across the room, pinning Gareth and nearly crushing Liz. She let out a musical shriek as Gareth was slammed bodily against the wall, crumpling to the ground, dazed.

Liz's fathomless eyes stared up at Mat. This was it, the moment to decide what kind of man he was going to be. Grounding himself, he tried to find the gale within him once more. He adjusted his grip on the hilt of his claymore and felt a roaring in his ears, like his pulse thundering.

"I made an oath to protect this woman, and that's what I'm going to do." Mat dug deep inside of himself, riding the wind as it picked up around him. He succumbed to his anger, a violence that hadn't been inside of him before. He couldn't contain it, wouldn't contain it any longer. He screamed as his wind tossed the Dragon's soldiers to the side, circling around his arms and torso. Mat leveled his claymore at the Dragon, bending the wind to his will.

"You dare challenge me!" the Dragon demanded, no longer amused at Mat's attempts to best him. Mat felt resistance now, something akin to lightning rumbling in the air. He pushed back against it, straining with all his might.

Tia was dead. Liz would be next. Liz with her living flame of hair, with curls that he loved to separate with his fingers. Liz who loved him against her better judgment, who would never have met him had it not been for his *brother* trying to murder her. Against all odds he'd found her, bound and dragged, her fair skin covered in mud. Her wrists still healing from that mistreatment.

"I won't let you hurt her!" Mat bellowed. Something within him snapped as his vision went white. High-pitched ringing resounded in his ears. He didn't know where he was or what happened, but he had fallen at some point. As he blinked, he realized he was sprawled on the floor. In the dust.

Someone shook his shoulder. He couldn't focus his gaze or stop the ringing in his ears. Someone strong pulled him to his feet. Gareth. Every bone in his body was on fire. His skin felt new and too sensitive, every sensation jarring. His blood boiled in his veins, and every soft touch abraded his skin.

"Liz." His voice still muffled to his ears. "Where's Liz?" He saw her copper hair out of the corner of his eye, blurry, but there. Some tension inside of him eased at the sight.

Then everything went black.

Chapter Twenty-Two

Liz's eyes were sore; her tears had run dry hours ago. Her voice ground down to nothing more than a garbled rasp. She couldn't breathe. Why couldn't she just breathe? The air was getting thinner, her inhalations more shallow. She clutched her knees to her chest, desperate to lessen the chasm of pain. She kept replaying it over and over in her mind. Unable to escape from the worst moment of her life.

She and Gareth fled, taking Mat and Tia with them and never once looking back at the wreckage of the manor. Hiding somewhere in the surrounding wilderness, in a cave. Far below them, the sea battered the cliffs. The ground was chalky and the air smelled of salt and brine. She didn't mind being tucked away here. Somewhere safe and high, out of sight, yet encompassed by the sea. She could almost imagine she was back in her room at the palace.

She would never be able to forget the way Tia's body lay broken and discarded on the dusty marble floor. Or the audible crack of her neck echoing in her ears. Liz's limbs had frozen in place, her mind numb to the world around her. She'd been unable to help Gareth as he wrapped Tia delicately in one of the dust covers from a settee that had been shattered by the Dragon's magick. All she could do was watch when he hauled her body and Mat onto one of the ponies before forcing Liz to ride away.

Liz told Mat a story about the curse on the house, but it was *her*. She was the curse. Everyone she loved died. She couldn't look at Mat. He had been unconscious for so long, completely unresponsive, wrapped in the Dragon's feather lined cloak. She'd tried yelling, shaking him, punching his chest, until she broke down into hysterical sobbing. She couldn't stop staring at the tall, willowy form hidden beneath a ratty dust cover lying too still in the corner of the cave.

Gareth placed his gloved hand over hers, but she jerked back, recoiling away from his touch. He knelt before her, reaching forward slowly. His grey eyes locked with hers, and the tepidness of his unyielding nature was a calm breeze on a turbulent sea. It soothed her. He breathed with her, and as he slowed his breathing, so did she. Her breath calmed, and the edges of her vision were no longer black. He led her back from the edge of madness.

A particularly nasty chill permeated the air tonight, worsened by the sea on the wind. Gareth must have noticed her shivering; he scooted closer, gripping both her hands between his own and rubbing them for warmth.

"When the Blood Moon has reached its peak,
The Red Princess will see unseen,
The threads of fate of two entwine,
Her blood, the magick, then shall bind.
The North Wind will meet the flame,
Magick shall return or forever fade,
One by one the pillars will fall,
He who weds her, will rule us all."

Liz spoke the words, the familiarity of them surrounding her, the threads of fate tightening around her neck and strangling all her false freedom from her. They resounded in her mind, growing louder ever since she witnessed the impossible. When she watched Mat wield the wind.

Every shadow reminded her of Rikard LaMonte's dark countenance. He hadn't been tossed away, crumpled and broken on the ground like his men. There were no signs of his presence, as if he'd turned into darkness itself. Perhaps he'd caught Mat's wind and taken flight, shedding the feather lined cloak in his haste. Somehow, it felt important for her to make sure Mat got it. After all, it belonged to his brother.

Once she finished reciting the prophecy, Gareth watched her, his eyes silently questioning. Liz was grateful for the way he spoke through his silence. She shrugged, her bottom lip quivering but her eyes holding fast. There were no more tears for her to cry anyway, even if she wanted to.

"I lived my life by that prophecy. Stupid words muttered by a priestess over a thousand years ago. Since the day I was born, the priestesses were so certain about everything. I had to be the sacrifice required because of my blood red hair. The Dragon had to be our savior, because he was the only sorcerer to emerge in a thousand years. The *only* one, Gareth." She looked over at Mat's sleeping face, his golden mane of hair slung sloppily across his brow.

"Not anymore."

Liz chuckled blackly in response, barely keeping the hysteria at bay.

"All this time I thought I'd run away from the sacrifice, that I thwarted the prophecy. What if, all I did was run straight towards it?" Liz clenched her hands so hard that her nails bit into the soft flesh of her palm, angry red crescents pressed into her pale skin. "What if Mat, not the Dragon, is the one meant to kill me after all?"

Her gaze rested on Mat's sleeping face with an unanswerable question playing on her lips. Gareth sighed, running a hand through his dark, curly mop of hair. He tugged her closer, wrapping both arms around her and holding her so tightly she heard the rapid beating of his heart against her cheek. She wanted to relax, wanted to let her guard down, but she couldn't.

"Before Lord Callum sent us on this quest, my brother paid me a visit," Gareth said, his voice cracking on the words. He trembled and Liz pretended not to notice. She couldn't tell if his trembling was in anger or fear, only that some invisible wall had lifted from between them, showing her a side of him usually kept hidden from the world.

"Isn't that a good thing?" she whispered, afraid Mat could overhear their conversation. This felt too personal to share with anyone else. Even Mat.

"He's broken in his mind." His hands shook and Liz held them to keep them together as he buried his nose in Liz's hair. "It isn't his fault. They broke him, our parents. They broke us both. Each in their own ways." She watched the muscle in his jaw jump as he clenched his teeth, gnashing down the memories and grinding them into nothing.

"It's also my fault. No one but Lord Callum knows, but I'm the eldest son in my family. Heir to my father's brutal legacy. When my father fell ill, I refused the responsibility. I just couldn't become him." Liz shifted so that she could better observe his expressions. No longer did he hide his pain beneath his silence; instead he wore it plain for her to see. It staggered her. "So, I left them."

"What did your brother come to speak to you about?" She shouldn't have asked. It wasn't her place. She knew it deep down, and yet, she'd been compelled to ask anyway, drawn to the possibility of unraveling the mystery of him. Tempted by the darkness always lurking deep within his grey eyes.

"He believes I'm still a threat to his position." Her mouth opened for a moment, but she couldn't bring herself to ask. She couldn't bring herself to twist out of his arms. "My little brother wants me dead. Part of me wanted that too, once."

Suddenly Liz understood. He knew how it felt to run from his duty, and to be wished dead for it. To wonder every moment if you'd done the right thing, or if you should have just died anyway. All this time, Gareth knew. They were the same.

When Liz left the palace all those weeks ago, she hadn't realized how messy and complicated life was. She didn't break her gaze with Gareth, quiet Gareth, who Tia had cared for. The man who'd kissed her when Mat wouldn't. She wanted to ask what had changed his mind about dying, but she already knew the answer. It was the same reason she fled the palace. Because no matter how messy, or hard, or heartbreaking... it's all they really had left. The fight.

"What should we do with..." His voice trailed off, but his eyes darted to the dark corner and the lithe, lifeless body of Liz's once vibrant best friend. Whatever pieces of herself she'd managed to knit together shattered again. *What should we do with her body?* Her bottom lip quivered, but she bit it hard enough to choke down her anguish.

"Her people, from the island she was born on, burn the dead and scatter their ashes on a strong southern wind." The words crawled out from her lips like knees over broken glass, each one slicing deep enough to make her ugly inside. Barely audible, hard to understand, but Gareth nodded.

He brushed his thumb over her cheek, tracing the fullness of her bottom lip. His eyes dropped to her mouth, and she could have sworn that he was going to kiss her again.

Then Mat groaned.

They pulled away from each other reluctantly, Liz twisting her fingers around the fabric of her skirt. She looked over at Mat's unconscious form for a long time. She should have been tired of kisses by now. How could she have almost kissed Gareth? She *loved* Mat. Every infinitesimal part of her was in love with Mat.

But, if she were being honest with herself, there was something magnetic about Gareth. Something undeniable. Liz had been drawn to him since she'd first met them both, pulled forcefully along by the threads that bound them, unable to resist. No, it was more than the threads of fate.

She bit her bottom lip, remembering the way Mat defended her back at the manor. How he'd shielded her from the Dragon. How he snarled at the most powerful man in the world. *Never.* Mat told the Dragon he would never have her. Until today, she was convinced of his devotion. She shouldn't begin to doubt him for things that may never come to pass. She hadn't allowed the prophecy to dictate how she lived her life yet, she wouldn't start now.

"I don't know what to be scared of anymore," she told Gareth, feeling his eyes searching her face for answers she couldn't give.

"Should I be scared of dying? Or of living long enough to watch everything I care about be taken away?"

"Princess." Gareth's voice was deep, his tone serious. "A lot happened today. But, if I knew Tia at all, she would tell you that life is nothing but taking risks, and if in the end you get hurt, at least you had the courage to take them." She thought there were no more tears to cry, but the mention of Tia's name sent them tumbling once more down her cheeks. It hurt to cry now, physically, her eyes red and sore.

But it did sound like something Tia would say. Something annoyingly optimistic. Irritatingly positive and snobbish and exactly what she needed to hear. She wiped at the salt tracks on her cheeks with the back of her hand.

"She had a soft spot for you. Did you know that?"

"I did." How did he remain so calm, so unaffected? Liz felt like she was unraveling inside.

"I think I see why now," she said softly.

Suddenly her vision blurred, and she gripped Gareth by the shirt, gasping as she fell into the mist that always accompanied her visions. She was aware of his hands on her arms, a distant voice calling her name. She tried to fight it, but the pull of the mist was so strong it tugged her swiftly and deeply under.

There he stood, dark and commanding. The Dragon. He didn't appear angry; in fact, an amused smile played on his lips. His green eyes looked her over carefully, inspecting every inch of her, looking for flaws.

"I see you better now."

"How did you do this?" She crossed her arms over her chest defensively, feeling exposed. She saw nothing but him and the familiar mist surrounding them. She'd never lingered in between this way

before; she had always stepped through the mist into her vision of the battle to come.

"I sensed it on your skin when I laid eyes on you before." His deep voice rumbled through her body and shook her spirit to the core.

"Sensed what?" she asked, realizing now that he'd summoned her into the mists somehow. He'd called her here. It wasn't possible. Sorcerer or not, no one had the power to control another's mind.

"Magick, of course." His words startled her, the truth of them ringing within her, a discordant note that left her trembling.

"Blessed by the gods or not, I will fulfill the prophecy. I will spill your blood, and I will gain the power I seek. My father's bastard can't stop me. If he aligns himself against me, he will fall." He stopped in front of her, holding his hand out to her face, his fingertips a millimeter from her skin. Not touching her, but desperate to.

"It's a shame you are so beautiful."

Liz snorted derisively. Her fear turning to fury in an instant.

"What do you want?" she asked, exasperated. Liz wanted peace from this man, she wanted to mourn. She had been broken, forced to run. She'd suffered loss and hunger, sacrifice and pain. He was the reason her parents were gone. He'd killed Tia. Because of him, she'd begun to question Mat's loyalty. His love.

No longer would she allow him to hold dominion over her life. Magick or not, he was still just a man. She stood straighter, tilting her chin forward in defiance. He smirked at her, looking down his nose straight to her bosom as it heaved at her chest.

"Quite beautiful. More so when angered, it would seem. Perhaps before I sacrifice you, we'll have a proper wedding night." His smirk grew lascivious, and Liz felt her stomach thrash and protest at the mere thought of his hands on her skin.

"You will never have me," she said, her eyes cold and unyielding. "Does it worry you that there's another contender to fulfill the prophecy?" A muscle twitched in his jaw, his green stare growing deadly. Sensing that she'd touched a nerve beneath his cold, unaffected cruelty, she pushed harder.

"You shouldn't have killed my friend." Liz's voice was raw but firm. "I will never allow you to complete the ritual, not while your brother can take your place." She meant it to hurt him, but it only seemed to amuse him further. His eyebrow rose at her words and he circled around her, studying her rapid breathing and her flushed cheeks.

"So be it."

There was a moment of darkness before she awoke, her eyes fluttering open to focus on Gareth. He was shouting her name and tapping her cheek with his palm. He clutched her to his chest wantonly as she regained her senses. She sucked in a sharp breath and twisted out of his arms. As if she were surfacing from beneath the waves after being under too long, she gulped sweet air in frantic relief.

"I thought I lost you too." His chest heaved, panicked. "What was that?"

"A warning." Her eyes wandered back over to Mat's still form. How long would he remain asleep? If she were to get a suitable distance away from the Dragon, it was possible Liz could keep him out of her mind. Or so she hoped. The urge to flee crawled down her arms and legs. Gareth didn't question her further, for which she was thankful.

Night fell quickly, and Mat began to whimper and grunt in his sleep. Liz curled next to him, wrapping her arms tight around his chest, only to have him jerk out of them several times throughout the night. Fitfully he slept, and yet she remained beside him, holding him to comfort herself as much as him. Eventually, she fell asleep, lulled by the sea beating violently against the cliff face.

Hoping to wake to a better world tomorrow.

Chapter Twenty-Three

When Mat woke, his entire body screamed in pain. The only exception was the side of his body where Liz's warm touch permeated his skin and soothed him. He groaned, long and low until she stirred. Her eyes cracked open, groggy and confused at first. Noticing his pained expression, she recoiled away with fearful eyes.

"Mat!" She brushed the hair out of his eyes with gentle touches. Her fingertips feathering over his sore skin. "You frightened me." Her voice was raw from her tears. The stained salt tracks had left rivulets in the layer of dirt and chalk on her cheeks.

"How—"

His throat rebelled, and his vocal chords throbbed as he fought to push the word past his lips. His head pounded at the cacophonous sound of waves crashing in rhythm with his heartbeat. Liz retrieved Gareth's water horn and pressed it to his mouth. He swallowed gratefully, moaning at the feel of the cool water against his dry, cracked throat.

"How long?" He struggled up onto one of his elbows. Liz shushed him, her gaze soft in the light of the dying embers of the fire and the scant grey dusk filtering in through the cave opening.

"One day," Gareth rumbled out, standing and peering over at him. "I'll be back by nightfall." Offering no other explanation of his intentions, he gave Mat a pointed look, motioning slightly toward Liz. Too slight for her to notice, but enough to illustrate his point. There were things he needed to discuss with her. She pressed the water horn to his lips and waited patiently, her eyes kind as she assessed him.

"Do you need me to help you up?" she asked, but he shook his head.

"How did we escape from the Dragon? How did we survive?"

"Well, you blasted the house apart."

His eyebrows furrowed at her words, not comprehending their meaning in the midst of the rampant throbbing of his temples.

"You swung your sword and the wind followed, an otherworldly gale force. I haven't seen anything like it since a hurricane hit the bay in Silver City three winters past." She didn't look quite as distraught as he thought she might after losing Tia.

Tia.

Gods, the guilt crushed down on him from all sides. It was at that moment he caught sight of her out of the corner of his eye, tied carefully in a sheet. He'd lain next to her body all night without knowing it. His fingers raked through his hair and pulled hard, his eyes watering against the pain. The wind whistled through the cave, an incessant breeze picking up and flapping the corner of the sheet to offer morbid peaks at Tia's arm, the skin grey-tinged and unnaturally pale.

"Stop that now," Liz commanded. His eyes snapped up to her face, and the wind died down immediately.

She held her chin high, giving him a defiant stare. That was good. She would need that strength to continue on to Fangorn. He didn't know how he got them into this mess, but he was desperate to fulfill his promise to Liz. To keep her safe. To deliver her to some form of safety.

He touched her face. They were alone now, after all. When he cupped her cheek, she leaned into his touch. Her eyes closed as she placed her fingers over his and sighed in relief. Some invisible weight lifted from her shoulders. He couldn't understand it. Why wasn't she disgusted with him? How could she stand to look at him now that she knew who he really was? He swallowed hard, but she spoke first.

"It doesn't matter."

"It *does* matter. I have magick." He shared the same blood, the same accursed blood as the man who wanted to murder her. That same malice could be hiding somewhere within him too, waiting to burst free, the way the wind surged from his fingertips when he lost control. What if next time, it was Liz who got hurt? He wouldn't be able to live with himself if that happened.

"You aren't him, Mat. You never will be." She grabbed his hand and placed it to her heaving breast. The rapid beat of her heart pounded against his hand. "We're all that matters, you and me. He can't break us as long as we're together."

His eyes grew hot thinking of the hateful words he last spoke to his mother. She'd been protecting him all these years. She had loved him enough to let him hate her if it was what he needed. He thought of Liz's eyes as Tia's body crumpled to the floor. Her strength astonished him.

He tangled his fingers in her fiery curls and pulled her into him. She whimpered into his mouth, and he swallowed the sound. There was an animal inside his chest, something feral and dark clawing to get out. The taste of her sweetness on his tongue and her warmth against his chest banished the darkness for a moment and he clung to that.

She pressed herself against him, allowing him to pull her deep into his embrace. Mat never wanted her to think he cared only about her body. He'd refused to let things go too far in the past. But now? Now, he needed to be close to her more than he needed to breathe. His hands wandered her curves, his lips kissing over her chin and down her neck. She gasped as he rolled her beneath him and pinned her with his weight. Her beautiful pale skin was like soft moonlight beneath his fingertips. It sent his pulse pounding an indecipherable rhythm in his ears.

She was the most beautiful thing he'd ever seen, splayed beneath him, every inch of her a mess. This was how he remembered first seeing her, a wild thing that appeared from deep within the Neither Wood. He wanted to see her this way forever. Eyes glazed over in passion, lips swollen from his attention. Freedom looked beautiful on her.

He pulled away just far enough to let the cool air temper the heat rising between them. She sighed as Mat slowed their kissing, both of them coming down from the wildness that arose between them.

"Please Mat," she begged.

"Not yet," he responded hoarsely, his fingertips making soft shapes on the pale skin of her shoulder. He never wanted to stop touching her. Not when he could taste his name on her lips. He knew that if he didn't stop now, he would never have the strength. So he pulled away, watching as she gathered herself. A furious blush crept up her cheeks, as though she were embarrassed to have lost herself so completely in his touch.

"I'm going to marry you first."

Her wide eyes flew to his, and he offered her a crooked grin. He pulled her hand to his heart, letting the steadiness of the beating thunder against her palm.

"I can now. Marry you, that is. Now that we know I'm the illegitimate son of a nobleman. It would still be frowned upon, but not impossible. We can be together now." She stared at him with incredulous eyes. "I want a life with you, Liz."

"Was that meant to be a proposal?" she asked finally, her ocean-blue eyes welling with tears and her mouth twisting with laughter. Mat couldn't help but chuckle in relief. In all truth, had things been different, they would have more time. He could court her properly. Attending chaperoned dinners, holding hands beneath the table. Dancing too often together at festivals and balls. Proving he could provide for her during winter months by offering bread and cheese eaten on a wool blanket beneath the stars. But they didn't, not now, not anymore. Not with the threat of the Dragon hanging over them.

"Yes?" he said, unsure of what her answer would be but determined to make his intentions clear nonetheless.

"That was awful," she admonished him playfully, tears rolling down her cheeks and her laughter lighting up the darkness roiling around within him. She was illuminating. Her radiance lifted him from his pain.

"It was bloody awful," he agreed, brushing a wayward curl away from her eyes. His voice lowered into a gentle rasp. "Will you marry me?"

"No. I won't."

Chapter Twenty-Four

"We'll arrive at the keep in a day or so," Gareth announced as Liz settled into the saddle. Mat's arms tightened around her as they had so many times before during their travels; his familiar heat encased her body, yet the distance between them was palpable.

"Good, the snow is coming fast this year," Mat said, staring at the black clouds gathering overhead.

Snow.

Her mind and soul were still beside Tia's meager pyre they'd lit that morning. She'd washed Tia's body, closing her still-open eyes and kissing her too-cold skin before folding the sheet carefully around her. Gareth had spent the last evening finding dried driftwood and arranging it neatly, so the flames glowed in a myriad of colors mimicking the sea. Blue and green and gold. As vibrant and colorful as Tia had been during her life.

Liz hadn't been able to find the strength to sing, not yet. She just stood there, her heart breaking, fighting the urge to throw herself into the beautiful flames and take Tia's hand the way they always did everything—together. When there was nothing left and the threat of discovery was too great, Gareth nudged her into stiff movement. Now she carried Tia's ashes with her in a small leather pouch tied carefully around her neck and tucked close to her heart.

Snow.

When the snow stuck to the ground, Mat's blood would stain it red. Her vision happened somewhere in the Black Mountains, exactly where they were headed in order to reach Fangorn Keep. She hadn't thwarted the vision after all, only delayed it for a little while. Tia died for nothing.

"Can we go to some other place?" Liz's stomach churned and thrashed inside of her.

"No. It's the closest shelter before winter sets in," Mat said, his tone indicating there would be no discussion on the matter. "Worry not, Gareth and I won't allow Lord Callum to turn you away, your majesty." The use of her title stung, but being turned away wasn't what worried her.

Gareth had been a new kind of quiet since he'd returned the night before. Now that they were nearing home, he seemed cagier than ever. They rode on, none of them wishing to speak of the events that transpired over the last few days.

When they stopped to eat, Mat sat across the meager fire from her, eyes averted and claymore leaning haphazardly against the base of the nearest tree. She knew he meant no offense, but his distance stung. They carried on this way until Liz could stand his silence no longer.

"We'll meet with the others once we've returned, at least." She smiled, hoping to start a civil conversation. "I wonder what trouble Smitty has gotten poor Wallace and Finn into by now."

Mat fixed her with a blank stare. The absence of warmth in his gaze only served to isolate her even more than before. The oppressive silence blanketed them once again, leaving her with nothing but thoughts rife with images of impending blood and death. Images of Mat, lying listless in the snow, a halo of crimson staining the pristine white surrounding him.

Liz shouldn't have provoked the Dragon in her dream walk with him. If the Dragon could pull her into the mists, perhaps there was a way to call him to meet her. Maybe she could reach out to him and make a deal. There had to be a way to avoid the bloodshed. If there was anything she could do to circumvent Mat's fate, she would take the risk. Now, more than ever, she knew that her visions were given to her for a reason. To save him. Mat was the only other person in the world that could wield magick like the Dragon. Besides, she wasn't strong enough to lose another person she loved.

That night, as the men lay sleeping, Liz wriggled from beneath the warm furs and took a small dagger normally hidden in Mat's boot. She didn't know how to call the Dragon, but perhaps a blood sacrifice to the goddess of moon and tides, Sierah, would give her the insight she needed. Just as in the prophecy, she would need three things; a source of water, moonlight, and her blood.

She remembered seeing a lake not too far away. She hiked through the dark forest with purpose, hurrying so the others didn't wake to find her gone. When she arrived at the lake, a chilly mist clung to its surface, the reflection of the moon a hazy halo in its center.

The water, like the rapidly cooling air surrounding her, would be freezing. She pulled off her cloak and her boots, unlaced her bodice, and pulled the thick brocade dress over her shoulders. She would go in nothing but her shift and pray to the gods that she knew what she was doing. Invoking the gods to commune with the Dragon across the countryside was dangerous. She prayed they would not punish her for blaspheming.

She stepped into the water, pressing the palm of her hand over her mouth to stifle her cry from the bite of the cold. It seeped inside of her as she kept walking, sapping her strength. She was submerged to her knees now, her steps slowed by the freezing temperature.

Now at her waist, her teeth chattered so hard she thought they might break. When she reached the center, submerged all the way to her chest, her breath came sharply. She was afraid she wouldn't be able to speak the necessary words. Slicing the dagger across her palm, she muffled a cry with her fist as she let the blood pool in the water before her.

She squeezed her eyes shut, holding the blade of the dagger and offering her sacrifice to the goddess. She mumbled a quick prayer beneath her breath and then entreated Sierah to hear her.

"I've never asked anything of you before," she said to the night air. "You've demanded so much of me, and I haven't asked for *anything*... until now." Even now the words echoed in an otherworldly way. They sounded wrong, as if the sound were being swallowed down a long tunnel. "Please," she begged. "Allow me to see beyond the mists again. Help me find the Dragon wherever he is and bring him to me."

Nothing happened.

"Why give me these visions if I wasn't meant to stop these things from happening!" she shouted, but no one responded. She sighed, feeling all her fight draining away in the frigid water. "I can tell this is my last chance to change it. Please, just give me the chance to *try*." She cried out as the mists surrounded her, her vision blurring as she was pulled somewhere dark.

She saw no one. Nothing but darkness and mist. Had the gods been angered by her request? Then she heard him, breathing behind her. She didn't turn. He meant to startle her, so she stood there. Trembling, but holding fast.

"Why did you call me, little lamb?" His deep voice echoed endlessly in the void around them. She swallowed hard, trying to find the courage to ask for what she sought from him.

"I wish to offer you a deal." Her voice sounded tinny and whining compared to his.

"What kind of deal?" he asked, still there behind her, his voice rumbling through her ear.

"I'll give myself over, stop fighting, stop running. I'll marry you. I'll be your willing bride sacrifice." It was the only thing he wanted, the only thing she had to offer him.

"And your price for such submission, lamb?" His voice feathered against the pulse pounding in her neck, a seductive whisper in her ear, slithering over her skin. She suppressed a shiver of revulsion.

"Mat. I need you to save him."

He laughed at her, a booming sound that unsettled her. She skittered a few steps away. At least now she could see the monster in the dark, his grin wide and predatory as his eyes ran over her wet skin.

"Save him?" His green eyes roamed over her body again, and she realized why. She was in a wet shift, and nothing more. He could see through it clearly to her nakedness beneath. She tried to cover herself with her hands, but he clucked his tongue and shook his head in disapproval. "Save him from what?" His disinterested drawl surrounded her in the dark.

"From you." She twisted her hands as she shielded her curves from his ravenous eyes. He studied her with a detached curiosity,

peering at her face as she worried her bottom lip with her teeth. Until the amused smile returned to his lips.

"You saw something, didn't you?" As loathe as she was to admit it, he was right. She had seen something. Mat's immediate future, and it was bleak. The storm clouds were gathering in the horizon and it wouldn't be long now. His laughter thundered around her again, her silence confirming his suspicions.

"I cannot change the will of the gods or the threads of fate, ever weaving around us. You should know that better than anyone. Whatever you've seen will come to pass. Should he stand against me, he will fall. You will be mine, either now or after I hunt you down. It makes no difference. You have always been mine."

She felt it too, in her blood and on her skin. One day those uttered prophetic words would come to pass. One day even sooner, the vision that haunted her through the mists would come true. But it wouldn't stop her from trying to save Mat or stop the Dragon. Not until there was no hope left.

"My vision showed me that your soldiers killed him. Call them away, and you won't have to hunt me down at all. Keep Mat safe, and I will never stand against you." She was desperate now, her breath catching at the thought of Mat's laughing green eyes going dim and unseeing.

"Liz!" She heard Mat's voice echoing around her in the nothing and mist. The Dragon contemplated her offer, but she felt a tugging in her mind. A sharp pull away from this accursed place.

"Please! Tell me we have an accord and I'll do anything you wish!" she shouted, but the Dragon had drifted too far away. She was left only with the image of his too wide smile, glinting ominously in the night.

"Damn you, Liz!"

 LAUREN SEVIER

She called out again, but he was too far gone. Another strong tug on her mind and suddenly she was falling faster and faster, the mist choking her.

Lurching forward, Liz's eyes sprang open, spluttering, choking water from her lungs and clutching someone's wet shirt in her hand. Her lungs burned, her body a mass of prickling flesh, painful everywhere from the cold. She couldn't stop the chatter of her teeth or the involuntary shaking of her body.

"By gods, Liz, what the bloody afterworld were you thinking?" Mat's mouth captured her shivering lips for a moment. He didn't ask anything else; he just wrapped her in his worn wool cloak and picked her up out of the mud, carrying her back to the campfire.

Gareth was turned away, seemingly asleep, though Liz doubted it. Mat brushed her wet, dirty curls from her face ignoring his own wet clothes to set about warming her up. He stoked the fire and knelt in front of her, gripping her trembling hands. His hands were still warm, though he'd swum through the same icy water. She took a few breaths, her teeth chattering less than before. Enough for her to choke out a few words.

"Why did you stop me?" she asked him, and he fixed her with an incredulous glare.

"When I found you, your lips were blue. You had no breath. If it weren't for me, you'd be dead. How about you tell me what was so important that you would risk your life?" He brandished the dagger with which she sliced her palm. Blood sacrifices were common even on household altars to local gods.

He reached for her, but she recoiled against his anger. His eyes softened and he dropped the dagger in the dirt at her feet. This wasn't how she wanted it to be between them.

She couldn't stand this distance any longer.

"I didn't refuse you because I don't love you." His hands gripped into tight fists at his sides. "It was the prophecy. The prophecy says the man I wed will rule all of Aegis and murder me, so I decided I wouldn't marry. Not *anyone*."

"It was the prophecy, not me? You don't find me... lacking?" She shook her head, words failing her. He pulled her into his warm embrace, his hands tangling in her hair. Her teeth were still chattering, her breath shallow. "What did you ask the gods for?" he asked her quietly, his nose brushing against her cheek.

She couldn't tell him that she'd failed to broker a deal to save him. He'd only just forgiven her, she couldn't tell him that he was going to die, and she began to weep. He shushed her, pulling her face into the crook of his neck, rubbing her back until her weeping slowed to a stop.

"You wouldn't understand," she whispered. She kissed his neck as her body warmed enough to stop shaking, easing the pinpricks of pain along her pale skin.

"I'm trying to." Mat was trying to protect her, not knowing the price he would soon pay. "Listen." He tugged her chin up until her eyes met his. "I want you to have this."

She looked down as he pulled the signet ring off his finger, the one with the sigil proclaiming him a member of the Dragon's family. This ring meant too much to him. She couldn't accept it, couldn't let him part with his only link to his past.

"No—"

"Take it, Liz. It's the nicest thing I'll ever be able to give you." His words cleaved her heart in two. He worried about giving her gold and jewels; she could see it in his eyes. What a silly thing for him to worry about. "Please."

She allowed him to slide it onto her ring finger; it was too large and swung around loosely, much to Mat's chagrin. Liz pulled at the hem of her shift, ripping a long strand of it and wrapping it around the ring until it fit snugly on her finger. Mat offered her a shaky smile.

"Let's not call it a wedding ring. It could just be a promise between the two of us," he said, and Liz looked down at the sigil on her hand, the Dragon's family crest. Even though it was Mat's most prized possession, even in this, the Dragon somehow found a way to claim her.

"I love it," she said, not exactly lying. He brushed the wet curls from her face and helped her onto her feet. "I'll only be a moment." She gathered her dress and walked a few feet away into the brush.

She looked down at her hand, the weight of the ring there mocking her. She would never be Mat's bride, no matter how much he wished for it. Gripping her stomach, she pressed her palm against her mouth as she fought the urge to scream into the night, angry tears racing down her cheeks as her shoulders shook in muted agony. She mopped at her eyes as the cloak fell to the ground. In the scant, filtered campfire light, Liz managed to wriggle her way back into her dress. Her limbs were still heavy with cold, and dressing took longer than she expected. Her sliced palm was throbbing something awful.

She had to tell him about her vision.

She had to make sure he understood that he was risking his life, going back to the Black Mountains. But how? This was something Tia would have helped her with. Tia had been good at the messy, personal, emotional parts of life.

She, at least, had a chance to be young. A chance to fall in and out of love several times. She broke hearts and had hers broken. Liz didn't know how to do this. She needed Tia here to guide her, to give her advice. In a rush, Liz remembered Tia's mouth pressed against hers and feathered confused fingers over her mouth. The absence of her hit Liz like a wave of pain, crashing through her body. She turned back toward camp then, noticing Gareth staring at her, wide awake.

Had he watched her silent sobbing, her struggle for composure, her confusion about Tia's last moments? He didn't say anything. She let her fingers fall from her mouth, humiliated, but he didn't blink. Didn't waver. After another long moment, he turned away, not acknowledging her at all. There was something enigmatic about his apathy, some dark secret hiding within his eyes.

Squaring her shoulders, she resigned herself to tell Mat everything, from the beginning. Even if it took all night, she was determined that they wouldn't get a step closer to the mountains without the truth coming to light. But when she found him, he was already fast asleep. For the first time in a while, worry wasn't furrowing his brow. She couldn't bring herself to wake him. The truth could wait until dawn. Or so she hoped.

Tomorrow she would tell him everything.

Chapter Twenty-Five

The morning light filtered through the trees and reflected on the crystalline dew when Liz awoke. The chilly morning was beautiful, the first freeze of a true winter. The forest fruitlessly clung to the last vestiges of fall. She heard soft voices behind her, but didn't wish to wake yet. Before she left the palace, she wouldn't have imagined lying on the frozen ground covered in furs could make her feel safe. They reminded her of Mat, his scent clinging to the rough wool he'd been wrapped in last night.

She lingered somewhere between fully awake and dreaming, her eyes still closed as her ears picked up the chittering of songbirds overhead. If the birds had yet to leave for warmer climes, they still had time. Her eyes cracked open and she found Mat on the other side of the small fire, speaking in low tones with a lanky young man with a wide grin.

"Finn, is that you?" she asked, her voice slow and groggy from disuse.

"M'lady, it's good to see you." Finn's smile overcoming his whole face as she managed to rise from her place in the furs. He gazed at her knowingly, his eyes flickering from the furs on the ground to the empty spot beside her that Mat once occupied. A flush rose hot on her cheeks. Liz wondered why he was here instead of at the keep. She thought the men from the lodge would have made it days ago. She blinked and realized they were all here. Smitty. Wallace. Finn. The wagon was leaning heavily to the right, one of the spokes missing from the wheel. Gareth and Wallace were hunched over arguing above it.

Mat grinned that crooked grin that turned her whole world upside down. Liz stretched her arms above her head and walked gingerly toward him. She had to tell him about her visions. Before they went a step further, she would tell him everything. She just had to get him alone first.

Mat wrapped an arm around her waist and pulled her into his arms, burying his nose in her hair. She smiled, her cheeks flushing a pretty pink. Gareth only gazed at them for a moment, silent, before turning away. Exactly like the night before. He saw her more clearly than she'd ever seen herself. How was it that his silence spoke such volumes?

"What are you men doing here?" she asked.

Wallace replied, "Broke an axle. Been roughing it trying to get back to the keep. Gareth spotted us this morning on the road. So we dragged the wagon here to repair it." His penchant for keeping conversation short was as endearing as ever.

She just wanted to be alone with Mat, to convince him not to go back to the keep. How was she ever going to do that now that his friends were stranded and in need? He wouldn't leave them. These woods were dangerous; they all knew that first hand. Would she be able to forgive herself if she convinced Mat to leave and something happened to them?

"Where's Tia?" Finn's question was sudden and unexpected. In an instant her grief swallowed Liz whole and filled her to bursting, she let out a strangled cry. She was horrified by her own reaction. Pushing out of Mat's arms, she staggered a few steps away to distance herself.

"Sorry, I am so sorry," she said. "I didn't expect—"

"What happened?" Finn looked to Mat for an explanation.

"It's a long story." Mat held out his hand to Finn, but he slapped it away.

"I'm not a child!"

Mat held both his hands up as a gesture of peace. "I know you aren't." He wrapped an arm around Finn's shoulders, pulling him in and clapping him on the back. "There's a lot you don't know. I can't explain now, but I can tell you everything once we've returned to the keep. Soon the mountain passes will freeze over, and the Dragon's men won't be able to follow us."

"What the bloody hell are ye jabberin' on about that bloody sorcerer fer?" Smitty asked. Liz stayed silent and small. The buzz of conversation overwhelmed her senses as they spoke around her.

"You shouldn't keep speaking about him, Smitty. He may appear." Wallace said fearfully, his eyes glancing towards the foliage.

Finn scowled, seeming to think Mat was still condescending to him. He shoved Mat's arm away, his lip curling in an angry snarl. "Tia was my friend, and I want to know what happened to her." Finn never looked so domineering. With his back ramrod straight, Finn dwarfed Mat. It was clear now this wasn't an argument he would back down from.

Liz sucked in a shuddered breath between her teeth. It would be a risk to reveal herself to all of them now. How else could she explain why the Dragon killed her? It was Liz he'd been searching for, after all. Without the protection of the frozen mountain passes, they could still turn her over to the Dragon's men scouring the countryside. Mat would lose a friend to keep her safe, but she couldn't in good conscience let him.

"Tia was killed by Lord Rikard LaMonte, known to you all as the Dragon." Liz blurted out the truth before she could talk herself out of it. The men all stopped and trained their eyes on her. His name silenced them all. Her words rang in the cold air. Her fogged breath was the only discernible movement in the clearing.

"What the bloody afterworld would that demon want with a little slip of a thing like Tia?" Smitty asked.

"Nothing." Her voice was a harsh push of warm air fogging before them. Mat squeezed her, his heart pounding furiously against her back. "He killed her to punish me." They hadn't discussed keeping Mat's lineage a secret, but she wanted to give him a choice.

Finn studied Liz for a long time. She watched the moment it all came together in his mind. Realization flared bright in his eyes as his face suddenly paled. His mouth fell open, his hands clenched into tight fists at his sides.

"Gods be damned! Your majesty. My apologies for swearing in front of you." The others took longer, but one by one they realized who she was. Each man dropped to his knees with bowed heads and frightened eyes. She wished Mat's arms were there holding her up, but this moment was a solitary burden Liz would have to bear alone.

"Mat, yer can't mean to bring her to Fangorn. The Dragon's men are searching for her everywhere." Smitty's incredulous voice stilled the riotous beating of Liz's heart.

"I can and I will," Mat replied, his eyes hard, daring Smitty to try and stop him. Each man kneeling in the frozen mud before her held a place in her heart. They'd laughed with her, spun her in wild country dances, taught her to curse and to shoe a pony. Her eyes grew hot as she stepped towards them. Her hand reached out to Smitty's rough cheek, her fingertips brushing his jaw to lift his chin. When their eyes met, his fear melted away beneath her kind stare.

"Get up, you idiots." She gifted them each with a warm smile. "I'll not be that kind of queen." The echo of Tia's words in her own made her heart pang in bittersweet remembrance.

"Beggin' yer pardon, majesty, but I don't reckon ye'll be any kind of queen we've seen before." Smitty appeared so shy, a far cry from the loud offensive butcher she first met. He gripped her pale hand tight for a moment before pressing a rough kiss to the back of her hand.

"No, I don't suppose so," she agreed, wondering when she'd come to trust this band of roughnecks with her life.

"Nevertheless, I'll not be bowed to or fawned over. I'm still just 'Liz' to you lot, and we have work to do." That straightened them up, although Finn remained quiet as he regarded her. "What do you think, Finn?"

He didn't answer for a long, tense moment. Instead, he gripped the carved wooden talisman hanging around his neck tight in his hand. His fingertips traced the pattern on its surface.

"I think it's your fault Tia died, Mat lied to me, and we're all going to starve. So, if you want someone to bow to you in the mud, it won't be me." Finn's words sliced deep, the truth of them thudding into her chest like arrows.

"Finn!" Mat chided him, but the young man was shoving against Mat's shoulder hard enough to make him stumble before disappearing into the woods. "I'm going to that lad's ears until he can't stand straight anymore."

"Don't," Liz said, placing a calming hand on Mat's shoulder. "He's not wrong. I'll go talk to him."

She followed slowly, dreading this confrontation. Liz heard his sobbing before she found him, nearly folded in half sitting at the base of a tree. He had a lace trimmed handkerchief clutched in his hands. Without speaking she sat beside him and reached out to hold his hand.

"I'm sorry," Finn said after a moment, blinking at her through red-rimmed eyes.

"I know," Liz said, sighing deeply. "I cried for a whole day. My face was so swollen it throbbed all night. I still turn to tell her things, expecting her to be there." Finn stiffened beside her, his hand sliding out from her own.

"You don't *understand*." His words were hard and unyielding.

"Tell me," She said, desperation fraying her patience. What was she missing here? Why was this so hard? They both loved her, they both lost her. "Please."

"I lied to Mat." He said instead, putting the handkerchief to his nose and inhaling deeply. "I told him my parents died and that's why I came to Fangorn. That's not true. I got caught kissing a stableman's son and they told me if I ever came back, they would hang me from the oak tree in front of our family home."

Liz opened her mouth, then snapped it shut again. She had no words. Finn gave her the barest smile, an ironic tilt of his lips. She squeezed his hand harder.

"That's horrible," She said, settling for the most obvious thought in her head.

"Tia was in love with you." Finn said, startling her again. Unconsciously she lifted her fingers to her lips and thought of the kiss shared between them right before her death. They'd kissed many times over the years, on foreheads or cheeks, to comfort or tease. Tia had never kissed her on the mouth before that awful night. Still, the thought that her best friend who she knew better than anyone else had a secret from her of that magnitude... it was impossible. She shook her head, the words on the tip of her tongue. Unsure why she couldn't speak them aloud.

"She was like me. I don't know how she could tell, but she knew we were the same and she gave me *hope*. A squire who lived in the village where I was born moved to Fangorn a few moons ago. He's been blackmailing me and roughing me up for fun. Tia told me she would take me back to Silver City with her when she left. She told me about people like us who didn't have to hide at court. For a few weeks I thought I would finally be safe." Liz's mangled heart couldn't take much more of this. The whispered conversations and glances between Tia and Finn made more sense now, given context.

"You know you can talk to Mat, he considers you his family. He would do anything to keep you safe." Liz said but Finn was shaking his head vigorously.

"Mat is the only family I have left. I can't risk losing him." Finn said, his hands shaking. "She said she always loved you, but she knew you would never be able to return her affection. Not the way she wanted you to anyway. She wanted to confess her feelings at the lodge, but then you kissed Mat and she just wanted you to be happy." He handed Liz the handkerchief, embroidered sloppily with violets and Liz's name in crooked letters. She traced the terrible needlework fondly with the tip of one finger as she sobbed in earnest.

She didn't care anymore about being brave, her shoulders shook and she clutched the handkerchief to her chest as if it could somehow lessen the pain in her heart. Finn wrapped his arms around her at some point and they clung together weeping for their fallen friend. They could have been there for moments or days, she wasn't sure. At some point they pulled apart, breathing raggedly and wiping at cheeks and eyes.

"I wish she'd told me," Liz said after a while. "She wouldn't have lost me, the way you're afraid to lose Mat. I wish I could have... I don't know. Talked to her. Eased her fears. Anything." Finn stood then, offering her his hand. She let him pull her up onto her feet and brushed dirt and leaves from her skirts.

"Mat will come charging over that hill with his claymore if we don't return." Finn said, smiling softly and walking beside her. Liz always thought Finn was so young, but really he was only a winter or two younger than her. In many ways, he knew himself better than she ever thought she could. "I'm not ready to tell him yet. Will you keep this between us?" He asked and she nodded, leaning her head on his shoulder affectionately for a moment.

"I'll take you to Silver City if we all survive what's to come, and are ever able to return. You'll be welcome in my court." She offered, turning to face him. "But, only for a friend."

He smiled so wide it was a wonder his face didn't break in half and they walked together back into the camp. Mat and the others stood, looking warily between Finn and Liz as if waiting for a shouting match to start any moment.

"Never had a noble friend before," he said. "I suppose it doesn't hurt that you're royalty. At least, you should be able to stop Lord Callum from flaying us alive for being late." Finn said. They shared a secret smile, closer than ever.

"I can do my best." With that, everyone began going about their normal day as if nothing at all happened, as if she were 'just Liz' after all. The way she always hoped to be. With that settled, she tugged on Mat's hand until he followed her into the brush. With Tia's handkerchief tucked into her bodice near her heart, Liz was fed up with secrets.

"I should go help—"

Liz silenced him with a kiss. He groaned, all resistance gone in a moment. "I need you to listen to me. You cannot return to Fangorn Keep."

"Mmmhmm," he muttered clearly not taking her seriously.

"No, Mat, I mean it. You cannot return with the others. We should break from them and make our own way somewhere else."

"I see what's going on here," he said, and Liz sighed, relieved at last.

"You do?"

He gave her that crooked grin of his, the one that made her heart thud harder in her chest. "You want me alone, all to your-self." She groaned in frustration, but he didn't seem to mind as he captured the sound with his mouth. She pushed against his chest then, until there was space between them and he was forced to look at her.

"If you go to Fangorn Keep, you'll die."

Chapter Twenty-Six

Without warning, Mat began to laugh. His rolling laughter intensified each time he gazed upon Liz's serious face. She crossed her arms over her chest, unamused. He held a hand up in apology, wiping the mirthful tears from the corners of his eyes. Her red cheeks attested to her annoyance. He took a deep breath and pulled her into his arms, though she was stiff and unyielding. He kissed the top of her head, his eyes softening down at her as she continued to hold her grim stance.

"Keep laughing, please," she said acerbically, clearly hurt by his lack of consideration. It wasn't his intention to hurt her feelings, so he took another calming breath.

"Apologies, Liz. It's just that you're so serious. You must understand how it sounds." His nose brushed hers as she leveled him with a sorrowful stare. Sorrowful enough that his merriment faded.

"Of course I do. I wanted to tell you a thousand times. I almost did that night in the tavern. Gods, I sound *insane,*" she said, pulling gently away.

At that moment Mat felt the heaviness of her tone dropping into the pit of his stomach like a stone. *I've seen your fate and it's grim.* Liz, he noticed, had a tendency to put physical distance between them when she needed to keep her head clear. Her eyes held a warning and it trilled along his spine. The air grew stiff, and her attention fell to her boots in the mud. A queen who couldn't stand to hold his gaze. The gravity of her warning sank into his skin, sharp as knives. He pulled her chin up until her eyes met his own again.

"You can tell me anything. Anything at all," he said, bolstering her.

"Since I was a young girl, I could feel things, see things. I only confided them to Tia, no one else. Not even my parents. I was afraid of what the things I saw might mean." She took a deep breath and leaned against the tree at her back. Her arms fell to her sides, and she chewed on her bottom lip with her teeth. It was raw and nearly bleeding.

"For the last few years, the same vision came to me, again and again. At first, I thought it was a bad dream, a vision I would only fall into in moments of deep relaxation or meditation. Then I began to lose myself to the vision anytime at all. The longer I ignored it, the more persistent it became."

"What did you see?" he asked, genuinely curious. The things she was saying were impossible. Though a seed of doubt had taken root in his mind, unsettling him. As someone whose emotions were currently causing the breeze to bluster and ruffle Liz's unruly curls, could he really afford to doubt her?

"You." Her voice was devoid of all emotion. Her eyes were blank, lost in a far-off torment he couldn't comprehend. His breath caught in his throat. "I saw visions of your death." His jaw tensed at her words and he took a step back. They could both probably use some healthy distance for this conversation.

"My death?" Mat's voice took on a high, unnatural tone.

"Yes. I wasn't sure until I recognized your ring." She held up her left hand, where that same ring that predicted his death now sat as a symbol of their commitment to each other. The irony of it turned his stomach violently. "That's when I knew."

"Knew what?" he asked. Neither of them moved, frozen by the implication of his request. They both understood at that moment what he was asking for. Mat needed to know the details of her claim; he needed to know *exactly* how she imagined he would die. She twisted in on herself, her inner torment at the gruesome knowledge taking a physical toll on her. Her eyes grew hot and she bit her lip hard enough to make it bleed.

"I cannot take this back. Once it's said, I cannot unsay it," she said. He nodded, bracing himself against the impending news. "When the snow falls and sticks to the ground, it will be stained red with your blood." Plucked from the ether, ripped from the mists of the afterworld, the words held some ethereal power as they hung on the chilly air between them..

"How?"

Tears tumbled down her cheeks unhindered, dripping off her chin. She shook her head, but Mat wouldn't allow her to dismiss his demand. He gripped her arms, pulling her so close she couldn't look away.

"Don't make me say it," she begged. "Just believe me and don't go back to the keep."

"Damnit, Liz. Tell me how!" he shouted, shaking her until her silent weeping turned into racking sobs.

"A battle! Somewhere near the base of the Black Mountains. You stand against the Dragon's men and they cut you down." Mat was frayed at the edges, experiencing everything from a league away.

"I tried to stop it," she said. "I encouraged you to go to Wharton Cove because I thought keeping you away would avert it. I didn't know how to tell you that you would die soon. That I had not only witnessed, but experienced your death as if I were looking through your eyes. Over and over again. For years." Her words echoed around him, hollow. She had risked her life to save him. Her tears and her trembling were right before him and yet seemed miles away at the same time.

"We can still run," she said. "We can just run away together. Stay away from the Black Mountains entirely, then it will never come to pass."

He couldn't bear to face her, his stiff shoulders bunched into knots. From the first moment he laid eyes on her beautiful, furious face, the idea of the two of them together had been an impossible dream.

"If we go to Fangorn, I'll be at the base of the Black Mountains where your vision took place and I will die." He turned back to her, deep in thought now. He took the moment to memorize the curve of her pert nose and the pale perfection of her skin.

"Yes." No hesitation. No question in her mind.

"If we don't get to the keep before the first blizzard, we won't be able to travel along the mountain pass, and the Dragon will send his soldiers for you." Liz furrowed her brow at his words. Even now the new Queen of Aegis refused to understand the stakes for fear of the loss of him. That should flatter him, but it didn't.

"Mat, you can't worry about that. Not when your life is at stake. There's no other option." She mopped her face with the back of her hand. What he would tell her next would break her beautiful heart, of that he was certain. Yet, for her sake, he would break it all the same.

"I have to get you to the keep, Liz."

"I won't let you give your life for me."

"I swore an oath." His tone allowed no room for argument.

"Blast your oath to the afterworld!" She gripped the front of his tunic in desperation.

"So you're the only one who can run from a prophecy?" Mat asked. Liz's face crumpled, and she wavered on her feet. "I know you could order me to leave anyway, Liz. But, could you take away my choice the way so many people took away yours?" She shook her head.

He wrapped his arms around her slowly, purposefully, crushing her to his chest. His nose was buried in her fiery curls, inhaling deep the scent of earth that always clung to her skin. Her hands reached up to cup his scruffy jaw, his fingertips trailed along her neck and her collarbone. They stood there, mapping each other's skin in an attempt to memorize each detail.

"Don't ask me to watch you die, not again," Liz begged him, her voice a whisper against the pulse in his neck. He chuckled darkly, softly, as if the irony wasn't lost on him.

"Don't ask me to let you risk your life, again. Not for me." The words were a pale imitation of hers, bitter on his tongue, but he would not be swayed. Mat remained unchanged; his conviction held no room for sentimental pleas. In his mind, he was saving her life and the cost was his own. A price he was willing to pay, regardless if she was not.

They stood there for a long time, just holding each other. Knowing that soon, they would have to let go. Soon they would have to say goodbye forever.

But not yet.

Chapter Twenty-Seven

Mat's wind blew Liz's curls into a tangled knotted mess once again. He'd made a habit of practicing how to call it forth and control it on the long ride from the Neither Wood and they were approaching a main road into the valley split in two by the mountain pass. So he wouldn't have time to practice soon. He'd been careful not to do anything too noticeable, careful not to display his newfound power in front of Smitty or Wallace. They were so distrustful of magick and had already been asked to accept so many changes. Finn however was fascinated, asking whispered questions for hours.

More and more Liz felt a divide between her and the others widening. A boundary had been erected and though they were warm and kind, they weren't as boisterous or inclusive as before. What could she expect? Tia was dead and it was her fault.

A low rumble sounded in the distance, black storm clouds were gathering in the west and would be upon them soon. Those clouds were her salvation and Mat's doom, they would be through the pass soon and when the blizzards began Lord Callum would have no way to turn her over to the Dragon. He'd be forced to give her the support she needed to raise an army to help her reclaim her throne. Assuming, of course, that she could discover a way to change the seasons without magick.

The village was quaint, steepled roofs so close together they made the hills look ominously like rows of teeth. It wound down from the highest point in the distance, Fangorn Keep visible to all those in its shadow. Liz kept her shoulders back and her chin lifted as the pony's hooves clopped on the cobblestoned street in the valley village. She was acutely aware of the looks she garnered from the people on the streets; women who dropped baskets and children who stilled their playing as they caught the copper gleam of her plaited hair in the cold sunlight. The weight of her duty settled on her shoulders, heavy and isolating, as the whispering began around them.

Mat's leather gloves creaked as his grip on the reins in front of her tightened hard enough to stretch the material tight over his knuckles. She inhaled, filling her lungs to bursting and holding the air there to steel her nerves as the crowd began to gather.

"It can't be."

"Shouldn't she already be—"

"Red Princess..."

Some of the voices were angry, others frightened, most of them had the disbelieving tilt of wonder. Those voices unsettled her the most. Liz had spent the majority of her life locked away in the libraries and temples of the palace, rarely wandering amongst the people. There were, over the years, a few that were committed enough to subverting the prophecy that they tried to harm her. Those attempts only gave faces to the monsters her mother warned her of over the years, aiding in her capitulation to walk to her own slaughter.

Liz didn't want to be worshipped.

But she did want to see her people free from the tyranny of the Dragon, the fickleness of the gods, and the ravages of magick. They rode on, winding their way at a steep angle, weaving between the gathering crowd. Mat's breath feathered hot on her neck as he leaned forward to whisper in her ear.

"Not long now."

That was precisely what she was afraid of. The pressure in the air changed over the course of their morning ride. A palpable tang of foreboding indicating a blizzard on the horizon would soon break. She and Mat had spoken little since she confided the details of her vision to him. He'd been unusually quiet, though she couldn't blame him for needing time to process. She knew intimately the terror and inner turmoil of coming to terms with your mortality. Even after seventeen years, Liz still hadn't been able to reconcile herself to her fate.

"Matioch! Matioch Steele!" The high-pitched voice rose above the general din, and Mat groaned low in his throat at the sound. Liz turned to find the source of the voice and caught the guilt and regret knitting Mat's brows together. It was then that she noticed the buxom beauty the voice belonged to, pushing through to the busy street. Her dark hair and wide doe eyes lent her a natural sultriness that accompanied her delicately tilted nose and full lips to perfection. Liz's shocked eyes searched Mat's face for any indication of who this woman might be.

"Don't you *dare* ride away from me, Matioch Steele!" Her imperious tone garnered another groan from deep within Mat's chest that rumbled through Liz and left her unsettled as he pulled the pony to a stop. Gareth led his pony closer to the two of them, reaching a forearm out to Liz to pull her into the saddle with him.

"Come, majesty. You don't have any part in this conversation," Gareth said, grey eyes stormy as he read the clear tension between Mat and the dark-haired woman on the street. Liz wanted to be petulant, to demand answers that would settle the pit growing in her stomach. She stamped down her jealousy and allowed Gareth to pull her into his lap, hands so large they spanned the width of her waist.

She and Gareth led the men on the wagon a few yards away and waited. Another stormy rumble rolled over the mountain range and Liz twisted a curl nervously around her fingers. They weren't through the pass yet. Liz kept her composure and only stole a peek back at Mat once. When the clear ring of a slap rang out on the winter wind, her eyes snapped over to him. Mat had dismounted at some point and his hands were open helplessly against the vicious sadness the woman battered him with. She spat at his feet, her hair escaping her careful chignon to hang wildly about her face. Her angry gaze swiveled around to find Liz.

When their eyes locked, Liz sucked a painful breath between her teeth. In her alluring eyes Liz saw a heartbreak so profound that her own vision began to water. This stranger and Liz would soon be connected by this feeling. The stark, overwhelming joy of being loved by him only to mourn his loss from your life. Her stomach churned at the thought, and she forced her eyes away from the scene.

Moments later Mat rejoined them, refusing to lift his eyes from the path ahead. "We need to get through the pass before the blizzard. Come on, let's go," Mat said to the others, pointedly avoiding her. Liz wasn't brave enough to try to bridge the silence that settled between them. Instead she adjusted awkwardly into

Gareth's arms as they continued pressing forward toward the keep. The dark monolith sat as a predator, on the highest point peering down at the valley below in silent expectation.

In those quiet moments, she let her mind wander, imagining Mat's life here before she met him. Or what next summer would be like for him, if he lived to see it. Caught up in her musings, she almost missed the tension in Gareth's arms and the furtive glances between her two protectors.

Angry eyes crowded around them. Villagers blocked their path. Voices rumbling with the threat of violence lingered in the air. Gareth slowly reached his arm around her to grasp the hilt of his sword, tensed and ready to draw on them. Her hand rested on his, stilling him.

"Speak," she commanded a man standing before the wagon. She was doing her best to impersonate her mother's regal voice, equal parts grace and power. Careful to keep a mask of indifference from revealing her fluttering heart and pounding pulse, she waited for the tall man to step forward.

"Ye've killed us!" he shouted, earning encouragement from the crowd. "Yer a coward and a disgrace. My family will starve because of yer selfishness."

"Yeah! We've all heard about how you fled when the King was slaughtered!" A pink-faced woman shouted from the cover of an alcove further down the street.

Her carefully composed mask of bravery faltered in the face of her people, terrified and dirty in the street. In truth, many of them would die in the months to follow. They would not die easily, either. Starvation was a slow death, painful every moment until the end. Liz condemned many of them to this. She couldn't run from it any longer. She shifted in the saddle until she was able to dismount, sliding to the cobbled street.

"Get back on the bloody horse!" Mat whispered harshly, but she ignored him.

She stepped forward gently, the tall man wavered at her approach. He towered over her, too thin, with scared eyes sunken into the hollows of his face. Her nearness sent the people around them fidgeting in nervousness, clutching makeshift weapons in calloused hands. She could feel the energy of fear and violence surrounding her much like the pressure change in the air.

"Yes," she said, her eyes fixed and unwavering on his. "Many of you will die." Sudden stillness from every wary watchful villager bound her tight. "I was ready to die for you. For all of you."

"Then why didn't you?" He asked.

"Because The Dragon isn't the right man to rule this kingdom and you all know it. He burns people to incite fear in you, and it's worked! You're all too scared to even call him by his name. You really expect a man like that to *save you*?" Liz asked and when she looked among the villagers gathered, they couldn't seem to meet her eyes.

The man folded in on himself, shoulders slumped, bent beneath the weight of his sorrow. Familiar sorrow. Liz could no longer hold back the rising tide of pain. *This* is how the Dragon would leave her people. Bent, broken, hopeless. She remembered the smoldering bodies displayed gruesomely as a warning to others. Their burned away smiles haunting her even now. She thought of Tia and her unwavering faith in the queen Liz could one day become.

"Magick isn't the key to saving Aegis, only we can do that by making the right choices. He isn't the right choice." Liz said, holding his gaze long enough that his fear and desperation welled in his eyes. The man gripped her hand and fell to his knees in front of her, weeping openly as he held her tight.

"I don't want my children to die."

Her eyes grew hot and the world in front of her blurred as she clung desperately to her control. Her mother always kept her composure, to keep the people's confidence in her ability to rule. But Liz was not her mother. She lowered herself onto her knees in front of him and pulled his hand into both of her own.

"Fight for me. Help me reclaim Aegis," she whispered, her lips trembling as the words crossed them. "So that if we survive this winter, they don't have to live as slaves."

A woman approached them, holding an arm out to Liz, offering to help her up from her knees. "His soldiers burned my sister's house to the ground. Her little girl died in the blaze." She said.

"I heard he conquered the people in the western seas!" Another shouted.

"Our grain stores were raided by his men." Said another.

Back on her feet, Liz gazed over the assembled crowd, and each person met her eyes before bowing deep.

They parted before her, hands over their hearts, some reaching blindly toward her. Whispers of "majesty" and "my queen" followed her on the short walk past them as the barricade folded away allowing them to pass. She clenched her teeth so hard she thought they might break beneath the strain. *Majesty*. Tia first called her by the title. It'd been offensive to her then, but now?

The people began to fill in behind her, behind the ponies and the wagon, people joining in her march to the keep. She had the urge to turn and look back at Mat, to see if he approved.

She didn't. Instead she marched forward, acknowledging each villager who bowed to her, hand to heart, as she approached the shadow of the portcullis that kept her from entering Fangorn Keep.

"State your name," a soldier bellowed from atop the wall, shifting nervously from one foot to the other at the sight of the parade approaching the gate.

"My name is Elisabetta, the Red Queen of Aegis, your sovereign, and you will open this gate."

Chapter Twenty-Eight

Mat attempted to stamp down the trepidation clawing up his throat as the clanging of the portcullis reverberated in the air around them. He dismounted quickly, his fingers twitching as he stood close behind Liz's confident shoulders. If he reached out with his hand, he could tangle their fingers together. Being here, back at the keep, changed things between them. She openly proclaimed herself the Queen of Aegis, and in this place Mat remained a bastard bladesmith.

The incredulous and confused stares of the soldiers he'd known his entire life as they observed him standing next to her reminded him of how far apart they remained in social standing. He hated the part of him that was connected to the Dragon. Unless he acknowledged it openly, publicly, to these people he was still nothing. Still no one. He didn't know if he was ready for the suspicion and hatred that would come from telling the world his lineage. They faced a gathering of armed soldiers awaiting them as they made their way into the bailey.

"Your majesty!" The knights parted and let a man in shining silver armor sporting the royal crest, a crown atop cresting waves, through. Mat bristled as Liz, who had been oddly composed and stiff, choked out a sob and broke into a run toward him. She threw herself into his arms and he wrapped her in his embrace, lifting her off her feet.

"Killian," Liz said, her voice breaking as he set her back onto her feet and his eyes roamed the rest of the people who accompanied her. "How did you find me?"

"Where is Tia?" he asked, his eyebrows knitting together in worry. Mat felt impotent, standing sentry, watching as Liz's features screwed up in pain. At that moment, Mat realized exactly who this man must be. He had the same dark ochre skin and honey eyes that Tia did. He took a step forward as Liz struggled for words, her hands held out helplessly in front of her. She shouldn't have to explain away the tragedy of Tia's loss. The knight, Killian, gripped the hilt of his sword tight when his eyes swung to Mat as he approached them.

"She didn't make it," Mat said, his voice even and deep. Holding out a hand, Killian looked between Mat and Liz for a moment before clasping his forearm tentatively. "Killian, is it? I'm Matioch Steele. We ran into the Dragon and a battalion of his soldiers in Wharton Cove. Tia didn't survive the encounter."

Killian's eyes filled with unshed tears and his jaw clenched. "Do I have you to thank for getting Lisbet here safely?"

"Among others," Mat said, motioning to Finn, Smitty, Wallace, and Gareth. They had all dismounted and stood further back, at attention.

"Did my sister suffer?"

His sister. Mat's eyes dropped to the stones beneath his feet. He suspected as much; they favored each other. Both had a unique warmth and clearly cared for Liz. As if they were all family by blood, not just love.

"No." Mat cleared his throat and raised his eyes to Killian's. He owed him that respect. "It was quick, but honorable."

"Her body?"

"We built her a pyre." Liz said stiffly. Killian's face paled. Liz gripped the leather pouch hanging from her neck, her knuckles white. Killian took a knee in front of her, his head bowed.

"Your majesty, Silver City has been occupied by the Dragon's soldiers. With no clear line of succession and the ceremony left incomplete the Royal Guard was divided and slow to act. We fought the insurrection to the best of our ability and experienced heavy casualties. When it became clear that we could not over-power the Dragon's army, I led a small group of trusted soldiers here to find you. The late queen managed to get a message to me. There are still many in the royal legion loyal to you and your family." The strangely neutral expression Liz adopted since that morning returned to her face, hiding the emotions Mat could normally read on her expressive face.

Before she could respond, the neatly arranged knights parted for the liveried Lord Callum, panting in exertion as he came to rest before Liz. Mat stepped forward to greet Lord Callum, bow-ing in deference before realizing the nobleman wasn't aware of his presence. His eyes fixated on Liz, his mouth opening and closing in a gaping motion reminiscent of a freshly caught fish. She raised an expectant eyebrow, and he bent his large girth into a bow so low he nearly fell over. If the impending blizzard wasn't enough pressure on Lord Callum to support Liz's cause, the Roy-al Guards presence certainly seemed to be.

Liz settled her skirts as the rest of the soldiers followed the Lord by example until none but Mat, Gareth, and the hunting party remained standing. The lord mumbled a string of incoherent apologies, which caused the corner of her beautiful mouth to twist into an amused smile.

"Arise, my lord. It has been a perilous journey, and your men are to be commended for ensuring my safety. I am in your debt." Lord Callum scrambled to his feet, kissing Liz's hands and clapping a grateful hand on Mat's shoulder. He tried to fight the smug grin curling onto his lips, but failed.

"Your Majesty, I had little hope of seeing you after hearing the accounts of events in Silver City after the blood moon ceremony." Mat wanted to reach out and touch Liz's hand, wanted to offer her the comfort of his touch as her blue eyes hardened into deep pools of ice.

"We were under the impression that none of the royal family survived."

Liz was the picture of the perfect royal, all poise and no sentimentality, as she responded. "I am the last."

With no response except his mouth pressing into a harsh line, Lord Callum ushered Liz inside to continue the conversation in comfort away from the cold winter air. She stunned everyone by holding a pale hand out to Mat, inviting him to go inside with her. His skin prickled from the hundreds of eyes boring into him from every direction. A considerable distance had grown between them since Liz confided the details of her vision to him. Since returning home, back into the bosom of society, he wondered if she'd realized how ill-matched they were.

He tangled his fingers with hers and her touch unburdened him considerably. He made gentle circles on the back of her hand with his thumb, and she squeezed his hand softly in response. His Liz was still there, inside this detached and poised queen. That's all he needed to know.

He let her lead him through the outer corridors of the keep and into the innermost halls. This was the most ornate and beautiful part of Fangorn. A fire roared at the end of the hall in an ironwork grate as massive and sprawling as the valley below. Radiating warmth down the length of the hall, it dispelled the chill so that it was hard to believe winter had come.

Lord Callum offered them food, wine, and rest. He kept glancing at Mat and Liz's entwined hands and didn't stop talking long enough to take a breath. He reminded Mat of a bee in summertime, ever buzzing, flitting from flower to flower in a meadow. Liz stood stoic, silent, her eyes assessing the hall and coming to a stop at Lord Callum's hip. There sat a bejeweled sword, the hilt composed of silver and sapphires. Mat recognized it, an ornamental piece that he had worked on last summer.

"Give me your sword, Lord Callum," Liz commanded, her voice stronger than Mat remembered ever hearing it before. Lord Callum sputtered, a high-pitched giggle wrenched from his throat.

"M-my sword, your majesty? I can assure you, the keep is the safest place for you. You will not meet harm here." Liz smiled, but it didn't reach her eyes.

"I need a sword to appoint a knight."

Chapter Twenty-Nine

Liz hadn't seen Mat's clear green eyes appear so vulnerable before, stripped of the laughter normally residing within them. He knew what coming here meant. Mat made his choice and she wouldn't rob him of it. His dream was to become a knight of the realm. This, at least, she could give him. Truthfully, she couldn't imagine anyone more deserving of a knighthood. He dropped her hand and stepped away from her, his breath shuddering as Lord Callum unbuckled the sword from his belt and held it out to Liz.

The ornamental scabbard slid free and clattered uselessly to the floor. Liz pretended not to notice Lord Callum's grimace. She trembled as she tilted her chin up, motioning fluidly for Mat to kneel before her. His golden hair and green eyes seemed godlike in the scant rays of the setting afternoon sun. The light filtered through the grated windows to kiss his handsome face and carve the hollows of his cheeks.

In a slow, lithe motion he knelt before her, head bowed in perfect obedience. The thrum of his rapid pulse resonated between them. Her vision narrowed until the onlookers faded from sight. Until she and Mat were left alone, this ceremony binding them to one another. After all they were bound in every other way that mattered.

"Matioch Steele." Her voice, much like the night she spoke to him of his fate, plucked the words from the mists beyond time. "Do you acknowledge me as your true and rightful queen?"

"I do." The words slid over her skin, his voice raw, until her hands shook in the fading light. She gripped the hilt of the silver sword tightly enough to quell the tremors.

"Repeat after me." She cleared her throat, images of her father speaking these same words over Killian's shoulders running through her mind. She'd been no more than thirteen winters old when Killian won his knighthood by saving her life. She thought his elevation of rank had been a sign that her father loved her, that he'd accepted Killian and Tia as her companions and elevated them so that she wouldn't have to live her life alone. As she grew older, she realized the assassin wanted to divert the prophecy, and that her life was no more than a coveted object. Killian had been rewarded for keeping her alive so that she could die at the right time, in the right way.

"I, Matioch Steele," she began, her eyes never wavering from his bowed head.

It warmed her bones, knowing that Mat's knighthood would be bestowed for the exact opposite reason. Better that she rule by love rather than fear. She would not be the kind of monarch her father had been or the Dragon would be. No, she had a responsibility to be better.

"Do solemnly swear to pledge my life and my sword to Queen Elisabetta of Aegis."

It's what Tia challenged her to do. What her mother sacrificed herself for. What her people suffered in the name of. What

Mat was going to die for. The chance that she could make a better world. Liz represented that hope, and she refused to fail them.

"To defend and obey her until my death. In the hallowed name of the gods and goddesses, as they are written in the Halls, I vow to uphold the honor of my knighthood and defend the rule of my sovereign." Mat's deep voice repeated her words, rumbling through her like a chord struck and lingering in the air, setting her senses alight. Liz took the hilt of the sword in both hands, her arms straining to hold it steady as she placed the flat of the blade gently to his left shoulder.

"I dub thee, Sir Matioch Steele, Knight of Aegis." She tapped the flat blade on his other shoulder, then held the sword to him as his eyes, wet with tears rose from the floor. "I gift this sword to you." Lord Callum coughed behind her but she ignored him. "To be wielded in my name. Arise, Sir Knight."

Mat rose then, seeming taller than before. He wrapped one callused hand around the hilt of the silver sword, sheathing it in the ornamental scabbard and buckling it to his side.

When his eyes met hers, no air remained in the room between them. The tension pulled her tight, threatening to snap her composure into thousands of fractured splinters. A servant bent to Lord Callum's ear and he straightened, clearing his throat to garner her attention.

"May I present my children, your majesty?"

She nodded, breaking the stare that threatened to consume her. She offered a conciliatory smile as Mat was ushered out of the hall by Killian, who beamed a brilliant white smile and demanded he be outfitted with his armor right away.

Liz sat then, her legs quaking from the force of emotion unexplored between them. Her back was ramrod straight as Lord

Callum's children, easily her age or older, were announced to the room.

"Danyl Callum, my son and heir, recently returned from the Royal University at Silver City." Her eyes shot to the young man of average height, pristinely dressed, hair combed to flop attractively in his eyes. Clearly, he'd learned much from the courtiers at the palace.

She wanted to ask him about his studies, but her attention was stolen by the woman seething beside him. Her ebony skin and sculpted features were the most beautiful Liz had ever seen. Fearsome and awe-inspiring.

"My daughter, Anibel Callum."

Anibel exuded regal entitlement, her eyes hard and assessing as she raked them over Liz's features. Her steely confidence made Liz feel the same way she had as a child when caught trying on her mother's tiaras and diadems, the crowns slipping over her ears and slung low over her brow. Ill-fitted to the position of queen.

Anibel walked forward, a slick glide Liz could never mimic, as graceful as a panther stalking her prey. She bowed her head, the motion so slight her chin barely dipped. The nobles at court wouldn't dare to disrespect her in such a manner. Liz's mouth turned up as she fought the urge to smile.

"You're wearing my mother's gown," she said, and a smile curled onto Liz's lips. Her fire reminded her of Tia. She liked the fearsome woman immediately. .

"Apologies, I thought it inappropriate to arrive in my corset. Not very regal, at least," Liz said, her tone teasing. Danyl, seemingly aggravated at being upstaged by his sister, cleared his throat and stepped forward to speak. Liz's eyes hardened, impatient already with his impertinence.

"You look ravishing, majesty. Almost as beautiful as when we last met, at the palace."

Liz's eyebrows knit together at his polished words. She didn't remember him, but he looked like many of the other nobles prancing about court. While Liz attended some functions, she wasn't an active part of court activities. Too studious to withstand the debauchery and revelry of the wild parties often frequented by courtiers and noblemen. Her father forbade any activity that would've threatened her reputation as the perfect sacrifice.

"Forgive me, Danyl, but I don't remember our last encounter. Could you be so kind as to remind me?" she asked. His ears went red in embarrassment, stumbling over his next few words until finally falling silent. Liz had the distinct impression Danyl was unaccustomed to being forgotten. She raised an eyebrow and he cleared his throat before speaking more slowly.

"I ran into you, on your way to the temple. You were with your friend."

Tia. The reminder of the long, hazy summer days they'd spent walking to temple together past the young nobles hiking the chalky white stone path to the cliffs of Morr, where they jumped from heights and drank wine until they could no longer stand and danced around fires of bleached driftwood. Liz remembered being jealous of them not so long ago. Her features lit in remembrance, seeming to catch the lingering scent of salt and chalk in the warm air.

"You dove from the cliffs?" she asked and he nodded.

Lord Callum leveled him with a dark glare. "You *dove* from the cliffs of Morr?" His chastising of Danyl earned a sly grin from Anibel, one that Liz answered after unwittingly outing Danyl's dangerous activities taking precedence over his studies.

"You and I will be good friends, majesty," Anibel said, her dark eyes warmer than before. For the first time in a long time, Liz believed she could grow to be happy here. Movement from the corner of her eye stole her attention away from the Callum family, cold dread splintering suddenly through her bones.

It was snowing.

Chapter Thirty

"You'll want a finer mail than that, at the very least. Too heavy and you won't be able to move quickly in battle." Killian had been running through the finer points of armor for the last hour. Grateful for the distraction from his tumultuous thoughts, Mat sat on the roughhewn armory bench, head in hands. Half clad in fine chainmail, he wrestled with the emptiness he felt from his elevation in rank. Hadn't this been everything he'd worked for?

Staring down the narrow barrel of time, and his lack of it, he found himself wishing he'd wasted less of it pursuing knighthood. In fact, he found himself thinking of his mother. He wanted to speak to her one last time, but he wouldn't get the opportunity. He would write her a letter, if only she could read it.

"I thought Tia was a refugee," Mat said, cutting off Killian's lecture on the benefits of scale armor versus plate armor. It wasn't until he recognized the offended expression in Killian's eyes that Mat realized he'd spoken out of turn. Killian took a deep measured breath, realizing Mat meant no harm.

"We were refugees. Our parents were killed in a raid, and the prince of a larger island planned to execute all of us that remained. With the help of family, we were smuggled onto a ship coming to Aegis to seek asylum," he said, as he put away the pieces of armor he'd pulled down previously.

"Tia and I were lucky enough to have each other. Many people seeking asylum are still separated from their families." The strain in Killian's voice contradicted the easy stare he leveled at Mat. Suddenly Mat felt like an idiot for even mentioning it. He sat next to Mat, his silver armor clanking loudly.

"How did you become a knight?" Mat asked. Curious about the man who appeared to have known Liz all her life, who'd become such a close friend that the princess flung herself into his arms.

"Years ago, there was a dedicated faction of extremists who wanted to avert the prophecy. They made several attempts on Lisbet's life. One of them got all the way into her bedchambers with a dagger. Had I not been checking on Tia, I wouldn't have been able to stop him in time." The tale was delivered flatly, a sign that Killian was humble as well as brave. Mat decided he liked him.

"The king awarded me a title for what I did for his family, and my knighthood for what I did for Aegis."

Mat ran his hands over his face, pulling absentmindedly at his hair. There were still so many things he didn't know about Liz. Things he would be able to discover if only he had more time. His stomach thrashed inside of him, threatening to spill his meager breakfast on the flagstones at his feet. Killian didn't stop him when he turned from the room to wander through the familiar halls. Halls he'd walked his entire life as a lesser man, eyes downcast, his presence a stain on the very stones beneath his feet.

He found himself back on the training grounds, across from the forge where he used to live. In a little back bedroom, covered in soot and hay. He took a deep breath and the scent of sweat and iron steadied him deep down. The clang of swords and thuds of arrows finding home in padded targets blended into a rhythm that defined him. This, he realized, was the rhythm that formed the song of *his* life.

"Come for a rematch?" Mat didn't think he'd ever heard Gareth's voice so light. He grinned, his hand resting on the ornamental silver scabbard, until Gareth noticed the ostentatious glimmering of sapphires and whistled low.

"I'd beat you again anyway," Mat said with a shrug. Gareth leaned against the dark stone at his back, looking out with wary eyes over the others training. They stood together in silence, a quality Mat had grown to appreciate. In the silence, Mat found a stillness that began in his chest and with each beat of his heart spread down his legs and arms.

When the first tufts of white snow began to lilt down from the sky, floating on the winter wind, Mat didn't feel dread. Instead he was filled with a deep resignation as the din of training slowed to a stop. The men halted to acknowledge that winter had come and the blizzard was breaking in earnest. Mat turned to Gareth, his voice hard.

"I know you love her." Gareth didn't respond; he held Mat's level stare, neither man needing to acknowledge the truth as sharp as the chill in the air. "I need you to swear something to me."

"Asking favors of me, bastard?" Gareth tried to adopt a light hearted tone, but it didn't suit him. Mat dropped his crossed arms and clapped a hand on the man's shoulder.

"Swear to me that should anything happen to me, you won't leave her side. You'll keep her safe. From everything, even herself if necessary."

Gareth's eyebrows knit together; his grey eyes grew stormy at Mat's imperious tone. "I had no intention of leaving her side. Some men don't need to declare public oaths to do the right thing." Mat opened his mouth, prepared to argue his point. "But, for you bastard, I'll swear it." Gareth said. As long as he'd known Gareth, he swore to no one and nothing. No one but a bastard, it would seem.

Mat choked out a laugh, wondering when he came to like Gareth Black enough to trust him with the person he loved the most. Clenching his jaw against the jealousy he refused to acknowledge roiling in the deepest part of his mind, he held out his forearm.

"Thank you, my friend."

The next hour passed in a blur. Mat could see nothing but the soft white of the snow falling harder as each minute passed. He sighed in relief when his new squire came to lead him to his newly appointed chambers by order of the queen. He knew the most esteemed knights resided within the keep, but walking into rooms more spacious than the entire forge he'd toiled away in, Mat struggled to believe this was his new reality. As if he were suspended under water, or somewhere between waking and sleeping. He had the distinct impression he had unwittingly stepped into someone else's life.

The squire laid out tunics with gold thread and thick brocades, gently pressing him to wash and shave. The lad spoke incessantly but every word fell on deaf ears. He allowed the boy to pull a linen shirt over his shoulders before taking a deep breath and waking from his self-imposed stupor.

"Lord Callum will not tolerate tardiness at her majesty's feast."

"Feast?" Mat asked, tying his sleeves closed and tucking the shirt haphazardly into his breeches. "No, Liz wouldn't approve of that. Not at the start of winter and facing food shortages. Take me to her rooms."

The boy balked at his order, stammering at his casual use of his pet name for the queen.

"Now," Mat growled, and the boy hopped forward nervously, leading the way down the twisting corridors lit by sconces crackling with flames that threatened to consume Mat whole. He needed to see *Liz*, not the Red Queen.

The boy stopped outside of an ornately carved oak door and knocked. A maid answered, and the boy began to speak, but Mat pushed past him, flinging the door open wide as he barged his way past. He didn't know how nobles put up with servants always in their way. The maid screeched and began cursing at him to leave at once.

He ignored her as his eyes fell on Liz's pale shoulders and long, elegant neck. She sat demurely, looking every bit as divine as a goddess in the soft candlelight. She smiled at him, fine lines appearing at the corners of her eyes. Lines he imagined would deepen sweetly with age and laughter. Neither of them cared about her state of undress; after all, she wore more now in her corset and many layers of undergarments than when they first met.

"Leave us," she said, silencing the maid's hysterics until they were finally alone. He watched her shoulders relax and breathed easier as her expression became less strained.

"It's snowing," he said, his voice breaking in the air between them.

"I know." She stood and closed the distance between them, her fingertips reaching to his jaw and caressing his smooth cheek. "We should have run."

She swayed on her feet, inching closer to him. Her body arched unconsciously toward him, and his arms reached out to cradle her. Her fingers stroked his clean shaven jaw again, her nose brushing his as she restrained the tears in her eyes.

"We were an impossible dream, Liz," he muttered against her hair, his hand buried in the newly brushed curls that shone in the soft light. Violence and passion warred in the vibrance of those locks he loved to separate with his fingers. Her lips ran over his pulse, pounding heavily in rhythm to his cacophonous heartbeat.

"I would have found you," she whispered against his skin. "No matter the circumstances." He pulled away to look in her dazed blue eyes. Darkened by a fierce longing that mirrored his own.

"I feel you in my bones, Mat. The world bends beneath my feet and sends me stumbling towards you. Wherever you go next, I will inevitably follow." Each word was a husky whisper that fell hot on his lips. He couldn't contain himself any longer; he clung to her desperately. His mouth came down hard on hers, swallowing her whimper.

The night was young, but Mat didn't have any more time to be indecisive. In moments, she'd pulled the fabric of his shirt over his head, her eyes devouring the sight of every dip and hollow from the curve of his neck to the tops of his breeches.

Mat gathered her up in his arms and tossed them both on the bed, tangled inextricably together. His hands and mouth wandered, tasting and feeling every inch of her porcelain skin. Her musical cries begged him for everything. Everything he couldn't give. He pulled away enough to let the cool air temper their rising passions.

"I won't ruin you." He pressed a finger over her open mouth, which was already prepared to argue with him. "I can't be like my father. I can't, Liz." Her eyes widened in understanding, her mouth soft beneath his touch.

"But I don't have to ruin you to satisfy us both." He couldn't stop the grin twisting onto his mouth as she rose to meet him, both of them ignoring the snow gathering steadily outside the window behind them.

Chapter Thirty-One

Incessant rapping on the door startled Liz from her deep slumber. Lulled by the steady rhythm of Mat's heart beating beneath her cheek, she groaned at the interruption. When she stirred, he gripped her tighter, rolling to pin her in his steel embrace. The rapping increased in intensity until neither of them could ignore it any longer. Mat cracked open bleary eyes, his hands wandering over her pale skin, mapping the terrain with inquisitive fingers.

"Tell them to bloody leave," he grumbled into her hair before the shouting began behind the door, forcing an annoyed snarl from between his clenched teeth. Liz giggled at his reaction, wishing for more time. Her lips caught his grumpy frown, and he buried his hands in her hair, separating the curls at the nape of her neck. Before they could sink back down into each other, the rapping started again.

Liz struggled to disentangle herself from his arms as she padded on bare feet to open the door, her hair flung wildly over her shoulders. The maid from the night before, Mat's squire, and three outfitted soldiers stood at attention as Liz waved impatiently at them.

"Well? What is it?" she asked impetuously. Their eyes fell away from her irritated expression as Mat approached behind her, shirtless, sliding an arm around her waist. The maid's face turned a strange shade of violet, and Liz realized how scandalous it must seem for she and Mat to be caught in the same room together with hardly any clothes on.

"Your majesty, Lord Callum calls for you urgently. The Dragon's soldiers have been spotted marching toward the pass."

Like the winter winds howling and rattling the windows in their grates, Liz couldn't keep her thoughts from tumbling and shattering within her mind. She turned to Mat, and he nodded, confirming her fear that the time had finally come.

"I'll meet you there," he promised, pulling her close and pressing a soft kiss to her stunned mouth. She nodded, unable to speak past the lump in her throat. She wasn't ready for this. It was all happening too quickly. He grinned at her, the same impish grin she loved so dearly, and followed his squire down the hall to his chambers.

Her red-faced maid shuffled inside, pulling out a dark green velvet gown and curling her lip at the broken stays of Liz's corset discarded on the floor. As she dressed, the air of urgency permeating her chambers kept her on edge and jittery. Her maid refused to meet Liz's eyes, and appeared to delight in pulling her corset too tight. The girl's vigor to pin her curls into a neat chignon had pins scraping viciously at Liz's scalp. Liz had to put her hand up to still the vehemence with which she fought her wild curls.

"Let me save us both some time and pain. My curls are not tamed quickly or easily. This will suffice," Liz said, her voice acerbic. The maid grunted, sneering at the sight of Liz's tousled sheets on the bed. She sighed, turning to face the woman full on.

"I think I can manage on my own from here." Clearly dismissed, the maid curtsied and shuffled swiftly out the door. Standing and assessing herself in the looking glass, Liz recognized how much she favored her mother. She was a shadow of the former queen.

After another urgent summons, Liz steeled her nerves, whispering a prayer to Sierah the goddess of moon and tides beneath her breath. She marched purposefully into the main hall to find familiar faces gathered around and speaking in fearful tones. Lord Callum and his son Danyl stood over a map of Aegis spread along a large table. Mat and Gareth stood speaking with their friends from Fangorn, catching them up on recent events. Smitty seemed the most confused of them all. She was glad Mat remembered their conversation late last night and summoned them. She wanted to make sure they were rewarded with honors, much as Mat had been knighted, so that the people of Fangorn knew of their loyalty and bravery.

"Your majesty," Lord Callum said, bowing low before sweeping a hand to usher her over to the map spread before them.

"The Dragon has a battalion of soldiers marching toward the pass, here." He pointed to the narrowest point between the mountains and the only entrance to the valley below. "They'll be there before the blizzard has enough time to impede their progress. At this rate, he'll make it here with a thousand armed men before nightfall."

Liz took a steadying breath, acknowledging the trepidation in Lord Callum's eyes. This was a test of her strength and resolve. She proclaimed herself queen and asked the people to fight for her. How she reacted now would prove to them if the faith they'd placed in her was justified. Her eyes fanned over to Mat and Gareth, waving them forward. Killian stood at her right shoulder, stone faced. Danyl scowled, annoyed by their presence.

"What are our options?" she asked, opening the room to offer solutions. Killian pointed to a low area beyond the pass and traced a path from there to a shipping route leading to the sea.

"We can flee this way, if we leave now we may be able to outpace him long enough to board ships. But, with winter approaching the tides will be more unpredictable than ever. It may be just as dangerous as trying to defend our position here." Killian explained.

"I won't leave these people undefended. They trust me." Looks were exchanged, confidence in her ability to rule was waning amongst them. Gareth fidgeted, and she turned to him, raising an expectant eyebrow. Instead of answering her, his grey eyes flicked to Lord Callum and then away from the group assembled.

"I care less about titles than lives. If you have a suggestion, speak it." She commanded.

"I know how to stall the Dragon, but you won't like it, majesty." Gareth cleared his throat, looking heavily between Mat and Liz. A muscle twitched in Mat's clenched jaw.

Danyl stepped forward then, his brown eyes alight with an idea. "If we can stall the Dragon long enough to let the pass freeze, we can keep a standing army through winter. After your arrival at Fangorn, there have been peasants offering to train as soldiers. We'll have all winter to train and outfit them." Liz's head began to spin with the implications of what they were discussing.

"You mean to imply, when winter ends, we would have the means to stand against the Dragon?" she asked Danyl nodding solemnly in response. "To be clear, we're talking about starting a civil war in Aegis." No one spoke. "We're talking about defying the prophecy and the will of the gods."

Though Liz had tried at every turn to defy the prophecy, fate seemed determined to bend her to its iron will. For so long it'd been only Liz, Tia, her mother, a handful of others who even thought it possible. With the support of the people in this room, an army, she could finally turn the tides. The silence blanketed her, suffocating and taut. No one dissented. Squaring her shoulders, she nodded slightly, the motion carrying grim consequences for millions of people. A long moment followed, appropriately grave as each person in attendance acknowledged the severity of the next few moments.

"Gareth," Liz said, her voice strained. "How do we stall him?"

"We don't," he said, his grey eyes sliding over to Mat once more. "He does."

Mat turned, dropping his crossed arms as he regarded Gareth. Liz knew it was coming; there would be no way to stop him from meeting the Dragon in battle. The sharp sting of loss twisted dagger-like in her chest and splintered into chasms of pain too wide to cross. She wasn't ready for him to die. Isn't that exactly what her mother said that night before the blood moon?

"My wind," he said, breathing out the words with a sardonic grin on his lips. "I can't make any guarantees. I've only used it on purpose a few times. But it may be possible for me to use the wind to help the blizzard come on faster." Killian put a comforting hand on her shoulder as she fisted her hands at her sides. The nails dug into the delicate skin of her palms leaving angry, red crescents behind.

"I'll need someone rallying loyal soldiers to our cause beyond Fangorn if I stand a chance in open war." She fixed her calculating gaze on Killian then, resting a hand over his own. "Two hundred men will ride out to meet the Dragon's battalion. Matioch will lead the charge and spur on the blizzard. Killian will use the battle as cover and make his way back to the southern shore." His answering smile reminded him of Tia's; it wrenched the chasms of pain open wider within her.

"Your majesty," Wallace said, startling Liz from her thoughts. He'd never spoken with such intent before. His normally downcast eyes bore straight into the heart of her. They were a warm brown, and reminded her of the moment his fingers brushed against his cheek where Tia kissed him. "I will go with Matioch."

She opened her mouth to refuse but found herself speechless. Instead, she nodded mutely at his request. She couldn't reconcile his gentleness with the brutality of battle. But then, she'd seen his fate along with Mat's not long ago. She was foolish to expect him to leave Mat's side.

"Aye, I'll follow the bastard as well." Smitty's grunt came as no surprise.

"Where you go, Mat, I follow," Finn said, standing tall beside his friend. Mat's eyebrows knit together in worry, fearful for them all.

"Let it be known," Liz said, her voice carrying through the hall. "That in Aegis's time of need, it was a stable hand, a butcher, a kitchen boy, and a bladesmith that answered the call." Her vision blurred with unshed tears, hot and insistent as she tried to memorize each man's face.

"Let it be known that these are the heroes of Fangorn. We will sing your songs with honor."

Time moved strangely in the aftermath of the war plans. Once decisions were made, orders were shouted and people scurried to heed the shouting. Though time passed too quickly, it also dragged forward. A sense of anticipation and fear warring for control. Liz stumbled on numb legs back to her chambers. The closer the time came for them to ride off, the more numb she felt. It was as if winter itself, a living thing, began to seep in through the chasms of pain where she broke open and froze her from within.

She gripped the rough wool of Mat's borrowed cloak tight in her hands, inhaling his scent to stave off the numbness and its poisonous spread. Leather, iron, and something indescribably *him*. A knock sounded at her door, and her maid allowed Gareth inside, striding on silent feet. Liz refused to acknowledge him for a long while.

"Was it cowardice, callousness, or opportunism?" She fixed her swollen eyes, sore from weeping, on his ambivalent face.

"I don't—"

"Were you too afraid to fight alongside him?" Liz asked.

Gareth sighed, pulling at the high collar of his shirt nervously.

"Did you care so little that you couldn't be bothered?" She continued.

He tugged harder, until the cravat loosened considerably.

"Or were you biding your time until he died to make your move?" She finished spitefully. His eyes turned flat then, steel resolve residing within them. The barely contained violence roiling off his tensed shoulders heated the air around them, flickers ready to turn to flames.

"I came to tell you they're leaving," Quiet contempt laced each word as he turned his back on her and left her alone. She tried to stand but stumbled and caught herself on her bedpost, wracked with pain and numbness mingling in a strange cocktail of emotion that paralyzed her. Her maid came to her aid, but she shooed her away, gritting her teeth against her own rising weakness. She could order him to stay. But, what was the point? He would die in the pass or here at the keep if the Dragon managed to get through. And he would resent her for taking away his choice.

If she loved him, she had to let him go.

She strode calmly down the halls, each step forcing cold apathy further through her body. Gareth stood sentry as she made her way into the courtyard, the sun glaring down between dark, low-hung clouds. The garish light haloed Mat's handsome face, statuesque as he handed the reins of his new stallion to his squire.

"Thank the gods," he breathed, dismissing the furtive glances from the other knights as he wrapped her up in his arms and crushed her against his thick armor. In his arms, she couldn't pretend to be strong. Instead of sending him off with a smile, she wailed into his neck and clawed at the metal plates, desperate to find purchase to his skin beneath.

"I cannot do this without you." Without his arms, she would have crumpled to the muddy snow sloshing thick beneath their feet. "Don't go. You'll die if you go. I *can't* lose you." She couldn't breathe. Why couldn't she breathe? He shushed her, sniffling as he buried his nose in her hair and inhaled deeply. Her hands trembled as his mouth found hers and he kissed her languidly, savoring the taste of her for the last time.

"Avenge me," he whispered against her mouth, his green eyes steady against the blinding whiteness. The moment her arms fell away from him, numbness took possession of what little remained of her heart. Unable to move, she stood watch as all two hundred men stampeded from the courtyard, shouts of "for the Queen" and "No blood, No glory" ringing on the sharp winter wind. One step in front of the other, she climbed the steps to the rampart on the southern wall. Carefully she held her skirts aloft until she climbed so high that she could gaze upon the soldiers as they rode all the way down the valley, twisting and rushing ever onward, a river of lives sacrificed for her.

She stood so long that her body began to shiver. Gareth attempted to move her, but she refused to budge while they were still in sight. She clenched frozen hands on the battlement as she leaned to keep them in sight. Mat's gold signet ring stood stark against the bone-white paleness of her hand.

She watched unblinking until the company of men were no more than specks of light on the horizon. Until the cold chilled her to the point that she could no longer feel her fingertips digging into the stone beneath her palms.

Closing her eyes, she reveled in the frozen wind lashing her cheeks, howling over the ramparts to whip her curls furiously around her face. Mat's wind. Tugging open the leather pouch at her neck, she watched as Tia's ashes swirled to the south to greet the coming storm. She stood to face it the way she was always meant to. She stood until the snow fell so hard that the world was washed white. Until she realized that this too would be a new beginning.

After all, there were songs to be sung and a war to be won.

Acknowledgements

Wow! I never thought I would be here, writing my thanks in the back of my very own book. But, here I am and I definitely didn't get here on my own. I have so many people I want to thank for their support, encouragement, advice, and effort. Without each and every one of these people Songs would be an unfinished dream in a computer file.

Firstly I want to thank my amazing husband for believing in me especially when I didn't believe in myself. He has been a constant source of strength and perseverance throughout this process. I would have succumbed to crippling self-doubt and imposter syndrome years ago if it weren't for his unfailing faith in me. I am so blessed to have him in my corner. Along the same vein I want to thank my son, Bellamy, for being the inspiration behind the premise of this book and the motivation behind seeing this through to the end. Everything I do is for the two of them.

Next I need to thank my darling beta readers and critique partners who suffered through many drafts of this book, pointing out each inconsistency and flaw in excruciating detail in an effort to help me make this story the best it could possibly be. So, hats off to: Meagan West, Nicole Mckeon, and AS Howell. (Also my mother, but she'll get her very own shout out.)

My family, more specifically my parents and sisters, have been so instrumental in developing this book. Weighing in on marketing decisions and cover art. Listening to me ramble on, ad nauseum, about fictional people and their fictional problems as if they existed in the real world without rolling their eyes. A feat, I'm sure. Thank you for being patient and kind during these last years as I found my author's voice and a story worth pursuing.

Bethany Robison, my editor, went above and beyond the call when she took on this manuscript offering resources and gentle criticisms that made it possible for me to focus the character voices and make them really sing. I couldn't have asked for anyone better to work with. She was so intuitive and plugged into the character's motivations and the themes of the book. She has my eternal gratitude and respect.

Finally, I want to thank Asha Hossain, cover artist extraordinaire. She took on the task of developing the brand for not just this book, but all the books in this series and her eye for aesthetics and attention to detail are unparalleled. I couldn't be happier with the work she did on this cover and the cover for book #2. Even though I was barely coherent and rambling about obscure ideas for the cover art, she was able to somehow translate that into something better than I imagined.

Of course I always want to thank you, dear reader, for going on this wild journey with me. Without your support there would be no one to write for. I am truly humbled by your support and patronage.

~Lauren

Don't miss out!

Visit the website below and you can sign up to receive emails whenever Lauren Sevier publishes a new book. There's no charge and no obligation.

https://books2read.com/r/B-A-WFUJ-ASEDB

BOOKS 2 READ

Connecting independent readers to independent writers.

About the Author

Lauren Sevier lives a simple life in small town Walker, Louisiana with her family and two mischievous dogs. She's a proud firefighter wife and mother to her miracle son, born through IVF after an eight-year battle with infertility. She works full-time for a non-profit hospital in Cardiology caring for the elderly and low-income families all over the state of Louisiana in satellite and outreach clinics. Writing and being in the service of helping others are her two passions in life.

She started writing song lyrics and poems on the front porch swing of her family home nestled amidst a 200-year-old pecan tree orchard that was once part of a Civil War plantation. She's inspired the most by Shakespeare, the Bronte sisters, Jane Austen, and JK Rowling. Her background in Theatre introduced her to classic British literature, playwrights, and poets from a very young age. This helped her to understand story concepts, dramatization, and character development the way Shakespeare once did, as an actor.

Now her biggest inspiration for writing is her son who, like all children, learns by example. Lauren is determined to set a specific example for him; to live simply, work hard, and to never stop chasing her dreams. Because, one day, you just might catch them.

Read more at https://www.laurensevier.com.

www.ingramcontent.com/pod-product-compliance
Lightning Source LLC
Chambersburg PA
CBHW021111110726
47900CB00007B/2137